T0065201

TOKEMA

TOKEMA

ANIE ZINTER

ARCHWAY
PUBLISHING

Archway Publishing books may be ordered through booksellers or by contacting:

Archway Publishing
1663 Liberty Drive
Bloomington, IN 47403
www.archwaypublishing.com
844-669-3957

ISBN: 978-1-6657-5513-9 (sc)
ISBN: 978-1-6657-5512-2 (e)

Library of Congress Control Number: 2024900075

Print information available on the last page.

Archway Publishing rev. date: 01/12/2024

And with an ember glow, a fiery haze, back
to hell which forth it came...

———⁕———

It's a rare thing. An unusual thing. To feel this way about someone. A feeling in which you don't even realize that it is happening. It develops slowly. Creeping up on you like falling asleep. Something you don't even realize you are having until you are dreaming, or suddenly awaken. To love someone in such a way that you are willing to sacrifice everything. And yes, it was worth it. To know the truth. To know what to do. But only love can hurt like this. I know it's love. The only patient I have ever loved. And it ends like this? Pity really. But I know it's what's best. Best for everyone really. I'll miss you...

———⁕———

The room was hot and reeked with a musty smell of old papers, cigarettes, and wood. The fans, while fluttering, did little to help the heat. Each drag and puff of a cigarette made the room even more hot and unbearable. The bodies all squished together in the seats, balcony, aisles, and down the hall were of no help either. The smell of sweat was heavy. However, through the chattering voices, grunts, and heaves, Doris did not notice a thing.

Nine... there were nine of them. I think... I remember nine. There was the beggar, the screamer, the... the... oh no what did he say? I missed it.

1

They don't believe me. I know they don't believe me. I wouldn't either if I was in their shoes. They are probably going to throw me in jail. The death penalty perhaps. Would that be any better? I think, maybe. But I don't want to die, but I can't keep living like this. I don't want-

Doris Draker sat in a wooden chair and stared blankly ahead waiting to hear the decision. Her lawyer forced her into pleading insanity. He knew it was the best option for her, even though he couldn't believe her story. He was assigned to her because she could not provide her own attorney, and no one would take her case even if she could. She could hear the chattering behind her as they all waited eagerly to hear the decision.

Doris looked down at her chair, she could see chipped and splintered wood from her nails. She had been scratching at the armrest, and it was not until now that she realized there were little pieces of wood underneath her nails. It didn't hurt though. She examined the wood pieces, trying her best to ignore the voices behind her. She picked at them, removing splinters one by one.

She heard one woman behind her saying, "I hope she rots in jail." She heard a priest praying, "If you make the Lord your refuge, if you make the Highest your shelter, no evil will conquer you; no plague will come near your home. The Lord says, 'I will rescue those who love me. I will protect those who trust in my name. When they call on me, I will answer; I will be with them in trouble. I will rescue and honor them. I will reward them with a long life and give them my salvation." Psalm 91:9-10:1416. Doris knew the passage well. She had been to see many priests. And even had an exorcism performed on her before she could no longer control herself. Although she had been wary of that priest. Nothing helped. No matter how many times she went to church, no matter how many times she prayed, no matter at all. *He* was with her.

The courtroom fell into a hush when the judge returned to his chair. "All rise for the honorable judge Devan Thomas." The judge was a man most likely in his 50s, not much older than Doris herself.

Devan had faded red hair that was neatly combed back. He styled it in a way that made him look much younger than his face. Doris had seen the style on a few young men while she had been out and about not too long ago.

"Will the jury foreperson please stand?" A man stood. He looked to be much older than Doris and held a stern face. His hair was gray, and he looked tired and worn from his days serving on jury duty. And no one would blame him with a case like hers. His eyes were cold, and they seemed to stare right through her, as if trying to avoid her body being there. But obviously, she was there. She was the whole reason for every one of those people being there. He could not avoid it. His eyes seemed to say, 'If I pretend not to see her then she will not see me. She'll pass me by.'

"Has the jury reached a unanimous verdict?"

"Yes, your honor" His voice cracked, and he handed the verdict to the clerk who passed it to the judge. He stared at the paper, face unchanging, and let out a low sigh as if he agreed with what the jury had concluded, but did not want to admit that. He handed the form back to the clerk.

"The jury finds the defendant not guilty under reasons of insanity..." Doris could hear the clerk continue reading but it sounded the same to her as if she was underwater. Slowly sinking further and further into darkness. The voice in her head began to laugh and suddenly *he* was there. Standing before her, same as everyone else in the courtroom. Only no one seemed to notice him, as he leered at her. Doris tried her best not to look at *it*.

They do believe you, congratulations.

"Shut up!" Doris whispered.

You're going to rot in there. No one will come for you.

"I said shut up!" Doris whispered again. Only this time the clerk paused, raised an eyebrow at Doris, then continued to read. The room was booming with noise. Protests, shrieks, crying, it was all there.

But we're not insane! We're not. Just you.

"Please no..." Doris's hands began to shake. She could feel the tears welling up. "I'm not insane!" She screamed; the room fell silent.

"What are you doing? This is what we wanted," her lawyer snapped, grabbing her arm.

"Miss Draker, please contain yourself in my court," The judge said harshly, eyeing her from above his spectacles.

"I'm not!" Doris whispered and began to cry. "I need help..." She sobbed.

"And that's exactly what you're getting!" Her lawyer barked, "We got what we wanted, now shut it!"

"Contain yourself or else I will be forced to have the bailiff do it for you!" The judge pointed his finger in warning as Doris sobbed in her chair.

Once the clerk wrapped up the verdict the room began to explode once more. People were shouting, "She deserves the death penalty!", "Let her rot in jail", one person even spit at the back of Doris's neck. She was just thankful no one flicked a cigarette butt in her direction.

"Order! Order!" the judge yelled, "There will be none of this in my courtroom! Now, Miss Draker, I find your crimes heinous, horrendous, and evil. But it is clear to see that you *are* deranged. Whispering to yourself about voices in your head, and even getting physical. You are remanded for life in Tokema State Hospital, and I *hope* it does you well, court adjourned." The gavel cracked like thunder. Doris jumped at the sound and covered her ears.

"No... no... no!" She murmured. Doris began to scream, throwing herself at her lawyer, "I'm not insane! I'm not! He- it- *whatever he* is here, why can't you see him? That *thing* is right there!" She pointed, shaking at her lawyer, "Don't let me go to that place. Have you heard? Do you know what they do there?" She felt a sharp pinch hit the side of her neck. She could hear whooping and hollering as it faded away.

—⁂—

Wha- what's happening? Where am I? Doris's head was heavy as she tried to flutter her eyes open. She went to rub them out of habit but soon noticed she could not feel her arms, nor was she capable of pulling them forward. *Wha- oh my god I'm in a straitjacket. They think I'm truly insane.*

"Well, what did you expect, Doris?" She looked up to see the man, or more appropriately, creature, she so feared sitting across from her. She tried her best not to look at it. His skin was gray, like the ashes that lay ignored at the bottom of a fireplace. She turned herself away so she would not have to look at his face again.

"Where are we going?" Doris choked out. She began thrashing about. "Where are we going?" she asked again.

"My, my, my. You don't remember now do you? You're insane! We're going to our new home." Doris could hear the blood rushing into her head and could hear her heart pounding.

"I'm not crazy, I'm not... You're right here" Doris whimpered, as she half-heartedly gestured as best, she could behind her back.

"Shh...we can still have fun there too." And with that he disappeared without a trace of its presence ever being there.

The drive to Tokema was a long and slow one for Doris. The truck in which she was in had no windows for her to see out of. There was, however, a small window at the front of the truck which had crisscross wires and was just big enough for one person to look through. Doris could see yellow light shining out, but when she went to peak out a large hand slapped across the metal. Little bits of cinders fell from his cigarette, landing on Doris's lap. With her arms still bound behind her back she did her best to blow them out.

"Get back you dirty bitch!" a man yelled. Doris yipped and shrunk back into the darkness of the car. "God she's awake, I was hoping she would stay out the whole trip" he rolled his eyes and looked out the window. Another man snorted,

"They never do," he replied. The road to Tokema was flat and dusty. The sky seemed to stretch on as they drove closer. Nothing but farmland traced their path and it all seemed to repeat itself. "I tell ya one thing, she's my last one."

"You say that every time Freddy."

"Nah, well this time I mean it! She's the last fucking one after what she did. Can't even look at her" he said, hitting the wired frame again. No one else was on the road as they drove. There were no lights to stop at, no turns to make. They had reached a straight shot and were headed right for the tree line that surrounded the facility.

The forest surrounding was thick and bunched close together. The leaves were beginning to change, and they made the grounds look almost pretty. They excelled at doing their job of masking the horrors that were encased within them, Tokema.

The grounds were really quite breathtaking. There was a large yellow brick building with matching yellow brick leading the way up the path. It reminded Doris slightly of the Wizard of Oz. *Follow the yellow brick road, follow the yellow brick road, follow, follow, follow, follow the yellow brick road. Follow the rainbow over the stream, Follow the fellow who follows a dream, follow, follow, follow, follow, follow, the yellow brick road. We're off to see the doctor, the doctor of the Tokema home!*

In the center of the path was a fountain. The fountain was three tiers high and spirted sparkling water in the light. The grass was cut neat and clean and there were large rows of bushes that lined the outside of the building. The bushes had lost their flowers, but Doris could tell that in the summertime they would turn into beautiful rose shrubs. The main building had two large balconies and a wraparound porch. There were no chairs for someone to sit outside and the balconies only hit the second and third floors. From what Doris could only guess she assumed there were to be 5 or 6 floors. She counted the windows up. Doris could see more buildings behind the main ones as it stretched far out of either side of the property and seemed to make half a moon. Almost creating outstretched arms for an unwanted welcome around those who entered. A welcome, which Doris feared, would snuff her out.

The car pulled to the front of the main building. The two men who drove Doris walked on either side of her, marching her up the yellow brick road. It seemed to match perfectly with the fall leaves that danced their way around Doris's feet. She longed to stay outside, to walk amongst the trees and the woods. Even if she was being forced to spend her days out here, let her spend them outside. Anything would be better than crossing through those doors. Doris held her breath as they approached closer and closer. It was a double-door entrance, with white crisp paint on the wood. The doors would be rather handsome to make a grand entrance through.

Ah yes, throw those doors open wide boys. Here comes the new queen of the nut house! Doris Draker in the flesh! Run for your lives everybody, this party is about to get started!

The two drivers escorted her up the stairs. Waiting by the door were two men who Doris assumed were facility workers, each took a handle and opened the doors for her—holding them wide open for the small group to walk through only to follow swiftly behind the three as they entered. The room in which the five of them now walked was rather bright. It hurt when first entering, it was the kind of strain on the eyes that lingered for a bit, even after adjusting. The kind of light that took you back for only a moment. Everything in the room was white brick, there was a desk and a glass screen about halfway in the room. Behind the glass were two doors, one on the right, and one on the left. Directly in the center of them was a swivel chair in which a small woman sat. She looked up as soon as the party had entered.

She had a thin, heart-shaped face, bright red lipstick, and chestnut brown curled hair.

"Well, hiya boys!" she smiled as they walked in.

"Morning Angela, we have someone here for you," said one of the drivers pushing Doris forward. Angela's smile faded with the sudden realization of whom she was looking at.

"Oh yes… We heard you were being sent over to our facility. We will need to wash you down, change you, get fingerprints, blood sample -"

"Why a blood sample?" Doris interjected.

"Because that's protocol!" Angela snapped, "We will show you to your room and explain the rules once we have all that we need. Thank you, boys," Angela motioned for the two drivers to leave, and for the two workers to follow her. "First, wash down. Follow me" Angela stood and held open a door for Doris and the two men to walk into. Passing her desk Doris could see Angela and some man standing side by side smiling by a lake. It seemed to be sunset.

"Is that your husband?" Doris asked, motioning with her whole body over to the picture. Angela turned and slammed the photo down.

"It's rude to snoop," she said, turning with her nose in the air, "I can tell you that won't last long here." Angela walked through the doors first, followed by one of the men, the one with yellow hair, Doris, and the brown-haired man pulling up the rear. They entered a long hallway with doors on either side. None of the rooms were labeled and Doris wondered to herself how anyone knew where anything was.

Surprisingly there was no sound. The hallway in which they walked was eerily quiet and possessed only the noise of Angela's clicking heels. "Through here," Angela swung open one of the doors that opened into a large showering vicinity.

⸺◦/◦/◦⸺

Doris loved coming to the YMCA at night. She always loved to swim to end her evenings, and even better no one seemed to come as late as her so she could shower in peace. She turned on the hot water and stepped into the small cubicle-like shower, pulling the thin, white plastic sheet behind her. She hummed as she rinsed her hair and squirted shampoo into her palms. It was then that she heard a slight click. At first it could have easily been mistaken for someone opening the door. Doris froze, straining her ears to hear the sound once more. There it was again, a slight click. Only this time it sounded as if someone's bare feet were smacking against the tile floor. It was this second click that caused her mind to open, that brought on the painful realization of who was in the changing room with her. The patter of the claw-like feet against the tile floor began to grow louder and louder.

"Go away!" She shouted. "Get out of here!" She could hear the slight thumping of the bare feet coming closer, pitter, patter, pitter, patter. Until they stopped directly in front of the curtain. She could see the shadowed blurred figure as it stood directly in front of her on the other side of the curtain. Even without fully seeing the figure she knew. "No, no, please, no" Doris cried and shrunk down onto the shower floor as if hoping to become small enough to disappear down the drain.

"Doris, Doris, time to have some fun!" She heard the voice say from behind the curtain as his fingers slowly wrapped around the white plastic, pulling it back to reveal the man-like creature with his ashed skin smile. His lips split, curled, and twisted around his gums, and his eyes were nothing more than bloodshot pinpricks. "Doris" he cooed and stepped closer, into the shower. She could see his sharpened teeth rise forward and out of his mouth. The water turned to steam as it dripped down to his shoulders. It seemed to roll off in a way that a small fog encased around him.

"Go away!" Doris shrieked as she hurled a bar of soap at the man. But this did nothing to him. Not only did it not faze him, but it didn't even leave a mark. The soap simply went through, landing loudly and slipping across the floor and into another stall. The monster began to laugh. And as he laughed, he opened his mouth wide, his jaw began to click and crack, distorting out of place, allowing his jaws to grow, Doris could see the rows of his sharp, shark-like teeth, and could even see all the way down into what appeared to be his stomach. Deep red, a putrid smell rolled out from within him, across his tongue, and into the air. But despite all this, the worst part was the darkness that seemed to fester inside him. A black hole of oblivion seemed to creep closer and closer the larger his mouth became. Doris shrieked again and tried this time to run between the demon's legs.

As she lunged forward, he grasped her. Holding on so tightly to one of her ankles she could almost feel it break.

"Please, please stop!" She whined in her last attempts before what happened next. And oh, how she knew all too well what was about to happen next. Doris' fingers clawed their way across the tile, hoping to catch hold of anything at all before he drew her in.

The man hoisted her up into the air, as if she was nothing, and dangled her in front of his mouth. His limbs seemed to grow, cracking and popping as they extended out of their original resting place. Then he forced her down. First her head, then, her flailing arms, her pulsating stomach, and lastly slurping down her kicking legs.

"There," he said, "don't we look fine?" The man with ashed skin turned to face the mirror at the end of the hall. There, standing in the reflection was Doris. Bare, naked, and slightly deformed-looking Doris. Her eyes were a milky pink with pinpricks for pupils, her stomach extended and bloated, her arms hung lazily, her jaw open and dislodged hung from the side of her mouth, and her skin, lumpy, wet, so very much like a sock on a puppeteer's hand. Ill-fitting, and knowing something more laid underneath.

⸺◈◈◈⸺

"Doris! Doris!" Angela cried, "Snap out of it!" Doris turned around, she had not realized they took her arms out of the jacket and stripped her naked.

"What…what happened?"

"Get in the stall! It's time for a wash down." Doris stumbled her way into the stall. She had not taken an actual shower since her encounter that day with the demon. She had stuck strictly to baths and that seemed to do the trick in avoiding him there. Doris stood dumbfounded in the shower. There was no handle or nozzle from her to turn to rinse down with.

"Where do I-" Before she could finish, she was being hosed down like a dirty dog that was too stinky and filthy to be allowed the decency of the family bathroom. The water pounded against her skin with such force that she could tell it would bruise. After about 5 minutes the pounding stopped, and a bar of soap was chucked at her.

"Scrub yourself down." Angela barked. Doris took the bar in her hand and began to make little suds, working their way from her face, down to her chest, buttocks, and legs. Once she had finished and was covered in tiny bubbles Angela began the hose again. It went on like this for some time, hosing down, getting lice shampoo thrown at her, hosing down, lice conditioner, hosing down, etc. Once Doris was deemed clean enough for the asylum's standards, she was given a faded gray towel to dry herself off with. It felt like sandpaper rubbing across her skin and even brought about red marks where she had brushed it up and down her body. Then Doris was given a gown and some socks with rubber soles on the bottom, so she would not slip.

"Next are prints," Angela sneered, "Hold out your arms" She began to pull the straight jacket up.

"No, no, please. I'll be good" Doris begged. Her shoulders ached at the thought of placing them back in.

"We keep you in the jacket until you're given your first round of meds. Now arms up!" Doris slowly raised her arms. *Perhaps if I can cooperate, they will see me as not a threat, and maybe they will reconsider their sentence and get me some real help.* Doris thought to herself.

Fat chance Doris… The voice crooned; *you'll be stuck in here, forever. We all know it. You know it deep down. Or, perhaps, not so deep.* The jacket was tighter than before. It irritated her exposed back and the buckles seemed to dig into her arm, despite being on the outside of the garment. Doris twitched and fidgeted her way down the hallway and into the next room. Angela led the way and the two men, one each at Doris's side.

Once the four of them entered the fingerprinting room they were greeted by a man behind a desk. Doris immediately recognized him as the man from the photograph in Angela's office.

"Hey, Eddie!" Angela sang, "Here she is, in the flesh!" Angela motioned around to Doris. Showing her off like a child would with a new toy. Eddie was a short man. Shorter than the picture led on anyway. He had black hair that was slicked back like one of those greaser boys. His eyes were a siren blue and made Doris feel like he was looking inside her when he looked up from his magazine.

"Angel-a! Good to see your doll." Eddie seemed to ignore the 'Here she is, in the flesh!' And just focused on Angela. His eyes glittered and gleamed at her like she was the only girl he had ever seen in his life. "Who's-..." Eddie's voice faded when he actually looked to the right at Angela where Doris stood. Doris knew then that while his eyes seemed to look inside of her, they failed him with false perceptions. Eddie did not continue his sentence but instead stood slowly from his desk and roughly grabbed at Doris, forcefully ripping off her jacket. She could see in Eddie's face that he got a sick pleasure from causing her pain, and it took almost everything she had to not give in to that satisfaction by crying out.

Once Doris was relieved of her jacket Eddie yanked her over to the back of the room where there was black ink, a small leather book, and a pen. If Doris did not willingly follow, Eddie's force would surely have pulled her arms straight from its socket, and she had the feeling that no one would bother to pop it back in. Not even the doctors she was soon to meet.

Eddie pried open Doris's fingers one by one, shoving them into black ink and rolling them down onto the paper. Once he finished with both hands he labeled them, "Doris Draker - left" and "Doris Draker - right". Doris's fingers were covered with black ink that made them stick together and made a small *pith-like* sound and she tapped them. Next, Eddie handed her a small damp cloth to wipe her fingers with, then slipped her back into her straight jacket.

It went on like this from room to room. Angela would greet whichever person they saw next, they would realize who Doris was, and make sure whatever was being done to her was as painful as possible. When collecting blood, the nurse purposely missed the vein each time, and even dug the needle around a little. Doris however held her tongue through each encounter. She never said a word, a sound, or even a twitch to indicate how she was feeling. She could not give in to them like that. She would not allow them the pleasure of seeing her suffer. She had been through enough suffering, in the past few months alone, to last an eternity.

The final few stops for Doris were meeting her doctors. First, she met Dr. Freude who would be her primary care physician and her gynecologist. Despite Dr. Freude 's name, he was the opposite. He was a cold, thin man, with short black hair that clung to the side of his face. When Dr. Freude saw Doris he said, "Vhat do vee have here? Small blume, ripe vor zee pluckings?" Next, was Dr. Tablani who was to be her dentist. Upon meeting him Doris could feel her skin crawl. He was short, large in the middle, and very wrinkled. He eyed Doris as if she was a new plaything for him. Slowly starting from her head and working his way down. He smiled at her with a wide, yellow tooth grin and remarked, "I was hoping I'd be your doctor" as she turned and left.

Lastly, Doris met Dr. Vernirelli, her therapist. Dr. Vernirelli was a tall man, old in age, around the late 70's or early 80's she would guess. He had powdered white hair, a big toothy smile, and a large hook nose. Despite his demeanor, Doris felt safe and relieved around him. Although she was only with him for brief introductions, she did not want to leave his side. She would be having sessions with him every Monday, Wednesday, and Friday for 2 hours. While most patients only received an hour, Doris was determined to be a "special case." These would soon become the days she looked forward to most.

—————

Doris was taken to the 3rd building on the left from the main center. It was slightly behind all the other buildings and was known to keep specific, "exceptional" cases. Although, those were not the only cases in the building. It ranged from slightly looney all the way to whack jobs. While Doris was considered to be dangerous, she was also considered to have a most fascinating mind. While doctor Vernirelli was her main psychiatrist there were plenty who wanted a chance at a sneak peek into her thoughts. The very idea was enthralling upon itself. There had been various students, doctors, and specialists who wanted a chance of cracking her open, and while Dr. Freude and Dr. Talabi did not mind others gawking at their sessions, Dr. Vernirelli would have no such thing.

The building in which she resided was one that was lined with filth. Doris had always been a relatively clean person, up until now. Cleaning every day, keeping her food in Tupperware, and covering her furniture with plastic so it would not stain. But here, the common room had human feces in the corner, people whipped their boogers and spit along the walls, and there would be random clumps of hair, which Doris believed the truly troubled individuals would rip out his or her own head, leaving behind (in some cases) chunks of skin.

Doris's room was where she found her sanctuary in this revolting and contaminated hole. Luckily for her, she was not given a roommate, her walls were lined with padding, and she had a small bed and scratchy sheets. While the conditions were by no means luxury, they were the best option provided. True, the walls and floors were nowhere close to her standards of cleanliness, but no feces or fluids were decorating her walls. She was not allowed anything more in her room for fear of manipulating it into some kind of weapon. She was not even given the simple pleasure of a pillow or a haircut. Scissors were considered to be extremely dangerous, even in the hands of a professional. During her time in jail, sitting trial, and being here Doris's hair had grown remarkably fast. She wished she could pull it back into a tight braid, similar to the one her mother used to make her wear as a child. Anything would be better than the stringy, tangled mess that continued to make its way into her eyes. She would attempt to braid it, but without a tie, the braid would often unravel and make its way to the arch of her back again.

"Real ladies always maintain order, and that includes a proper hairstyle." Her mother would say as she stretched and pulled at Doris's scalp. She always hated the feeling of her hair on her neck and had kept it short until now. "You look like a boy," her mother snapped the first time she came home from college. With the newfound freedom of college and being away from her parents she was set off into the wild to make her own decisions. And this included how she wanted her hair to be.

Doris would often reflect on the days with her mother while she was forced to sit in the common room. She would think of how her mother would yell at her, for not being thrown in the nuthouse, but for how her posture slouched. Or, how she would slurp her soup during lunch instead of sipping. The soup was never served hot here anyway. It was always cold, for the nurses feared someone might have a fit and throw hot soup on themselves or someone else. Apparently, this happened once or twice before.

The common room smelled and would often make Doris become sick. Instead of blaming her sickness on the rotting fecal matter in the corner, the nurses on watch would simply say it was a side effect of her medication. Which it could have been as well. But as to how the nurses did not gag themselves was something Doris could not comprehend. Were they so numbed to the filth around them that it hardly seemed to matter? Were they so desensitized to the fact that the conditions they were in, were not only dangerous for the patients but also themselves? If they did not care to even that capacity obviously no one else would.

Doris stared down at the little red, yellow, and blue pills she was obligated to take once a day at lunch with her cold, room-temperature soup. She was not sure what they gave her, and when she asked, she was greeted with a slap across the face from Dr. Freude, "Vee do not ask such sings. Noisy Madchen" and with that Doris did not bring the matter to light again. The pills to her almost looked like candy.

Time for your candy! She would think, *Come on, it's not so bad. You like candy. This one is cherry, that one is lemon, and this one is blueberry.* Popping pills one by one. It would be about 20 minutes before she could really feel anything. But every day, without fail, when 1:00 o'clock rolled around it would slowly begin to drip from the face of the clock, and the ticking hand sound appeared too slow making a *tiiiccccckkkkk* sound… *Hickory Dickory Dock. The mouse went up the clock. The clock struck one. The mouse went down. Hickory Dickory Dock. Tick tock, tick tock, tick tock, tick tock…*

※※※

"So, tell me, Doris, how is your day going so far?" asked Doctor Vernirelli. He sat in a cream-colored chair, which matched the couch on which Doris was laying. His office was painted lime green and while to some that might cause a headache, she found it comforting. Just like she found him to be. The lighting in his office was low, just how she liked it. Every other room in the vicinity was too bright for her with its white walls, bare with the exceptions of the stains smeared across, and painful fluorescent lights. The room even has a potted plant, which was quite a delight for Doris to see. Pots were considered to be a weapon here, but Doctor Vernirelli told her he insisted on having them because it brought him peace to see a living thing each and every day while at work. When he mentioned this to Doris, it had taken her by surprise,

"But you see people every day?" she remarked.

"Well, yes that is true, and while technically the people I interact with are alive, they are not living." This is what Doris liked about him. He was not afraid to not bullshit her. He did not tiptoe around the fact that Tokema was not a place for people to get better, not really anyway. He, just like Doris, and everyone else for that matter, knew this place was to lock up those who were so far down Alice's rabbit hole that they would never be able to climb out. *We're all mad here.* And even if by miracle one person did make it out, what then?

They would still be trapped in the never-ending tea party of the Mad Hatter and the Hare. He knew just as well as anyone else that people sent to Tokema were not truly living lives. They were mere husks of their former selves. Hollowed out in attempts to make them as bearable as possible to those who were considered to be, "normal". And for this reason, he had gained her respect.

"I am feeling fine today. The clock dripped again."

"Yes, it tends to do that."

"I don't like the medicine I am on… I no longer like the taste of cherry, lemon, and blueberry."

"I was not aware the pills had flavors," Dr. Vernirelli said, chuckling a little.

"Oh, they don't. But that is what I think of them as. Makes them easier to swallow."

"Yes, telling little lies to ourselves does make things easier to swallow." he remarked, "Have you had any more visions since arriving here, like that one in the shower on your first day?"

"No. But I hear him. Not all the time. But he is very witty and likes to make remarks and references."

"I see. Would you like to talk about that?"

"Isn't that why I'm here?" Doris glared, "You know me Doc. I will be an open book with you because I am *not* crazy! I told you that on the first day, you met me."

"I know that, Doris. And while you do not seem to have any issue in talking about this demon-like man with ashed-colored skin, you do, however, rarely talk about the things he forced you into doing. We talked about your memory, yes, but we did not talk about what happens next."

"I don't like remembering it," she stated as she rolled on her side, away from his gaze.

"These sessions are for you Doris. You can direct them anyway you'd like."

"Okay then..." she exhaled, turning back, "I have some complaints about this place."

"By all means," he motioned for her to continue.

"I don't like cold soup every day. They say that it is an issue of safety, but I think they enjoy robbing us of small pleasures. They don't clean the common room and I have to smell literal shit every day. I don't like that I have to sleep with a light one, and I hate that I am forced to take stupid cherry, lemon, and blueberry pills every gott damn day!" Doris was almost shouting now. Her chest heaved up and down. Doctor Vernirelli smiled from behind his notes,

"Let me see what I can do about that. I was not aware of the 'literal shit' smell. Although, the medication I can't control. But perhaps I can prescribe some of my own."

"Oh yeah. It's not here in the fancy front buildings that they show off to the crowds in the papers, but have you ever made your way to my building? It's all over in that place. People pull it from their pants and wipe it on the walls like it's no big deal."

The doctor held his hands to his nose. As if he could smell what she was talking about here in his office. He sighed and shook his head, "Now that is a real issue. I don't normally visit the buildings my patients are in."

"Well, if you care to take a gander, be my guest."

"I trust what you have to tell me, Doris."

"Also, I don't want more medications, I want less."

"Trust me, you'll like this one."

—⟨ø/ø/ø⟩—

The next day in the common room Doris looked around. She did not feel sick today. In fact, there was something almost sweet in the air. She looked around and saw sitting on the nurses desk a bottle of air freshener. It smelled like laundry. She turned to the corner in which she often avoided and saw there was no more poop or pee piled up. Instead, there was a group of patients scrubbing away at the walls and floors. And when it was time for lunch, she was not met with a cold bowl of soup, but instead a turkey sandwich on rye with extra mayo, her favorite. Although the sandwich itself was nothing to write home about, she found it to be a great improvement. And placed down next to her sandwich were her pills, cherry, lemon, blueberry, and today a lime was added.

Doris plucked the little green pill from the cup and stared at it. *What is this?* She thought. Then Dr. Vernirelli's words came back to her, "Trust me, you'll like this one." She popped the "candies" into her mouth all at once and followed them with water. *One pill makes your larger and one pill makes you small. And the ones that mother gives you, don't do anything at all...* Doris hummed to herself.

She lazily went about her business looking out the window and onto the forest leaves as they continued changing color and becoming barer. She enjoyed looking outside. She would occasionally see a small squirrel or bird about and wished she was able to join them. She sat this way for a long time before turning back to the face of the clock. The time was 1:13 and the face had not melted away. She jumped to her feet and instead of feeling slow, like walking through sticky Jello she felt light on her feet. Like she could dance.

...I need you so that I could die, I love you so and that is why, whenever I want you, all I have to do is dream, dream, dream, dream, dream... All I have to it is a dream by the Everly Brothers played softly on the vinyl. Doris closed her eyes and listened to the music. She never realized before that music came on in the common room after lunch. Several people got up to dance, and some patients even held each other close.

"D-does music always play after lunch?" Doris asked the woman sitting next to her. The woman smiled, shook her head, and said,

"Always, you've never noticed?"

"No, I guess not." Doris closed her eyes again and listened.

———◦⟨❀⟩◦———

"You know they played music in the common room?" Doris smiled at Dr. Vernirelli.

"Why yes, sometimes I can hear it when I go for strolls outside."

"I noticed it for the first time yesterday. Also, the clock did not melt. I think it might have had something to do with the little green pill you gave me. That's lime by the way." The doctor smiled.

"Yes, I thought you would like it." he nodded.

"I also got a sandwich yesterday. And today I was given warm soup! Not hot, but still, enough where I needed to let it cool a little first. And the lights were dimmed by a significant amount in my room when it was bedtime. Thank you."

"The pleasure is all mine, Doris. We sometimes forget that our patients are human and need a little humane enjoyment. Of course, I could not make all the requests happen, but hopefully they were enough." He smiled.

"More than enough. At least you care about us enough to try and make a compromise."

"Compromises are indeed something that goes on a lot here, not always involving our patients." Doris traced her fingers along the lining of the couch.

"Do you think we could have a session outside today? Before the weather gets too cold?" Doris asked. She thought back on the squirrels and chipmunks she had seen outside and could feel the sun shining on her skin. Being outside was hardly ever in the cards for Doris. Not really anyway. She did have to walk to and from her building to get to the doctors' offices, which were in the main center. But she was always in a straitjacket, and always was escorted by a guard and one of the nurses.

Dr. Vernirelli glanced at the clock on the side of the wall, 3:15. He scratched his chin and clicked a red button on the side of his desk.

"Oh no, no, please. I didn't mean to upset you" Doris begged. She knew the button called the guards in. It had been a button only used on her once, by Dr. Freude, when she refused to let him see "vat's happening" between her legs. Yes, he was the gynecologist here, but she always knew he looked at her with more than just medical needs in mind. The guard that day had beaten Doris until she submitted. Leaving her with a bruised eye and a busted lip. A man in a gray uniform and a nightstick quickly entered the room,

"What's the issue?" he said, eyeing Doris.

"There is no issue," Dr. Vernirelli replied, "We are going to be having our session outside today. Such a lovely day for a walk don't you think?" The guard nodded,

"Let me get her straitjacket" and he turned to leave the room when Dr. Vernirelli caught him,

"No, I do not think that will be necessary. But you can follow us from a distance with the on-call nurse to make sure everything is going alright." the doctor winked at Doris. The guard opened his mouth to protest but Dr. Vernirelli jumped in, "And I believe the on-call nurse is Camillia, yes? Such a lovely girl to know." Doris had seen the way the guard had previously eyed Camillia. She had never seen him talk to her, but she did see him attempt to make an introduction several times before becoming too shy, changing his mind, and slinking back to the corner in which he stood.

Watching the staff interact at Tokema had been one of Doris's ways of entertaining herself. It was like its very own soap opera. While Doris never really found herself watching such things at her real home, she did find them to be one of the best ways to pass time here. She learned that Angela was Eddie's fiancé, although she suspected she had been cheating on him with one of the male nurses, Dan. Doris had seen Angela sneak back to building 3 several times, and go into the nursing station, shortly to always be followed by Dan. When the two of them left the room, they always left separately, and one time Doris noticed that Angela's blouse had missed a few buttons, and her lipstick was smeared.

Doris missed that most of all, the thrill of meeting someone new, that first kiss. That first time making love to a stranger, only with a similar interest in unattached sex. She had not been promiscuous by any means, but she did enjoy a random stranger now and then. Doris had never married, and therefore could not fantasize about a husband to come home to. She was, after all, only in her late 30s. Yes, unusual for a woman of her age to still be single, but she did not care. She was not sure if she even wanted to get married, however, with being here it was pretty much set in stone that she would never marry.

The air was crisper out than Doris initially thought, but it still felt nice. She lifted her arms and let the air flow below them, the breeze running its way across her body felt almost nostalgic. Again, something as simple as a breeze was missed.

"How are you liking it out here?" Dr. Vernirelli asked.

"It's lovely, thank you" she nodded. He nodded in return.

"A bit nippy for my taste, but these old bones could use the air every now and then." he chortled. Doris gave a small smile in return.

"Fall is my favorite season, you know Doc. It's cool, everything is changing, and it always means Halloween is right around the corner."

"Are you a fan of Halloween?" he asked, making a note in the small pad to be brought along with him.

"Oh yes. When I was little, I loved to dress up. I was 12 when the Wizard of Oz came out. That witch was the scariest thing I had ever seen..."

Doris looked at herself in her mirror in her bedroom. Her hair was pulled back into one long braid that hung directly behind her back, brushing just above her buttocks and she was smearing green paint across her face. She had on a long black dress and could not wait to show her mother her costume. She had been working on it all month.

"Doris, come downstairs! The neighbor kids are here for trick-or-treating!"

"Coming mother!" Doris yelled down. She was almost finished with her makeup, and just needed a few final touches. As Doris wrapped up with the green paint, she grabbed the black hat she had made. She put it on and smiled at herself in the mirror. She looked just like the Wicked Witch of the West. Doris gave a cackle, imitating the laugh as best she could, "Fly monkey's fly!" she laughed.

"Doris!" her mother shouted again. Doris grabbed for her broom and headed down the stairs. Her mother stood at the bottom, when she saw Doris's face she gasped, "Doris! What did you do?"

"I'm the Wicked Witch from the Wizard of Oz."

"I see..." her mother shook her head, "When you said you wanted to be someone from the Wizard of Oz, I thought you meant Dorothy. Not, this Satan worshiper."

"It's Halloween. I wanted to be someone scary." Her mother stared at her, eyes narrowing.

"Holly, Hannah, go on without Doris, she needs to change her costume."

"No mother please!" Doris cried, "I worked so hard on my dress and hat, please let me go with them."

"Why don't you wear that nice clown costume from last year? It will be a little small, but everyone loves a clown" her mother smiled. Holly peaked her head from around the corner.

"Wow, Doris, you look so scary!" Holly smiled. Holly was dressed as a cowgirl. She had a small silver pistol around her hip and a hat that hung from a string on her back. Hannah, Holly's sister, popped her head around too. She was dressed as an Indian, with feathers in her hair and red makeup smeared across her face.

"See, Doris, Holly and Hannah have such nice costumes. Why can't you change into something like that?" Doris's mother motioned.

"Mother. I want to do something scary this year." Doris stepped closer to Holly and Hannah. "What do you girls think?"

"We think you look great, don't we Hannah?" Holly said, looking at her sister.

"Very grand!" Hannah agreed, "We loved seeing that movie, and you look just like her Doris." Doris smiled up at her mother.

"Please?" she clasped her hands together. Her mother rolled her eyes.

"Oh alright. But if I hear one word about this from the gals at church saying how inappropriate that outfit is I'll be sure to-"

"Thank you, mother!" Doris jumped up and down, clapping her hands together.

"-burn it" her mother finished.

"And how was that Halloween for you?" Dr. Vernirelli asked.

"We three had a great time. That was my last one. My mother claimed it was because I was getting too old, which I am sure is partially true. But I think it was because of that outfit I fashioned" Doris laughed.

"This is amusing?" the doctor asked, raising an eyebrow.

"A little," Doris replied, "I love my mother very much. But she was always concerned with what the church girls thought. Bunch of hens, clucking with their gossip. I'm sure they pecked her to death once people started catching on to the things, I was made to do..." Doris became quiet then. She looked at her hands and then quickly put them behind her back, as if not wanting to see them.

"What are your hands saying to you?" Dr. Vernirelli asked.

"What?"

"I said, what are your hands saying to you? You are looking at them like they are something shameful. So, what did they say to make you hide them?" Doris gulped, pulling her hands back to her front and staring down at them. She had long fingers she had at one point used to play the piano, and her nails were down the nubs. She was not allowed to keep her nails in this place, because they were considered to be "threatening."

"I don't know. I don't know if they are saying anything. But I don't like to look at them."

"Why not?" the doctor asked.

"I couldn't control them when the time mattered, and looking at them was always the first thing I did when I came back out. And cleaning them off was always the hardest part." She could feel her eyes welling up, and small round tears fell onto her palms.

"Come out of where? Blackouts?" the doctor asked, continuing to scribble on his small pad.

"No, come out of his mouth" Doris began to cry. Dr. Vernirelli stared at Doris for a second, taking in what she had to say. He slowly placed the notepad and pen into his breast pocket.

"I remember from your trial, I even showed up once. I had a feeling you might end up here and I wanted to see what I was potentially going to be working with. One time when you were called to stand, you claimed this man-like thing with the ashed skin would take over your body. But what do you mean, 'come out of his mouth?'" Doris let her silence grow, contemplating whether or not to continue down this path of conversation. While she was very willing to talk about the ashed-skin humanoid, she was not so sure if she wanted to talk about the crimes, he drove her to do.

Doris stuttered and stammered through what she said next, whispering even, "When… when he comes. I can hear him. I hear the click of the pads of his feet. And nothing, from what I can tell triggers him. He just comes when he feels like it. But he will grab me and force me down his throat. He eats me. He eats my soul and presses me into becoming a part of him. But no one sees this. It's never happened in front of a person before, but he does it when he knows I am going to be around people. I know… I know how it sounds. You are not the first person I have mentioned this to."

"Who else have you told?" the doctor asked.

"I've seen therapists before you. I've gone to confession."

"And what do they say?"

"Nothing. Nothing helpful anyway. They think I am crazy. Of course, I could never mention the murderers. That was kept a secret. But I say I thought I was possessed at times. I wasn't even able to say that for a long time. But of course, they thought the possessions were nonsense. Just like how I am sure you think too." Dr. Vernirelli smiled at this statement,

"Doris, I do not think you're crazy. In fact, I'll tell you a secret, I don't think most people here are. I think a majority of you are very misunderstood creatures, and it is my job to try and understand you, when society fails to see." This had not been what Doris expected to hear. She knew from the start that there was something rather unique about Dr. Vernirelli, and it was this something that drew her into liking and trusting him in the first place.

Maybe I should open up more? Doris thought to herself; then she felt it. That chill that strikes you so strong and intensely, that it makes you cold all the way down into your bones. The numbing feeling in which there was no relief of heat unless held under hot water like a lobster being thrown into a pot. Doris's heart started to pound. Thumping against her ribs, making her whole body seem to shake in response.

Doris... he said, *Doris...*

Doris looked frantically around; she could hear him but not see him. She turned to the edge of the woods and there she found what she had been searching for. There stood the ashed skinned man. He was not in his demon form, yet he looked sickening and dangerous. He hid amongst the trees, just barely visible, more of a shadow than a man.

"Doris, Doris what's the matter?" the doctor exclaimed, reaching out for her arm, but Doris pulled away.

Don't open up Doris. Not just yet. Think about it. Or maybe we'll have another incident.

"No," Doris murmured.

"Doris what's wrong?" Vernirelli yelled, this time shaking her arm as if trying to wake her from a trance. The man with ashed skin smiled at her, his eyes began to narrow into slits, and he held long, pale, crooked fingers to his lips. Then he was gone. As if never even there. Doris shuttered and turned to the doctor. She saw the guard approaching, reaching for the stick that rested on his hip.

"N-nothing. I'm fine. I want to go back inside. It's too cold." Doris turned away from the trees and began walking to the building. The air no longer felt nice on her skin. It stung and made her feel heavy. It was hard to keep her head up as she trucked on. Her feet felt like they were stuck in the mud, and with every step she took she could feel herself sinking a little further into the ground. The doctor walked beside her, keeping pace with her slow steps.

Once they were back inside his office, Dr. Vernirelli closed the door. "I know our session ends in a few minutes" Vernirelli said, slowly turning back to Doris, "And, I know something happened to you outside. We do not need to discuss it. Again, you are in control of these sessions, and you do not need to share more than you wish. I just want to remind and encourage you that the more we are open and honest with each other, the more progress we will make." He smiled at her and patted her shoulder.

I wish I could be open and honest. I really do. But I am afraid. Doris thought as she hung her head.

※※※

Dr. Vernirelli sat in his office. He glanced at the notes from which he took when he and Doris went out walking this afternoon. On the 5th page, underlined was the word, "trees". When Doris went into her trance, he could see she was transfixed on them. Perhaps it would be a wise thing to take Doris outside again for her next session. Maybe subtly steering her towards the trees that lined the facility. There seemed to be something amongst these oaks, pine, and beech that Doris found to be rather interesting or more so, unsettling.

He noted too that during several of their meetings she mentioned trees before. She talked about sitting in the common room and watching the trees. Perhaps there was something out there that soothed her amongst them? Or, another likely conclusion, something that scared her. Either way, Dr. Vernirelli was determined to see which it was. He looked at the clock on his wall, 12:34.

Shoot, another late night.

He stacked his notes together and walked over to the cabinet that was behind his desk, he pulled open A-D, and in the very back of the drawer rested his notes under, "Draker, D." There had not been as many notes as the rest of his patients. Yes, Doris was the newest still, but also, she was the toughest nut for him to crack. He was used to having his patients open up to him rather quickly. And while she did in some aspects, she also kept others close to her chest.

When he was young and a new up-and-coming doctor there was no issue at all. He had been an attractive young man and all the female patients especially liked to open up to him. There were several, in fact, who even tried to seduce him. And if he swung that way perhaps, he would have given in to one or two. He is, after all, human. But luckily for him, God did not tempt him with a woman's touch. And the young men at the time never even tried to make a pass. When they did now, of course, it was always in secret.

As Dr. Vernirelli wrapped up in his office he heard the drifting sound of music. A rather unusual event for this time of night. ... *I need you so that I could die, I love you so and that is why, whenever I want you, all I have to do is dream, dream, dream, dream, dream, dream, dream, dream.* He wandered into the hall but could see nothing there. The corridor was not as bright as it was during the day. Only a few lights every 10 or so feet were on. Just when one light seemed to fade, at the edge of its beam, another one took its place.

"Hello?" he called out. There was no response. "Hello?" he called again and still nothing. He grabbed his briefcase, turned and locked the door, and headed down the hall. *Dream, dream, dream...*

the melody played on, getting slightly louder with every few steps he took until he heard it rather loudly in the main entrance. Dr. Vernirelli pushed the doors open wide and stood in the circle room. There was no sound. Not even the sound of wind from outside. He looked around and then popped his head back into the hall. *Perhaps the music was coming from another room?* But again, he was met with silence. During his 60 years here at Tokema he had indeed encountered a few strange instances like this. They were few and far in between, but not unheard of. They usually took place when something was about to happen.

⸻ σ/σ/σ ⸻

Doris looked out amongst the large courtyard. She was outside where she and Dr. Vernirelli had been earlier that day. The trees were now completely bare, and she noticed she was in her bare feet. She looked about but could see no one, *am I alone?* Doris thought. "Hello?" she called out. No one answered. She walked out a little further, this time approaching the fountain. "Hello?" she called again, a little louder.

"Doris," a man said, "Doris hurry. I must show you something" She looked towards the direction in which she heard the voice, by the tree line. "Doris, please!" The man called out again. She slowly approached,

"Who are you?" she yelled. But there was no answer. She continued to walk forward and suddenly found herself to be in a small circular clearing amongst the trees. *How did I get-?*

"Doris!" the man yelled, "Doris, please" She turned and saw a man slightly taller than her amongst the trees. He was dirty, his hair was long, and what were the remains of a ripped and burned shirt clung loosely to his chest, covered in burnt holes that still seemed to still glow. But much more than this his skin was completely charred, head to toe. Doris held her breath, fighting the urge to scream and run.

"Who are you?" Doris managed to croak, sounding braver than she felt. The man held out his arms as if to hug her and then began to scream. Doris flinched back, covering her ears to block-out the awful sound. She swore she could hear crackling amongst his cries. The man continued to shriek in pain, still extending his arms toward her. He bunched his hands into fists and seemed to be thrusting into the air. His eyes rolled back into his head and his body shook. Then, just as quickly as it started, he stopped.

Doris gently began to lower her hands, still afraid to let them fall entirely in case he began his tortured howling again. His back slowly un-arched itself making him stand erect. As if he were a soldier. She could hear his spine cracking as he did so. His arms fell to his side and his head upturned. He stood like this for some time. And then, he fell. He fell perfectly straight and smacked the ground, but instead of his body remaining there was a small plume of gray smoke and cinders. As if he had never been there at all. Doris could hear a distant sigh of relief and she screamed.

Doris screamed so loudly that it jolted her. She was back in her bed, covered in sweat. She clung to her sheets and looked around her small room. Her lights were dim, and she could see nothing out of the ordinary. Then she heard it, ... *Whenever I want you, all I have to do is dream, dream, dream, dream, dream, dream, dream, dream.* Doris got to her feet and slowly approached her door. There was a small window whose purpose was for the guards to glance into her room at any given time. Doris stood on her tiptoes and looked out. She could see nothing except for the clock in the hall, directly adjacent to her room, 12:34. She turned back towards her bed and slowly started to get under her sheets, and that is when she saw it. Her feet were caked with mud.

Doris began to panic. She quickly threw on her socks and walked to her door, "Hello?" she cried, "Hello, I need to use the bathroom!" She heard shuffling in the hall, she knew there was always a guard there to check in on the patients, and sometimes if they were nice enough, they would let the patients get a cup of water or use the bathroom at night.

A man appeared at the window, Doris had not recognized him and guessed he was a newer guard. Most new guards received a nightshift since it was the easiest time. He had red hair and a freckled face. He stared at Doris for a minute, scanning inside her room.

"Hold up your hands." he barked. Doris slowly raised her hands for the guard to see. "Alright," he said, pulling out his keys and unlocking the door. "Let me get your jacket." He reached over to the wall and grabbed her straitjacket. She obediently held out her arms for him to wrap her. Most guards did not bother wrapping patients when they needed to use the bathroom, but it was protocol for "unique" patients to be wrapped whenever transitioning from one place to another. And Doris was as unique as they came.

The guard slowly walked behind Doris as they neared the bathroom. Once they approached Doris turned back for him to unlock her.

"What? What do you want? Get in there!" He raised his voice and reached for his stick; Doris flinched.

"I...I can't do my business, with my jacket on," she whispered. The guard looked at her for a second, and then his face began to soften.

"Oh yeah, of course not" he placed his stick back in its holster and undid her bindings. Once she was free Doris turned and quickly ran into the stall. She tore her socks off and stuck her feet into the toilet. She would have used the sink, but the guard stood right outside, where he would have seen. She dunked her feet in the slime-covered toilet over and over again. Frantically rubbing at them with toilet paper. Once she deemed them to be clean enough, she flushed the stall and hurried over to the sink to scrub her hands.

The guard turned to her when she was finished, "Ready to go?" he asked. She nodded, allowed him to strap her back in, and the two of them walked back to Doris's room. Doris scanned the hallway as they walked. Looking at the ground to see if there were any signs of her footprints. She saw no traces of dirt and sighed with relief as they approached her door.

"Thank you," Doris said to the guard as he slipped her back out. She crawled back into bed. She lay there for a few minutes, straining her ears to hear more music. She heard nothing in the hallway when she went to the bathroom. She stayed very quiet, closing her eyes to see if that would help. But she heard nothing. Doris sighed and rolled onto her side. She thought about the man from her dream that she saw in the woods. She tried to think if she had seen him anywhere before, but nothing came to mind. Of course, she could not be sure, his skin was completely burned after all. She had not looked at him for more than a few minutes anyway. It was very unusual for Doris to have dreams in which she did not recognize the person. Sometimes it was someone she knew and was close to, or sometimes it was someone she had seen in passing, but she was certain that she had never seen this man before, despite his smoldering complexion.

As Doris lay there, slowly drifting off to sleep she thought about her mother, and what she might be doing on a night like this one. Her mother had not spoken to her since she had first been arrested, who could blame her? She had not bothered to visit her since she came to Tokema. She knew her mother was a religious woman, and most likely could not bother herself with a child of Satan.

The next morning Doris stared out the window in the common room, as she so often did. There was soft music playing on the record player and she swayed as it played on. Today's song was Walkin' After Midnight by Patsy Cline. Doris was rather fond of this song. She could never quite put her finger on it, but there was something calming, and yet unsettling in the lyrics. They seemed to touch her - *I stopped to see a weeping' willow'. Cryin' on his pillow. Maybe he's cryin' for me. And as the skies turn gloomy night winds whisper to me, I'm as lonesome as I can be. I go out walkin' after midnight.* Doris hummed along.

She thought back to the mud that was on her feet last night. She reflected on her dream. It seemed so real to her. The man, although she did not know him, felt connected to her somehow too. She felt as if this might be important information to share with Dr. Vernirelli at their session tomorrow. *Perhaps I should request to see the Doc every day. I'm sure he wouldn't mind.* Dr. Vernirelli really was the only person Doris could and did talk to. Yes, she talked to the guards and to the nurses. And there were a few interactions with Dr. Freude and Dr. Tablani, but nothing led to full conversations. And true, it was Dr. Vernirelli's job to have conversations with her, but she had the inkling that even if he was not her doctor, they would become friends.

Doris continued looking out onto the trees. She was curious to see if there really was a small clearing deep inside them, like in her dream. Perhaps she could go for a walk today. There was a group of patients who spent the majority of their time outside. These patients were left to tend to the property. They were able to sweep, mow the grass, and rake the leaves. In fact, there were numerous jobs distributed in the complex, but Doris was deemed to not be stable enough for any of these jobs, given that they all involved some kind of "weapon." And what Doris meant by weapon was a broom, shovel, kitchen knife, etc.

There had been several times when Doris asked for work to keep her busy, but she was even denied basic entertainment, besides TV and radio, and everyone got those. She was allowed, however, to try fingerpainting, given that the class was only paper and paints. She found this to be a little juvenile for her taste. But did not rule it out completely. She might go again if she was feeling more nostalgic.

There was a slight possibility that this time could be different, however. Maybe she could simply just ask to join the group outside. Although, the staff might say no depending on who was working.

Doris had only been in Tokema a few weeks, but she knew well enough by now which guards were more reasonable and which ones were not. Of course, none of that really mattered when it came to her. She was considered to be sick, twisted, disturbed, and lethal. Doris sat there for a minute closing her eyes and reflecting on whether or not to ask to go outside when she heard someone approach her.

"Hiya Doris. Aah'm Donnie " she looked to see another patient sitting next to her. He talked with a slow southern drawl. The other patients hardly spoke to her at all. In fact, most of them avoided her as best they could. Doris looked the man up and down. He appeared to be in his 50s or 60s, grayed, with short hair and stubble on his face. She was surprised to see the stubble and short hair. Only the patients between level 1 and level 6 were able to get haircuts and shaves. Doris was classified as a level 9. And due to the lack of scissors and razors in her life, her pits and legs had become a tangled mess. Yes, she was washed down, but the quick rinses and lack of hygiene products hardly helped at all. She could hardly stand the smell of herself.

There were 10 levels at the hospital. Levels 1-3 were usually the more submissive patients. Patients 4-6 were typically the ones who threw their feces, or fluids. While they were not considered to be dangerous, they were disgusting and a health violation. Patients 7-9 were considered to be dangerous to themselves and others. A majority of these patients were in for some kind of murder. And lastly, patients who were considered to be 10 were for reasons unknown to Doris. She simply just knew that there were levels 1-10, and she was considered to be a 9. Doris was not even sure there was a level 10 throughout the hospital.

"Hi" Doris warily said to the man sitting by her side. She looked at his hands and saw no signs of smudges or stains. He smiled at her, his teeth were relatively white, and he smelled like soap. *Clearly not a poop thrower.* Doris thought to herself. And the fact that he smelled like soap showed to Doris that he was given more bathroom privileges then she was.

"Ah'm a level 3," Donnie said, "Aah can see you lookin' mah up and down tryin' to figures it out. Aah checked mahself in after mah wife died."

"I'm sorry for your loss," Doris replied.

"Ah that's okey. She been sick for a while and it t'was her times to go." Doris nodded. She wondered why he had come over to talk with her.

"Donnie, can I ask why you're here?"

"Aah's told ya. Aah check mahself in."

"No, why are you here, here. Talking to me?" she asked.

"Oh… well, ya sees. It's a lil embarrassin'. Yous kind o' like a celebrity 'round here. Aah's wanted to know how yous could continya doing what ya done? I did my wife and that were all I could bare. Had ta check the ol' noggin' in afta that. But don' tell nobody ya hear? When I check in I says it was for thoughts not actions' ' Donnie leaned in close, as if he had just asked her for baking tips. Like he was her close neighbor and wanted to know how to get a grass stain out of a shirt.

'What?" Doris whispered, appalled, "How dare you!" She quickly stood up.

"Aah aint's tryin' to steals yer thunder. Aah's just gits to know. How you bear it for so long."

"Well for your information I did not kill anyone!" Doris shouted, "It was not me! It was the man, demon, thing! And if you want to continue doing what you are doing then please, take him from me. Take him!" Doris lunged forward at Donnie, knocking him over, "Take him!" she shouted over and over again as guards from all directions went running at her. The first guard to reach Doris tackled her off of Donnie and onto the ground. It was a guard named George. George was a bigger man but light on his feet. He always seemed to be one of the more reasonable guards, according to Doris.

"Couple hours in the reconditioning room ought to help you behave," George said as he hoisted her up. A nurse quickly ran over with a straitjacket to put Doris in and pulled out a syringe from her pocket.

"No!" Doris cried, "No, I'll be good! I'll walk on my own and not fight. Please don't stick me!" but the nurse ignored her pleas as she shot Doris right in the neck.

⸺◦/◦/◦⸺

Doris had not yet been thrown into the reconditioning room and was not sure what she expected to find in there. Her head felt heavy, and her knees were weak. The room was pitch black and she could feel something under her. She was not sure what it was, it felt soft and slightly comforting. Doris sat up as best she could for not having the use of her arms still. Then she heard a click,

"Hello?" Doris called out. The lights came on and Doris shielded her eyes as best she could.

"Hello, Doris. How are you feeling?" a woman asked. Doris opened her eyes and looked around the room. She was in a black and white striped room with an orange shag carpet. She was sitting on an orange and green couch and across from her, sitting in what appeared to be a matching orange and green director's chair was a woman. The woman was older, perhaps 60s or 70s, and had her hair fashioned into a beehive.

"Who are you?" Doris asked.

"I'm Dr. Tracy." The woman said. "I'm one of the therapists here at Tokema."

"I thought Doc Vernirelli was my therapist?" Doris asked, concerned she was taken away from his care.

"He still is. But there are many of us in the facility, all equally qualified." Dr. Tracy smiled. "Do you remember why you are here?"

"Yes," Doris began, "I was talking to a man named Donnie."

"And?" Dr. Tracy leaned in.

"And... I yelled at him" Doris added.

"Now, why were you yelling at him? You kept saying, 'Take him, take him' who did you want him to take?" Doris grew very silent.

"He... he asked me how I was able to kill so many people when he could only kill his wife. But I did not kill anyone! I was not in control of my body, and I was forced to do those things. If Donnie wants to kill people that's his business. So, he can take the demon that's attached himself to me. I don't want him" Doris answered. Dr. Tracy sat there, taking in all Doris had to say, writing down each word carefully.

"Well, Donnie checked himself in here, he did not murder anyone. Let's get that cleared up. What do you mean by 'attached himself' to you?" Dr. Tracy asked, "He is not an actual part of you?" She raised an eyebrow.

"Makes sense you'd think that..." Doris mumbled "No, he's not. I have discussed this with Dr. Vernirelli before. I'd feel more comfortable talking with him."

"Ah," Dr. Tracy nodded, "I can understand why you'd feel that way. Let me ask you this, Miss Draker, do you know why we call this room the 'reconditioning' room?"

"Because I need to be reconditioned?" Doris sneered. Dr. Tracy let out a laugh.

"I like you. I'm sure if you weren't in this place, you'd be a hoot. But I can see you're scared. I can see you're walking on eggshells." Dr. Tracy stood and slowly began to walk about the room. Eyeing Doris as she did so. "See, I've observed you a few times in the common room. In case I ever had the pleasure of meeting you here. And throughout my few observations I notice before you speak you usually pause and will take a minute to think about how you want to respond. Just now though you were quick about it." Dr. Tracy snapped her fingers, "Had a little bite! See, my job here is not like all the other psychologists, my job is unique in the sense that I get to take that bite and break it!" She curled her hands into fists and mimicked snapping a twig or stick.

Doris glared at her wearily, "And what about my, 'bite' are you going to break? I have followed all the rules asked of me. This was the only incident. It won't happen again." Doris said, slinking into the couch as best she could.

"Well, that lip for one thing. You might 'follow the rules." Tracy raised her arms and made quotations with her fingers, "But underlying that is an attitude that Tokema does not appreciate. So, I've called in some nurses to help me." Dr. Tracy strolled over to her desk and clicked the red button on the side. Two nurses walked in, one had what appeared to be an IV drip on a stand, and the other one a bucket.

"Alright," Dr. Tracy clapped her hands together. "This is Olga and Sandy. They're going to be our helpers today. Olga has a little doodad that she is going to hook up to your arm. Now, this is a very special kind of medication. If I ask Olga to release this little plastic thingy…" Dr. Tracy pointed to a plastic clip that kept the liquid in the bag from dripping down the tube and into Doris's arm, "… It'll make you sick, hence Sandy with the bucket. Understand?" Doris nodded.

"Good! Now I am going to ask you some questions and I want you to not think about what you're going to say, just answer. If you answer in the correct, non-attitude way, you won't get sick. But if I sense an underlying quip, I'll have Olga remove the strip. Clear?" Doris nodded again at Dr. Tracy.

Sandy placed down the bucket and went over to remove Doris's straitjacket. Once free Doris hung her arms in relief and Olga grabbed one and stuck her with the needle and hooked her up to the IV. Doris sat up on the couch, bucket in hand.

"Okay…" Dr. Tracy began, "We'll start simple. Why are you in our facilities?"

"Because a demon has attached itself to me," Doris replied without hesitation.

"Tsk, tsk, tsk…" Tracy said, shaking her head, "Give her a little." Olga pulled the plastic tab and immediately Doris felt sick, she lunged over her bucket, heaving chunks of breakfast inside. Doris spit,

"What did I do wrong?"

"You're not in here because you think a demon is attached to you. You're in here because you're a hallucinating murderer," Dr. Tracy said in a slow mocking voice, as she jotted something in her notes.

"I'm not a murderer!" Doris yelled, and again Olga pulled the clip and again Doris vomited heavily.

"Yes. You. Are!" Dr. Tracy said, pausing after each word and leaning in close. "Now I'll ask you again, why are you here?" Doris glared up at Dr. Tracy. Sure, she did not wish to continue this form of torture, but she knew she was no killer. It was not her. Then Doris stiffened; standing behind Dr. Tracy, in the corner of the room was the demon-man with the ashed-colored skin. He smiled at Doris and snapped his fingers.

———◦/◦/◦———

Doris was back to where she was that first day, back at the YMCA. Her skin looked like it had been stretched and deformed as she stood there looking at herself in the mirror at the end of the hallway. Her eyes were bloodshot and crazed. *No.* Doris thought, *not back here, please not back here.*

Doris felt again like her body was no longer her own. She knew that she had been swallowed up by *him* once again. Only to use her as a fake facade to hide behind, that's when she heard it. There was a click, someone was opening the locker room door.

"Oh, hello there," a woman said, "nice night for a light workout, am I right?" The woman turned and placed her headset back on. She was young, in her early 20s, maybe. She stood at the opposite end of the hall with a small towel in hand, dabbing off her face. She had not seemed to pay much attention to Doris, given that Doris was still naked. The woman simply turned after her greeting and was busying herself in front of a locker. Gathering up whatever items she needed to place in her gym bag for home.

Doris's body slowly turned around to face the woman. Doris could feel her legs begin to move. They felt weighed down as if they were stuffed with lead. Her head hung on the side of her shoulder and her jaw remained open. Her body dragged itself across the room silently. Only the sound of Doris's bare feet on the tile floor made any noise. But the woman paid no mind. Her radio headphones were on and blasting.

As her body approached the young woman Doris could feel her arms slowly lifting, as if being moved by an invisible string attached to the back of her hand. She grabbed the woman from behind, quickly putting one hand over the girl's mouth. Although Doris's body left heavy, it moved quickly and precisely. Doris knocked off the woman's headset and grabbed the back of her hair. Twisting her head around until the lady's head was completely facing Doris. Then Doris let her drop.

The woman fell to the floor like an old rag doll after a child has thrown it to the side out of boredom. Doris crouched beside the woman. She stretched the woman's head back, exposing her slender neck. Doris' head shot forward like a snake. Her teeth bared, she ripped out the woman's throat and began to suck. The feeling was unlike anything Doris had ever experienced before. It was rejuvenating, almost climatic, and then... nothing. Nothing at all. Whatever it was that swallowed Doris up and now controlled her did not seem all that pleased. In fact, it felt almost disappointing. Just then it made Doris lift the woman's hand to her mouth, it suckled on the girl's fingers. Slowly pulling the meat off the bone, like one would do with a plate of ribs. This seemed to do that trick, it felt almost orgasmic as it continued to make Doris devour. After it had finished both hands, the demon finally gagged Doris back up, like a mother bird, regurgitating food for its babies. The demon-like creature had had its fill.

Once she was free Doris fell to the ground and screamed. She scrabbled backward into one of the bathroom stalls. Gagging for she could still taste the blood of the woman on her lips. The demon slowly began to morph back into a man, losing its extended limbs, its eyes flexing back to human instead of a serpent. Staring at the dead girl sprawled out on the floor, he sighed, "That was not as much fun as I was hoping. Oh well, next time I'll be sure to savor the moment." He turned back towards Doris. "Until next time" he smiled at her and was gone.

Doris was unsure of how long she laid there on the floor crying, not knowing what to do. How could she explain what happened to the cops? She would be thrown in jail. Who would take care of her mother? She could not afford a nursing home, her siblings were of no help, and her dad died a long time ago. Doris bawled herself up, rocking back and forth on her heels. Then, when she felt she was able, she turned on the shower, rinsed herself of the filth, put on her clothes and crawled out the window. Leaving the young woman on the floor.

See Doris, you left her. Just like you left them all...

"I was scared."

You left them all...

—————◦/◦/◦—————

"No, I didn't" ...

"Clearly she isn't even paying attention to the questions anymore, hit her again." Doris looked up, she was back in the office with Olga, Sandy, and Dr. Tracy. She could feel herself becoming sick and again, plunged her head into the bucket, which was nearly halfway full at this point. This went on for such a long time that when Dr. Tracy finally felt like they were finished Doris had nothing left inside her to vomit. No food, no mucus, not even any stomach acid. It was only breath.

When Doris was permitted to leave and walk back to her room with a guard and nurse it was dark outside. Not even stars seemed to light the path. The cool air, however, felt nice on her skin. Doris had not eaten, or even had a drink of water after her, "reconditioning" and it was difficult for her to keep her head up and walk straight. But the cool air helped her to drag on.

Right before approaching her room Doris turned to the guard and asked, "May I please use the bathroom?" the guard nodded, led her to the bathroom, and took her out of her straitjacket. Doris stumbled into a stall, closing the door behind her. She plunged her hands into the toilet, cupped them, and drank the water.

———◦/◦/◦———

Doris sat in Dr. Vernirelli's office. She traced her fingers along the couch.

"How are you feeling today, Doris? I heard you were sent to the reconditioning room yesterday." Dr. Vernirelli said; Doris nodded.

"I feel alright. Still a little weak from yesterday."

"Why were you sent there?" Doris knew that Dr. Vernirelli probably already knew that answer. *Is he testing if I learned from my reconditioning? Is there a trick answer?* Doris thought. She stayed silent for a long time. Dr. Vernirelli sighed. "I am not tricking you, Doris. I know what it is like in the reconditioning room. You are free to answer everything honestly when we have our sessions together. I just want to know your side of things." Doris eyed him up and down. This is another reason why she felt as though she could trust Dr. Vernirelli, he always seemed to know what she was thinking.

"I was sent there because I tackled another patient. He asked me about the killings, and I am not a killer..." Doris's stomach began to become queasy, as if she were going to throw up. Dr. Vernirelli nodded. He must have seen her expression, for he handed her a trash can. Doris held her head over it but there was no vomit. *My stomach must still be empty...* she thought.

"I see they hit you pretty hard with that medication. I still don't think that form of 'reconditioning' is right. But no one seems to care what I have to say about it." the doctor said as he handed her a tissue.

"Thanks," Doris muttered.

"Now, why did you tackle this other patient? That's not like you."

"He said I was a killer and I'm not. The demon man is." Again, Doris winced and leaned over her bucket.

"Yes, Doris you've mentioned. But, we have yet to discuss what it is he made you do. Perhaps if we were to dive into such things, we could get a better insight?" Doris knew the Doc was baiting her. But maybe opening up to him would help her. The last time she had that thought, however, the demon-like man with the ashed-colored skin had appeared.

Doris glanced around the room, she did not see him and there was no chill throughout her body, she sighed.

"Okay, Doc. We can talk about it..."

———ᴑᴣᴑᴣᴑ———

Doris walked down the street. It was late, past her usual work time, but the office needed her to stay late. She was a secretary, and her boss had some project he was working on finishing up. He asked her to stay with him so she could make copies, brew fresh coffee, highlight certain information, etc. He had offered to drive her home, but she insisted that she only lived a short walk away and would be fine.

Looking back, she had mixed feelings about whether or not his driving her back to her house would have been a good or bad thing. Maybe if he had nothing would have happened. She would have gone home, heated herself up a can of soap on the stove, read her book, and gone to bed. Or, if he had driven her home that night... The thought was too horrible to think about. Too horrible to even fathom. Not a family man who was the sole provider of five. Although, it wouldn't matter, not to him.

As Doris walked, she heard a noise. The streetlights above her began to flicker. The dull orange coming in and out. The light made a little sound that was similar to a bug smacking itself against a blub. She stared up at the light for some time before continuing her walk, and then she stopped. At the end of the street, in the middle of the road stood a figure.

Doris jumped at the sight. She was not sure who or what it was, but she did not intend to walk any further, with that thing ahead. Doris quickly turned on her heels and standing there, right in front of her was what she feared most. Doris shrieked, threw her purse at him, and began running as fast as she could back in the direction she originally planned to avoid. The figure was no longer there. Doris felt something grab her by the back of the neck and begin to pull her back.

"No!" She yelled as she struggled to get away. "Help me! Someone please!" She shouted looking frantically at the houses that surrounded the neighborhood she was in. "Please" she screamed. She threw her head side to side, in hopes that she would catch a glance of somebody, anybody making their way to the door. But most of the lights were out. The families already snuggled up in their homes fast asleep. She felt the creature-like man shove her head into his mouth. He bit down hard, and Doris yelped. He gobbled her up as if she was a long strand of spaghetti on the other end of a fork. Slurrrrrrp…

Doris heavied heavily inside her body. She tried to move her arms and legs, even though she knew very well she would not be able to. She must, however, try.

"Hey lady!" She heard someone yell. She could feel her body turning itself slowly around. Her arms hung like sacks of flour at her side. Her legs dragged and twisted around each other. Her eyes seemed glossed and hazy as she scanned around. That's when she saw him. There was a young man turned down the street. She later read in the newspaper that he was a freshman in college and was on his way to a frat house party further up the road, his name was Johnny.

Johnny turned the corner. He had been whistling, "I got you" by James Brown. He had heard it on the radio and thought it was a pretty groovy sound. And it summed up how he was feeling at that moment. He was on his way to see his new girl, Amanda, at a party the boys were throwing when he stopped dead in his tracks.

Down the sidewalk a little way stood a woman. She stood there, like her feet were a part of the concrete. She looked off, that seemed to be the only way to describe her body. Her head hung to her side and her hair was a mess and stuck out from different angles. Her knees seemed to buckle under her own weight, although she was not that big, not that big at all. Johnny thought maybe 5'4, 5'5 at the most.

"Hey, lady!" Johnny yelled. The woman slowly turned, and as she turned Johnny leaped back. The woman wore a grotesque, twisted grin. As if she knew something about him that he didn't quite know himself. Her teeth were sharp and pointed. She slowly unraveled her tongue, licking her lips. "He-hey, are you okay?" He asked. Hoping she would reply with, I'm fine. This is my house. And turn to go inside. But she did not do that. She just stood there, staring at him. He could hear her breathing. She was wheezing loudly and sounded like she had a bone stuck in her throat. The choke and chortle sound made her seem almost inhuman. She stared directly at him, eyeing him as if he was something to eat.

Johnny turned on his heels quickly. He headed to the sidewalk on the opposite side of the road. Holy cow! What a freak… He thought to himself as he made his way up the walk. The woman continued to stand slightly in front of him. She gawked in his direction still, watching him carefully. He tried his best not to look at her. Maybe if he ignored her, she would leave him alone. Nonetheless, he could still feel her eyes upon him. He swore he could even hear her drooling. The little plips of spit hitting the ground and the sucking noise she made when she tried to slurp it back up. He quickened his stride, and right as he reached the opposite side of the walk as her the streetlights began to flicker.

Johnny jumped at the light bulb beginning to twitch, spasming, like a rat trapped inside a cage. In the split second of darkness Johnny heard a shuffle and then that wheezing. That awful, horrible, unsettling wheezing. He feared for the lights to return. Knowing what would be standing before him. He tried to turn, but as quickly as they were out, they returned. And there she was, standing directly in front of him. That same sick and twisted grin plastered to her face.

Johnny screamed, lunging backward to try and escape the woman that stood before him. As he spun around, he felt a strong grip around his collar, *pulling him back. He looked up to see the face of what looked like a demon. The narrow slits for eyes, teeth razors, and fingers long and doughy all at once. Johnny whipped around, throwing his fist up in the air for a punch, but his arm was caught.*

The woman gave out a sinister laugh far too deep to truly belong to her. It seemed to be the laugh only a devil would possess. Her jaw clicked and unlocked as she did so. She turned his fist and forced it behind his back, breaking his arm. Johnny yelled out again, "Help! Someone please!" But no one came. In fact, no one even seemed to notice. Johnny could see through into some of the lit houses. While most were dark, he could see one family sitting and watching TV. He could see one woman bringing a young man a drink, but not one of them looked up from what they were doing. Johnny continued to howl out.

"No one can hear you, boy," the voice said. The sound of her voice made his spine shiver. It came from the pit of her stomach, so deep that it was the kind of voice that should never be spoken. Then she got a glint in her eye. She released his broken arm, making him stagger back. "Run..." she said smiling. Johnny did not hesitate, he turned as fast as he could, sprinting for anywhere, but here. He made it to the main road. Looking in either direction for a car to leap into. He ran further down the street in hopes of making it to a shop. Then, from far behind him, in what could only be described as a whisper, he could have sworn he heard the dark voice say "...I love a good hunt," as scrambling and quickened shuffling came after him.

⊰•◦•◦•⊱

Doris sat on the couch. Her head hung low. She had never told the stories of the murders to anyone before. She technically did not even tell them at her trial. She simply sat there as others related what happened to her, although they never had the full truth. She would only sit and shake or nod her head. She had refused to talk about them like she had any control in the matter. While yes, she was technically there it was not her doing these things. She only bore witness to these hideous, disturbing, acts. Forced to watch and partake. Sitting in the passenger seat as the driver drove them off a bridge.

Dr. Vernirelli sat there, looking at Doris. His face had not changed from the start of the story to now. He simply stared at Doris, listening contently. Once she finished, she had grown very silent, which was to be expected when releasing such a load of deranged trauma. She raised her hands and held her head. Ashamed to show her face to the doctor, to anyone. All Dr. Vernirelli had to say was, "I am very sorry that happened to you. Both of you. And I believe you Doris."

This was not something Doris expected to hear. There had been many times the Doc shocked her with his responses. But never one person told Doris they were sorry for her and what horrors she had to face. And completely on her own no less.

"You- you do?" she asked, slowly beginning to lower her hands, only to tuck them back to her face. The doctor nodded.

"Yes. For Doris, I believe that there are many things within this world that are unexplainable. Sometimes those things are wonderful. And create joy and happiness wherever they go. But then there are some things, dark, sinister, evil. These things only create destruction and pain. And there is not always a reason behind them."

Doris stared at the doctor. She truly felt that he believed what he had just relayed to her. She could feel her heart beating faster, she could feel that choking feeling in the back of one's throat when they know they are about to cry. She could feel her tears streaming down her cheeks. Dr. Vernirelli handed her a box of tissues. Doris lowered her hands grabbing one and wiped her nose. "Thank you," she said. The doctor nodded.

"Have you ever encountered this before, Doc?" Doris asked, eyeing him above her cloudy vision.

"I am not at liberty to discuss such things. But I can say you are the first to be swallowed by such a force. The first that I have ever encountered at least." Doris could feel her throat beginning to swell.

It felt as if it was starting to close. Becoming hotter and tighter with every second. All she could do was nod at Dr. Vernirelli's statement. She wanted to know more. Were there other patients like her? Perhaps. Were they here? But as the Doc said, he was not at liberty to discuss such things. And even if he was, Doris was not sure that he would freely admit them. Even if it is not from his own personal experiences the trauma and heartache of others can catch fire from one person to the next. And given Dr. Vernirelli's profession she was sure he had been caught in flames more than once.

Their session continued on after that. Doris told the doctor of how the situation made her feel. As if she were a helpless child. Or a doll in which a cruel individual would make her act out. Using her limbs and body at free will. Controlling her every move. How she only could imagine what that young man was feeling when it happened. She imagined he would have been frightened, confused, and felt just as helpless as she did. And she spoke of how the demon man felt as well.

"You had a sensation of his feelings too?" Dr. Vernirelli asked.

"Yes and no…" Doris replied, "…I could tell he was excited. I knew he wanted to torture the boy. He wanted it to last longer than it did with his other victims. Well… the victims he made me do anyways. I knew it excited him and he craved more. But I couldn't see into his thoughts. I did not know what was going to happen next. I did not know what he was going to make me do. I went in totally blind. Helpless." The last word came out mumbled and her voice trailed off.

The doctor nodded and continued to write as Doris reached for her braid. She stroked it, something about playing with her hair suddenly soothed her. Weaving her fingers in and out of each strand. Before, she hated having long hair and how it brushed against her neck, now it felt comforting and almost relieving in a way. She continued to fiddle as the doctor scanned over his notes.

"Doris, do you still see the creature that tortured you?" he asked, Doris froze. She had not freely admitted to the doctor yet that she had seen him while here at Tokema. She almost did not want to. Maybe, if she did not fully acknowledge him being here to someone else the creature would simply go away before he would only show himself when it was time to take someone. Now he was showing himself in the shadows of her mind, talking to her. Just a continued part of her imagination that had not been scrapped clean yet. Like gum as it sticks to the bottom side of a table or a shoe.

Vernirelli continued to eye Doris. She had not spoken for several minutes, and he could tell from her silence that she had indeed seen the creature before. He eyed her up and down. She almost looked like she had forgotten his question. Eyes glazed over, looking at nothing in particular straight ahead, clumsily batting away at her braid.

"Doris" Dr. Vernirelli spoke again, "Have you seen the demon-man since being admitted to Tokema?" Doris slowly raised her eyes, acknowledging that she heard him. She looked to the ground and slowly nodded. "Has he spoken to you? Or tried to coax you into doing things?" There was a long pause.

"He... he comes sometimes. Not like before."

"And why do you think that is?" the doctor asked. Purposefully trying to egg her on for an answer he already seemed to be fully aware of.

"Because... because he only comes when there is an opportunity. And the opportunities here are not as strong as they are out there. I think." Doris hung her head. Ashamed of her answer. The doctor nodded. He circled something in his notes, it read, *opportunity*.

Dr. Vernirelli glanced at the clock. Their session was up. *Boy time flies when the session is with someone like her*. He thought to himself. As Doris reached the door she turned and thanked Dr. Vernirelli for listening and believing in her and her story. That was the first time she ever thanked him after a session together.

Doris sat with a deck of cards in her hands. She was in the common room playing a game of rummy against another woman. The woman's name was Ruth. She had not spoken much to Doris, but one of Ruth's favorite things to do in the common room was to play cards. In fact, Doris was almost positive it was the only thing Ruth liked to do. She had never seen her without cards in her hand. Ruth had gone around to each person, aggressively shaking the deck of cards in all their faces, asking them to play. But given that today was Halloween everyone else was glued to the tv's Halloween specials, while the nurses handed out little unwrapped candies.

The Charlie Brown special was on. The other patients whooped at hollered at the tv in excitement, while Doris did her daily ritual of looking out the window, when she felt a tap on her shoulder.

"Rummy?" Ruth asked, holding the cards in Doris's face. Doris had loved rummy as a child and agreed to play. She had never been invited to play before. Doris glanced at the remaining cards in her hand. She only had a queen and an ace left. Doris looked up at Ruth, who had 5 cards left. She could tell that Ruth was on edge from not winning. Doris shifted uncomfortably in her chair as Ruth made her play.

Just as Ruth was about to set a pair of her cards down Doris felt her chair get pulled out from under her. She lay there sprawled on the ground in shock. Ruth screamed,

"Rummy, rummy, no, rummy!"

"Hiya bitch!" towering over Doris was Donnie. He had a crazed smile across his face as he looked down on Doris. His eyes were bloodshot, like he hadn't slept all night, his hair had grown some and his beard was starting to fill in. Doris could see there was a bruise in the crease of his arm, right where a reconditioning needle would go. "Now Ahh heard somethin' internestin'. You gone fucked up and tolds Dr. Tracy Ahh was lookin' for killin ti-" Just then Donnie was tackled by one of the guards on duty. Donnie swung his arms about like a crazed gorilla banging at his chest. He lunged an arm out at Doris, trying to grab her gown but she quickly shuffled back.

"Le meh go. Ahh gota beesness with 'er." Donnie screamed. He tried again to free himself, but the guard holding Donnie had him in almost what appeared to be a headlock, *it's like watching a wrestler's match* Doris thought to herself. Doris scrambled to her feet and ran to the opposite side of the room. She attempted to hide herself in the crowd of the patients watching the tv but all of them parted like the sea when she came in their direction. Doris watched as Donnie continued to yell out profanities and struggle against the guard. Two more guards came to help, and a nurse came running up with a needle.

The nurse plunged the needle into Donnie's neck and almost immediately he went down like a sack of potatoes. A few other nurses went running over with a straitjacket and shoved Donnie's arms inside. Once he was safely strapped up the guard dragged him out of the room. Like he was a dead body being taken away on a stretcher.

Doris let out a heavy breath and looked around the room. And to her surprise everyone went back to what they were doing, as if nothing had taken place at all. The patients watching tv returned to their seats. The nurses immediately went back to their station. Ruth walked right back up to Doris, shoving the cards in her face, "Rummy?" Doris took the cards from Ruth and returned to her chair.

Doris had lost her place. She fumbled with the cards in her hand. But Ruth had not missed a beat. She went on as if nothing had disturbed their game in the first place.

"Sorry about that," mumbled Doris. As she picked up a card.

"Rummy cards rummy," Ruth said, waving her hand as if she was saying, *think nothing of it,* or *happens all the time.* Ruth's hands moved swiftly as she laid cards down, creating a meld and then adding to Doris's. Soon all the cards were out of her hand. Ruth jumped up from the table and yelled, "Rummy! Rummy! Rummy!" she beamed up at Doris clapping her hands. Doris patted her on the back. Ruth scooped up the cards, quickly shuffled them, and held them back to Doris's face. Silently asking to play again, Ruth nodded eagerly. Doris shook her head,

"Sorry." She moved to the group of people watching the special and sat herself down at the end.

Well, another Halloween has come and gone.

Yes, Charlie Brown.

But I don't understand it. I went trick-or-treating and all I got was a bag full of rocks...

While usually Doris's days at Tokema were met with boring repetition and order, that was not the case for today. True, her morning did begin this way, but with a dash more excitement, as Donnie had rushed out at her, but luckily her day continued just fine. And tonight, would not consist of immediately being locked up in her room as soon as the sun set. Tonight was Halloween and the patients were allowed to pick a movie, eat popcorn, and get candy. Something so simple might not seem so enthralling to a person, but for a patient of Tokema, this was heaven.

Doris sat in her room patiently waiting to be taken to the movie. Everyone would be released out of their rooms at 8:00 and seated in the common room. Doris could see the time from outside her room, 7:56. *Only four more minutes* Doris thought to herself.

She fiddled with her fingers and played with her hair, a newfound comfort. She stared eagerly as the clock ticked, 7:57. *A watched pot never boils Doris. You must be patient. You must wait your turn like everyone else.* She continued to keep herself occupied by pacing around her room, something she normally tried to avoid, given that this was a clear sign of being insane, *which I am not!*

Just then Doris heard a loud creak from behind her, her door was open. She calmly walked to the entrance and peaked her head out. She could see others doing the same. Slowly walking to their door frame, looking around the corner to make sure it was safe for them to come out. Guards stood in the hallway, "Alright, the lot of you, make a straight line and we'll go to the common room for a movie" one of them yelled. Doris could see one down the hall had not been opened. She could hear slightly muffled yelling. *Someone must have disobeyed the rules and lost privileges...*

Doris obeyed and jumped in line behind another woman around the same height as her. Doris had seen the woman before but did not yet know her name. She had a different lunch time from Doris and worked in the laundry room. It was rare for Doris to see her at all, except in passing through the doors. The woman turned to see who was standing behind her, and when her eyes met Doris's, she jumped a little. The woman quickly stepped out of line and made her way to the back.

Doris watched her go; she had become used to this sort of thing. Many people avoided her at all costs. And since there were no straitjackets on anyone yet, Doris assumed that the woman might suspect she was fair game to Doris. *Ah yes, that's my plan. Get thrown in the crazy house, and as soon as I don't have a straitjacket on, I'll strangle the woman standing in front of me. Good plan, good plan. This whole thing has been a ploy, just to get to you random lady in here with me!* Doris rolled her eyes and stepped forward.

The guards led the group down the common room. It was decorated with plastic spiders and fake cobwebs. The chairs were lined up in neat rows for the patients to sit in, and waiting on each chair was a small cup of popcorn and a single piece of chocolate. Doris rushed over to the first row. She wanted to make sure she had a good seat when the movie started, if she was further in the back, she knew she would miss everything.

Once everyone was all seated and settled in, Dr. Freude walked up to the front of the room, it was surprising to see him there. Given that Doris had only ever seen him in his office. It never really occurred to her that Dr. Freude existed outside of it.

"Velcome. Ve have zree filme to vatch tonight. Nummer von, Zee Vogel..." Dr. Freude held up the film, *The Birds*, "...Nummer two, Carnival von zouls..." Freude held up, *Carnival of Souls*, "...Und, nummer zree, Hush... Hush Sweet, Charlotte. Vich von?" Immediately people started throwing their hands in the air, holding up the number of fingers for the movie they wanted. Dr. Freude took a long silver whistle from his neck and blew a sharp high-pitched noise. Some patients screamed and cupped their hands over their ears, while others grew quiet and wide-eyed.

"Ve do not yell. Ich, vill ask vich filme, you raise Hände". Dr. Freude raised his hand in a demonstration. Everyone nodded their heads, still afraid to speak. Dr. Freude nodded his head in approval. He held up the first film, a few hands raised, but not very many. Dr. Freude raised the second film in the air, more hands went up this time, Doris's included. Then, Dr. Freude raised the last film and a majority of the hands sprung up. Freude nodded his head again and turned to put the film on the projector. The film began to flicker on the white sheet. The black and gray lines started to make a picture and the film was rolling. *Hush hush, sweet Charlotte. Charlotte, don't you cry. Hush... hush, sweet Charlotte. He'll love you till he dies...*

Doris sat up in her chair, reaching for her small cup of popcorn when she heard, ever so faintly, just under the sounds of the movie, *Dream, dream, dream, dream. When I want you in my arms. When I want you and all your charms. Whenever I want you, all I have to do is dream, dream, dream, dream...* Doris slowly glanced around the room. Looking for wherever the music was coming from. But no one else seemed to notice it. They all just sat looking forward, excited to watch the film. Doris scanned, but as softly as she heard the music coming it was gone again. Doris returned her head to the film. *Perhaps someone is playing it in their office*, she thought and continued to watch.

Doris watched as Joseph Cotten played the piano. Slowly singing away *Hush... Hush, Sweet Charlotte*. There was something in his tone that made her feel unsettled and made her spine crawl. *Hush... Hush, Sweet Doris. I'll love you 'til you die...* Doris jumped up from her chair. "Sit down!" some patients yelled.

"Doris, take your seat or you'll be put back in your room!" One of the nurses threatened. Doris slowly sat back down again. Eyes glancing from side to side, no longer focused on the movie. She heard him. She knew he was close. Doris closed her eyes and prayed he would not come here, not now. She kept her eyes shut tight, drowning out the sound of the flick as best she could, only focusing on the low hum of the projector. She stayed like this for some time.

"Honestly Doris, I don't know how you do it" John smiled at her as she placed down the pot roast, she had in her slow cooker all day. The house smelled like meat and potatoes, and she had laid out a lovely spread of home-made baked bread, and candles were lit.

Doris smiled up at him, "Oh really it's nothing." She winked. John smiled back at her as he cut into the dinner. He asked her how her day had been, and what she had done. Doris kept up the conversation as best she could, but that voice implanted in the back of her head would not fully allow her to hold true exchanging of words. There's poison in the roast. There is poison in the roast, don't eat it you fool.

But John seemed not to notice that Doris was not herself this evening. All he saw was a tight red dress, a woman, and a pot roast made just for him. Doris's head hung on her side, her mouth slightly agape and she slightly licked her lips. The man-like demon seemed to fit inside her body better the more and more he swallowed her. This had been around the 5th time he forced himself upon her. And he had gotten quite good at passing her off. She no longer moved clumsily, she no longer had his eyes, her body moved more fluidly. Of course, it was not perfect. But it was hardly even noticeable now. Like a pair of jean pants that needed to be worn over and over again, until finally they matched the shape of the wearer. The demon hummed the farmer in the del as he watched John gobble down the dinner that Doris had been preparing most of her day, There's poison in the roast. There's poison in the roast. Oh, how you'll die tonight, there's poison in the roast.

Doris's face continued to hold its plastered smile as John tiddled on about his work, "...I told the guy, I told him not to send over the H-forms, but he did it anyway. So, you know what I did? Boom! Fired his ass!" John laughed as he shoveled more food in. Paying no attention to the fact that Doris had not even bothered to make herself a plate. "Listen doll..." John started, mouth still full, "...I gotta tell ya... woah, wait hold up..." John held a finger in the air, and made his other hand into a fist and coughed into it. There was a deep rumble from inside his stomach.

"Woah, I ain't feeling so good. Where's your bathroom?" Doris slowly stood, fumbling to make her way down the hall to show John where to go. Her walk had still not been perfected, she gently bumped and stumbled her way down, holding her hands gesturing towards the door. John did not seem to partake notice given that he was now clutching to his stomach and pushing past her to get in. He sprinted down in the direction in which she had pointed.

Doris's body stood waiting in the hallway. She could hear his coughs and gags. She could feel her legs slowly start to drag their way down the hall to where he was.

"Oh John?" she cooed. But the only response she was met with was the sound of his chokes and then there was a loud thud. Doris hummed and skipped down the hall, only falling twice. Soon it was just easier to crawl toward the bathroom. She peered in from around the corner. She could see his limp body hanging over the toilet. The man inside her laughed. He quickly scuttled her toward John and scooped him up. Slowly unbuttoning John's shirt. She stared at his chest, marveled by how much meat there was. Then her teeth began to grow and extend out, sharp and pointed, she took a bite.

———⟨o/o/o⟩———

Doris opened her eyes again. She was not sure how long she had her eyes and ears covered from the movie. But as she blinked them open the credits were rolling and most of the other patients had already stood and lined up. She placed her still full cup of popcorn back on the chair and got in line with the rest. The one little moment she had to try and enjoy a "normal" evening. And she had spent it trying to cower from the past.

Once in her room Doris pulled her sheets up high above her face. *Whenever I want you, all I have to do is dream, dream, dream, dream...* Doris jumped. She could hear the music again. She looked around to see where it might be coming from but could see no indication. She hesitated as she swung her legs over her bed. She crept to the door and looked outside. She could see the clock adjustment, 12:34. Doris peered out the little window, but saw no guard. No one was standing duty watching in the halls. She pushed her handle down, and sure enough the door swung open with a high pitched, *CREEEAK.*

She wandered into the hall, looking side to side. But no one was there, all the room lights were out, and even the light in the hall was lower than usual. "H-hello?" Doris cried out. But the hall was still. "Hello?" She called again, this time with more confidence in her voice. Again, there was no reply, except for her echo.

Doris slowly walked down the hallway. She glanced into the rooms of the other patients, but she saw nothing. All their lights were out, something highly unusual, given that security would keep the lights on at all times to check on all of the patients. Doris walked up to one of the doors. Cupping her hands to look inside. But it was too dark to see.

Doris grabbed the handle of one patient's room and slowly pressed it open. She glanced in the door, "Hello? Is someone in here?" she whispered. But there was no response. She stepped into the room, only to find that she was no longer in another patient's room but standing outside amongst the trees. She looked up, the sun had set, and she could see small stars sparkling their way through the bare tree branches. The leaves were all gone and only remained on the ground. She turned behind her, to go back inside and return to her room, but there was no door.

Doris grasped at the air, trying to catch something that was not there. Blindly feeling around for the door handle, in hopes that it was just a trick of the light, that the door really was there, and she somehow was missing it. But her fingers felt nothing except the cold air between them. Doris looked down and saw that her feet were bare. Her toes felt numb, and she began to shiver.

Doris...

When Doris turned, she could see nothing except rows of trees that led deeper into the woods that surrounded the property of Tokema. She squinted her eyes in hopes that it would help, but still she saw nothing and no one there.

Doris turned, walking in the direction in which she hoped her building was in. *Maybe I can somehow sneak in, and no one will notice I was not in my room.* She thought to herself.

Doris...

She jumped, this time the sound was closer to her, and she could feel hot breath on her neck. It made her skin crawl as she slowly lifted her hand to touch the back on her neck. Doris could hear heavy breathing from behind her, and she stiffly turned around to see a man standing there. It was the same man from a few weeks before... the dirty man whose shirt hung on him like old elephant skin. Small bits of ember still clung to his shirt. His skin was raw and shredded. She stared at him, wide eyed and frozen.

"What d-o y-y-o-o-u-u- w-want?" she stuttered. Her body was shaking as she looked him up and down. His eyes seemed empty, and yet so fixated on her, she was sure if she tried to run, he would lash out and grab her.

Watch... Doris... Watch... His lips did not move, he just continued to breath, hot, and heavily. But she could still hear him. His voice rang in her head like bells on a Sunday morning. She could hear it was full of pain and longing. He sounded tired and weak.

Doris took a step back but did not take her eyes away from the man. He stood very straight, as if there was a transparent string attached to his head, holding his whole body erect. Doris noticed something rustling behind him. She could see a blurry shadow making its way through the forest, but it concealed itself behind the man. As it came closer Doris could see that it was the demon-like man, only this time he was completely in his man-like form, the only difference was the color of his gray, ash skin. Doris shrieked and began to run. She suddenly found the courage in her legs that was not there before. *C-c-c-courage* she heard the cowardly lion quiver.

Watch... Doris... Watch...

Doris slowed her stride, she could feel her skin begin to prickle, her brow began to sweat. She did not wish to look back, but she could still feel that hot breath. She could still smell the dirt and burning flesh of the man. She could still sense the demon-man with his sickly gray skin. All so close to her she felt as if she were on a hamster's wheel. Running, round and round and making no distance at all.

She knew if she stayed and turned around that the demon-man would make her hurt this stranger. He would force her down inside of himself and make her do things she could not control. She cupped her hands over her ears. And ran forward as quickly as she could. Looking for the building in which she resided. But all she was met with were more trees.

Don't be afraid...Watch... Doris... Watch...

Doris continued to run forward as best she could. Ignoring the words in her head. She could see a clearing in the distance and forced her legs to pump harder. She huffed and puffed as she made her way there, but as she drew closer to the clearing what lay before began to solidify and she stopped. Standing only a few yards ahead of her in the clearing was the burned man and the demon still in his human form. Doris stepped back at this sight, but the rustle of the leaves beneath her feet gave her away.

Both men turned to face her, their heads snapping. The demon-man grinned at her; his teeth pointed in the starlight. But before she could turn back the demon-man lunged, grabbing the burnt man, hoisting him into the air and swallowed him.

Doris cried out, she wanted to run forward, to help the man who had just been gobbled-up. But could not move her feet. Her body seemed to be glued in place. She struggled against herself, but still her body made no efforts in moving forward. If she was forced to stand there, she would at least close her eyes. But to her dismay they would not. Her lids were paralyzed open. Realizing this the air began to sting at them.

Doris could see the demon-man slowly shedding into his true form. His jaw began to crack open, and something appeared to be crawling its way out of his mouth. Doris stood there; eyes fixated on what was happening before her in horror. The demon-man began to gag-up what appeared to be the same man he had swallowed only moments before. The man with the burned skin was crawling his way up and out of the mouth that so many times consumed Doris herself.

She could see him ripping and tearing his way out of the throat. Until, finally, he was out. Once he was out of the creature's mouth he stood perfectly still, then collapsed straight forward. His body still erect, face planting into the ground. All of a sudden, he convulsed, his body spazzing in such a way it almost looked like he was lit on fire. Flames that Doris could not see, smell, touch, or hear. Then he was gone. The only trace left was smoke where he once was. Smoke that only seemed to form once his body had disappeared. Doris gasped at the sight before her. Mouth hung open like a door on loose hinges. Eyes stuck to the wisp of smoke that remained. Then she slowly looked up. And to her surprise both men were gone, and she was no longer in the woods.

Doris was back in her bedroom, standing in the middle of the room. She shrieked, and jolted upwards, suddenly back in her bed. Doris jumped from where she was and ran to the door and looked at the clock outside her room, 12:35. She threw her head to the side, to see out the hallway. There was a guard standing only a few feet down the hall, same as usual. Doris slowly looked down at her feet. Once again, they were slathered with mud and dead leaves clung to her toes.

"Something strange has been happening to me lately Doc…" Doris said, sitting on the cream couch and intertwining her fingers between her hair, while absent mindedly looking straight ahead. Eyes not focused on anything in particular.

"And what would that be?" Dr. Vernirelli asked, eyeing her from over a mug of tea he was slowly sipping. He offered a cup for Doris as well, saying it would be their little secret, since she was still not allowed to have fully hot food or drink. Doris had accepted. Her chia sat next to her, untouched, but still steam was flowing over the rim.

"I've been…" Doris hesitated. She did not think Dr. Vernirelli would report her or get her into trouble for what was happening, but she was still not sure she could trust him with this knowledge. He could see her contemplating whether or not it would be best to share whatever information was laying on her shoulders.

"My dear. You are here for life. You will be having sessions with me until I die and then move on to another therapist until you are gone as well. It is up to you what to share and not share. But if something is concerning you, who is best to share them with?" He smiled. Doris nodded,

"…Yes. You're right. Something has been happening to me at night. It's not an everyday thing, but it has happened twice. I'll be in my room at night, and then something draws me out. I can't remember what exactly, all I know is that I do find myself out. And there is this man and he… darn I can't remember" Doris rubbed her head, trying to recall the events that only took place the night before. Like she stated, this event had occurred twice. But now she was struggling to remember what went down. Before it was in her mind's eye perfectly. She could recall every detail, but now it seemed almost like a fever dream.

"All I know for sure is I am outside at night and when I'm back in my room my feet are covered in mud and dirt. But I know, I know I can't leave at night. Someone would have seen me. So why is there filth on my feet?" Doris removed one of her socks, she had not washed her feet this time. Only threw on her socks, so she could show Dr. Vernirelli.

Doris looked at her foot. The bottom was indeed filthy and there was dried dirt underneath her toenails. She held it up for Dr. Vernirelli to see. He stared at her foot for a while, looked up at Doris and asked.

"Describe your foot for me, Doris."

"Oh, uh, well. It has dried mud, see? Like I stepped in a dirty puddle or something and it set in the night. And, well there's dirt under the nails. See?" She pointed to her nails. Dr. Vernirelli nodded and wrote something down. "You don't seem all that surprised Doc. I thought you'd have something else to say."

"What would you like me to say?"

"Well… I *thought* something along the lines of, 'Oh my how did you get out?' Or 'my dear this is serious,' I don't know!" Doris slumped into the couch, pulling her sock back over her foot. All the doctor did was nod.

"You must be uncomfortable if you can feel that dirt piled up in your sock." He finally said.

"Yeah, sure I'm uncom-" Doris paused, "What do you mean 'if'? Of course, I can feel it. My foot feels all dried out. But what did you mean by that?"

"Well, I was just concerned for your comfort level. Perhaps after our session you can request a shower? Although I suppose it's more of a hosing down" Dr. Vernirelli rolled his eyes.

"I can't do that; they'll see my feet and know I was outside."

"I don't think it will be an issue. You said this happened once before. What did you do with your foot then?" Dr. Vernirelli asked. Doris's cheeks became red. She was embarrassed to admit that she needed to dunk her feet in the toilet water. But what other choice was there? Take a beating from one of the guards, go back into the reconditioning room? No thank you. A dirty bowl of toilet water was better than those options.

"I-I put it in the toilet" Doris whispered. Dr. Vernirelli nodded empathetically.

"My dear, if you are uncomfortable, simply ask for a shower. No one will even see the dirt on your feet." He sounded so confident and sure of himself, "I promise." Doris sat there; arms crossed.

"You can't make such promises, and I am not about to be beaten for something I didn't even mean to do."

"There will be no beatings." Dr. Vernirelli said in a calm voice, "No reconditioning, no getting in trouble of any kind Doris." he nodded once again to reassure her.

"How can you make that promise?" She sat up a little.

"Because, Doris, I don't see any dirt on your feet." Doris just looked at the doctor. Unsure of what to say. Clearly, her feet were covered with dirt. Doris simply shook her head.

"Uh…no? See, look closer. I don't even know how you're missing it." Once again Doris took off her sock and held it up for the doctor to look at. Dr. Vernirelli stared at Doris for a little, he wasn't studying her foot, he did not immediately say, 'Oh I see it now, sorry, these old eyes!' He slowly moved his gaze down to once again meet her foot, he just looked at it. After a few seconds, he shrugged sympathetically and shook his head.

"I'm very sorry my dear, but it simply looks like a clean foot to me. I mean, a little dirty, yes. But it does not look like it has been through the mud." Doris continued to shake her head. How could he possibly be missing what she was seeing? It was clear as day. Doris scraped her nail under her heel, kicking up the dried-up dirt on her foot. There was a thick clump of it under her nail. She held it up for the doctor to see.

"Come on Doc, look. Don't tell me you can't see that!" But Dr. Vernirelli simply glanced and met her eyes. They seemed to be saying, *I'm sorry my dear, but once again there is nothing there for me to see.*

"Doris, just because I cannot see the dirt doesn't mean it's not there. There are plenty of things that happen in our world where some people can see things others can't. And that does not make them insane. It just means certain things in this world are purposely not meant to be seen by everyone…" Doris slumped into her chair,

"But you have something attached to you. You have something that *wants* you to believe you are losing your marbles, something that wants you to feel isolated. So, it could be that the demon-man is trying to make you feel alone?" Dr. Vernirelli said.

Doris could feel the hairs on her neck begin to stand on their ends. Her skin prickled and a cold chill ran down her spine. She looked around the room, listening for any indication that *he* was in there with them. But she neither saw nor heard a thing. It was simply just her and the doctor. Doris nodded her head in agreement with the doctor.

The demon-like man always wanted to cut her off from the rest of the world it felt like. He wanted her to be afraid. To feel small. To feel like no matter what she did or said she would always come off demented. Some days there were times in which she believed it to be true herself. But what the Doc had said made sense. When someone stands alone, they are much easier to tear down, than when someone else stands with them.

"You're right Doc." Doris eventually said, "I do feel alone. I have been alone ever since he ate up my soul. But I don't feel that way so much during our sessions." Her skin once again began to prickle, as if it were upset by something. As if she were a cat, arching her back and hissing at whatever threat had presented itself. Her skin crawled like bugs. Doris brushed at her arms, legs, and neck. Trying to get her body to calm itself down.

Dr. Vernirelli smiled at her, although he could see her visible discomfort. He jotted something down in his notes. Doris leaned over a little to try and see what he was writing, he did not hide his pad from her, but she could not read his chicken scratch of handwriting. She sighed, *doctors.*

—⦿⦿⦿—

Dr. Vernirelli sat in his office. His workday had finished not too long ago, and he was reviewing his notes from his earlier sessions. He flipped through various pages of different patients. Carefully examining and looking over his observations for each one. Tabitha was coming along nicely in her acceptance of having schizophrenia. Shawn finally made a breakthrough in discovering for himself that his emotional and abusive behaviors come from his father's parenting style. Doris... Dr. Vernirelli paused when he reached her.

Doris was still not opening up about everything she had to say or was experiencing. She was still considered to be a "new" patient, even though she had been admitted a few months ago. He sighed. Although he felt like he and Doris had established a solid foundation, he could still see there was so much she was holding back from him. *If only I could crack her open somehow.* He thought to himself.

Dr. Vernirelli was of course familiar with Doris's background, murder. Sick, twisted, tormented murder. And none of her victims were connected to each other. She had gone after both men and women. And in some cases, her victims were much larger and stronger than her. How could she over-power such individuals alone?

Well, she wasn't alone. She was possessed, remember? By some kind of satanic creation that she had described as a man and yet not a man, with his skin the same color as ash. The strength must have come from having him. And after having even a few sessions with Doris, the Doc could not even imagine her as someone who could possibly be capable of any crimes, let alone murder! *But I must get her to open up somehow. She is isolating herself without even realizing what she is doing. And yes, I can lead a horse to water, but I can't make it drink. That is something she must be open and willing to do on her own. She must be the one, I cannot prey it out of her.*

Of course, he did not want to use means like reconditioning, and he would never result in shock therapies. Perhaps hydrotherapy would help? Doris mentioned before how she had first seen this demon-man at Tokema when she was first subjected to the showers here. Perhaps something like that would jog a memory, or even cause *him* to appear. And what if he does appear Doc? What then? She'll be trapped in a tub, panicking. Or worse, she could get "swallowed" up and you become her next victim. Think Doc, think! Dr. Vernirelli shook his head.

He made a note of potential hydrotherapy in his book. He looked it over, rereading the note as if contemplating whether or not it should remain there. *Of course, I don't want to push Doris too far. If I expose her to a therapy that she does not necessarily agree with, that could cause a rift in our relationship, and I would be back to square one. But then again, it could not hurt to try and help by any means necessary, right?*

Dr. Vernirelli nodded to himself, *by whatever civil means necessary*, she needed a push to open up. The Doc circled the word, "Hydrotherapy." He would call in the morning to have it all arranged for their next session together. Soon the doctor gathered his things and began making his way to the car. The night sky was bright. Not a cloud seemed to be in it and the stars sparkled through that deep blue velvet blanket in the sky. Dr. Vernirelli looked up and smiled. He was feeling hopeful for the feature.

⸺⟨⊘⊘⊘⟩⸺

Dr. Vernirelli smiled at Doris, "Today we are going to be trying something different from our usual sessions..." Doris raised an eyebrow at him. It had been a week since he thought about giving her hydrotherapy and since nothing had changed in that time, he finally decided it was time to proceed "... We are going to try and do something called hydrotherapy. Do you know what that is?" Doris thought she may have read something about hydrotherapy in The Kansas City Star, but she was not sure. She eventually ended up shaking her head. Dr. Vernirelli nodded,

"Hydrotherapy was first introduced to the United States around the late 1880s. It exposes the patients to bathes of either hot or cold water for an extended period of time. This is supposed to create a calming effect. I am hoping to use it today to try and get you to relax and possibly open up more."

"You don't think I open up enough Doc?" Doris asked. The doctor smirked and let out a small laugh.

"I think we are making great strides in that direction. But sometimes things could use a catalyst to help get the ball really rolling. A snowman after all isn't just the bottom now, is it? It's going to need a middle, a head, teeth, arms, eyes...what we have right now is just the base. We need to help turn it into something." He smiled at Doris, and she nodded in agreement.

"Alright. Let's get to the tub."

—————

"How are you feeling Doris?" Dr. Vernirelli asked once she was all stripped down and inside the tub. The tub looked like a relatively normal bath, like how Doris expected. The only exception being that it had a lid that went over the open face of the tub, so her body was to be completely covered except for her head. The lid also had 2 small latches on the top and bottom rims, so it could lock in place.

Doris felt extremely hot, the water was boiling when she entered, so much so that it made her jump. Having the lid closed to keep all the hot steam in did not help. She squirmed around the bath uncomfortably, unable to really move. Her brow was already covered in sweat, and she was dying to itch it. But, like every other limb, her hands were tucked away neatly under the surface.

"I'm really uncomfortable Doc, not going to lie to you. How exactly is this supposed to help me relax and open up more?"

"Well..." the doctor began, "The extreme heat will dilate your blood vessels, this is meant to reduce stiffness. Reducing stiffness helps you to relax. While at the same time, extreme heat can cause some people to have hallucinations. Maybe it could even push your body into a fight or flight mode."

"And that's good? We want hallucinations and a fight or flight mode?" Doris squirmed.

"Well... maybe not necessarily those things, but..." the doctor hesitated, "Oh, well, let's just start by telling me what you're seeing right now in the room. I just want you to ramble off everything you're thinking and everything you're seeing. Even if you don't find it necessarily interesting or exciting. I still want to hear it all." The doctor took a seat on a small metal stool beside Doris. He crossed his legs and pulled out a small notepad, ready for whatever she had to say.

"Well..." Doris began, "I feel hot. Like so, so, so hot. I am uncomfortable and am not sure if I would be willing to do this again."

"Go on," the doctor said.

"My brow is sweating and all I want to do is wipe it. That's it!" The Doc pulled a small handkerchief from his breast pocket and dabbed at Doris's forehead. She moaned in relief, "Oh thank you Doc!" he smiled in return.

"Okay...hm... Well, it's throwing me off a little that there is no steam, I feel like my skin is going to be boiled like a lobster when I get out of here." Doris squirmed around some more. "I can't seem to get comfortable under this thing. I feel like I'm just a head, a floating head in a hot spring." The doctor chuckled a little.

"Keep going Doris, what do you see around the room?"

"Well, I see you, sitting on a stool. There are some windows, and it looks like it's snowing outside, there's some frost on the pane.

The floor was a grimy, yellowish tile. You guys should really send someone to clean in here more often."

"I'll make a note of that" Vernirelli smiled as he jotted it down in his notebook - *clean floors, "grimy, yellowish"* Dr. Vernirelli glanced down at the floors, they really were quite awful. He began to feel very sorry for Doris. Having to walk around in socks all day, no shoes. Her socks were probably stained an awful color and would probably seep through with whatever guck was strewn about. However, this was a non-negotiable thing for patients to wear socks. There had been too many severe incidents in the past where patients would use their shoes as a weapon. One man even beat another patient to death with his shoe when they still allowed them. That was considered to be the straw that broke the camel's back.

"The walls are kind of gross too. There are all these stains of... I don't know what." Doris remarked. Dr. Vernirelli then turned his attention to the walls. They were in fact, disgusting. He thought he could even see some kind of mold growing out of the corner in the ceiling. He made another note for the vicinity to be cleaned more often. Patients were supposed to be coming through every day and cleaning while being supervised. Clearly, they weren't doing a good job, or the more likely reason, no one was taking them to do it; because no one cared whether the patients had clean rooms to live in or not.

"I see you are noticing a lot of filth issues. Were you clean at home?" The doctor asked.

"Oh yes. My mother made sure I was always spick and span."

———✦✦✦———

"Doris!" Her mother screamed, "DOR-IS! Get in here young lady!" Doris came running into her room. Her mother was standing in the center of the room with her arms crossed. She glared at Doris, like she had done something so awful and horrific she almost could not bring herself to speak about what it was.

"Yes, mother?" Doris slowly walked in. Eyeing the room. Her bed was made, her books were all put-away, there were no clothes lying on the floor, and even her desk was as neat as ever.

"Doris, open your drawers." Her mother snapped, pointing to where Doris's clothes were tucked away. Doris slowly pulled one of the drawers open. Her clothes were not folded neatly like usual. Most of them were, but a few had just been tucked in and not properly turned over like they should have been. Doris gasped,

"I'm sorry Mother I didn't realize-"

"No, you did not!" Her mother shouted, "Cleanliness is what?"

"Close to Godliness," Doris answered.

"So, you are not?"

"Close to Godliness" Doris bowed her head.

"So, that means what?" Her mother asked, tapping her foot.

"Not going to heaven" Doris began to weep. Her mother sighed heavily and rolled her eyes. Doris truly did fear that she would not see those pearly gates she heard so much about on the Sunday services. Her mother told her herself; Doris would not get in because she was too messy. Doris would not get in because she talked to boys. Doris would not get in for her Halloween costumes 3 years ago. Doris would not get in because the girls who kept her company were not devoted Christians.

And if you did not get into heaven what would be waiting for you? Hell! The fire consuming your body, the demons poking at you with sharpened sticks, sins of your life forever haunting you, no rapture to bring relief.

"Well maybe you will think about that when you say your prayers tonight. Pray for forgiveness. I know I will pray for you. Wicked child." Her mother said as she patted her head smiling and left the room.

Doris pulled out the unfolded clothes, neatly arranged them how they should be, and put them back in the drawer. Then, she crawled into her bed and silently began to cry.

"Please God forgive me for I have sinned…"

"That must have been hard on you trying to keep everything in such order all the time," the doctor said.

"It was. Now I know what hell is going to feel like. It'll feel like being in this tub. Only, I am sure much worse given that my flesh will be falling straight off the bone and all." She tried to force a giggle but quickly fell silent, soon realizing that the doctor asked her to go on about any and all that she saw or thought.

"The sweat is starting to drip into my eyes Doc," she said as Dr. Vernirelli reached for his handkerchief but then paused.

"Perhaps we should let your body get to the extreme if we want this to work," he suggested. Doris huffed,

"If you say so but it's stinging my eyes really bad and making everything so blurry." Doris tried to twist and turn her head to get the sweat out, but nothing helped. She gazed around the room. Pointing out what objects she was able to make out to the doctor, although all were blurry. The room felt musty to look at. The titles all individually littered with grim. Doris went on and on about how she cannot stand seeing such things. If this filth was in her house, she would immediately be on her knees scrubbing. Perhaps she could join the cleaning crew, even though she knew it was not possible. Too many "weapons". And then she saw him.

Just a blurry shadow, barely in view. He stood in the corner. Not moving, just staring. He watched Doris in her tub, he watched her strapped in, unable to move. He watched Dr. Vernirelli scribbling notes on a pad. He saw it all. Doris wiggled and squirmed.

"Doc…" she whispered, "Doc, he's-he's in the corner" Doris nodded her head as best she could in the direction that the demon-man stood. She could barely see through her fogged up eyes, but she knew he was there. She could feel him. And soon her skin began to prickle in a way that not even the water could sooth out. Her blood turned cold despite the extraordinary temperature. The doctor slowly turned in the direction in which Doris was indicating. The doctor looked around.

The corner in which Doris had motioned was in the farthest corner of the room. It was dark, no natural light hit it. There was slime against the wall and the doctor could have sworn he saw a shadow of some kind, despite it being unlight. Was there truly something there? Or was this his imagination getting the best of him?

"Keep going Doris" the doctor said, encouraging her to push forward.

"He's standing there. He's just watching us." Doris gulped. She blinked trying to get the sweat to disappear, but it only made it worse. The sweat stung so badly it made her eyes water more than they were before. She closed them and kept them shut. After a minute or two she felt a soft dabbing on her eyelids, she sighed gratefully and opened them to find what she feared most grinning at her, inches from her face.

His teeth were sharp as ever, they were stained and yellowed. She could smell his breath and began to gag at such a putrid smell. One of rotten flesh and musk. His eyes bulge out, but he pupils nothing more than pin pricks that seemed to morph into slits.

Doris shrieked and began to thrash in her tub. Her thighs hit the lip so hard it almost unlocked one of the hinges.

"Doris, Doris!" She could hear the Doc yelling. But his voice seemed far away, he looked blurred, as if she was being pulled under water and looking up at him. She wished for him to drag her back to the surface, but she was falling. Deeper and deeper. And waiting for her in that dark murky water was *him*. She could feel him reaching towards her, waiting patiently at the bottom. She could feel his fingers graze against her, and she shrieked again. Opening her eyes this time.

The man-like demon reached for one of the latches, clicking it open. And then the other. He threw open the lid. Doris looked as if she had been cooked alive, and she felt it too. She tried to scramble to her feet. But he was waiting over her, like a vulture. He swooped down upon her, snatching her up to only swallow her whole.

The doctor watched in horror as Doris thrashed about in the tub. She was jerking so hard that the doctor feared she would throw the hinges off. He quickly held onto the latches as best he could, but they felt cold. Like ice had crept its way upon them. So cold that it made his hands retreat at the touch. Her eyes had rolled to the back of her head, and she looked as if she was gagging on nothing. She had clicked her jaw open and looked like she was eating the air, taking huge gulps, and forcing her neck forward like she was a bird choking down a rat. The doctor screamed her name, trying to snap her back into reality, but she would not listen. Could not listen. And then, almost as quickly as it started, it stopped. She stopped. Her body became very still, her neck seemed to lose the strength to keep her head up and it flopped to the back on the tub, smacking it on the porcelain.

"Doris!" The doctor lifted her head, checking for bleeding as it rolled to the front of the tub and into the doctor's other awaiting hand. "Doris?" He said again. But she did not answer him.

Her mouth was eschewed, eyes seemed to be glazy and yet so focused. Doris let out a moan. One that seemed to come straight from the deepest pit of her stomach. It buzzed on her lips like a cicada in the summer evenings.

"Doc...Doc..." she seemed to say, but her mouth wasn't moving, the noise just seemed to float out of her. It was deep and sinister. That buzzing joined in with her words, making the Docs skin raise in goosebumps. His first reaction was to run. But he could not leave her. He would not leave her. This is what he wanted right? For the man to come. To see Doris at her most vulnerable, and yet he almost forgot, her most dangerous as well.

"Yes, Doris?" the Doc said aloud.

"Let me out Doc." the floating noise said, "Let me out!" Suddenly Doris snapped her head in his direction. Dr. Vernirelli jumped back. Alarmed how quickly she was able to move and for still being latched in the tub.

"Doris, I think you need to stay in the tub longer." he eventually replied. His words came out like brittle, broken and sunbaked. All the saliva seemed to have dried up. His lips felt cracked, and his throat scratched. All the air seemed to be sucked out of the room. The only noise now, besides that awful buzzing was his heart, trying to thump his way through his chest, out of his ribcage, on the floor and out the door. Doris's body began to shake in anger. Her eyes rolled madly in her skull. Her lips pulled back into a snarl.

"I said, let me out you old fuck!" her voice was much lower this time. Deep, as if from her gut. Her words hung in the air. The doctor moved his chair back.

"Doris," he said, "Doris this is not you. This is your demon coming to claim your body. You need to fight it. You need to tell him that you're in control." Doris screamed inside her body. She yelled, *I'm in control! Release me!* But the creature only laughed. She could hear him echoing in her head as he made her wriggle and writhe like a worm on a hook. *Let go! Let me out. Let me out.* Doris began to claw her way within her own body. She felt like she was in a hole, so small, so tight. She was in what she called, "the hollow". The tight small area in which she felt like she just fit within her skin. It was constricted, hot, crowded, and worst of all she could see and feel everything that was happening to her, without controlling it. The hollow was so tight that she could not crawl her way out, but instead needed to inch out.

Doris pushed herself forward as best she could from within, she thrashed, and kicked her toes as best she could, wriggling her way up. "Fight it, Doris!" the doctor cried, "You're stronger than him. Think of all the terrible things he has forced you to do. Think of all he's made you lose. Don't give into him. You can break free." Doris pushed harder. She could feel her nails digging into what felt like flesh from within. The flesh of a mind-set, the one of darkness. Doris cried out again, *Let me out!* And then, she could see it. What looked almost like a cave, the walls were red, and pink, and squishy.

It felt wet as she continued to scoot and squirm herself up, farther and farther.

There was light and she could see the doctor. She reached for him as best she could, but her arms were not free yet to pull her forward.

"No!" The demon cried. She felt what seemed like tugging on her ankles. Something was trying to pull her back. Pull her back into the darkness. *Let go!* She screamed. Doris could hear the doctor. He seemed close. She could hear him encouraging her. Cheering for her to break free.

"Think of the family you lost. The families he made you tear apart. Think about having to wash off your hands. How he used and manipulated your body and mind!" Doris cried out again. She thought of all the faces. She thought how with all those people, her deranged, deformed face was the last those people ever saw. She thought about the mothers and fathers, sisters, and brothers he made her take way. She thought about them all.

Doris screamed out again, kicking off at whatever was pulling her down inside. She squirmed her way up, she saw the light, and could see the doctor. Then she knew where her inner self was. She was in the mouth. Doris reached a handout.

The doctor stared at Doris, wide eyed and afraid. Her head whirled back and forth, the way a roller coaster does when it whips heads about so effortlessly. Doris's eyes were nothing but white in her head and her mouth was beginning to foam. Dr. Vernirelli thought about clicking the button for a nurse's aide, the guard, anybody. Just so he wouldn't feel so alone in witnessing what was happening before him. But he knew that this illness Doris was experiencing could not be helped by medicine or brute force.

The doctor reached for Doris's head, attempting to brush the hair from her eyes. As soon as he held his hand out, she began to snap and spit at him like a dog with rabies would. He retreated. Doris looked as though she was going to throw-up. The doctor recalled how Doris had mentioned several times how the demon-like man would swallow her up, perhaps he would release her by vomiting.

"Doris, you're so close, I can see it. Keep going" The monster that was Doris's body screamed. It wailed as if it had been struck. Then it began to gag and choke on its own spit. Profusely foaming now. The doctor could see that she was crying. Tears, snot, and spit seemed to be oozing out of Doris, instead of just leaking. Forcing up something that he could not physically see but was hoping was there.

Doris suddenly broke her arms free from within. She gripped her fingers around the edge of the tub and pulled herself out as hard as she could from what was holding her in. Suddenly, she was back. Doris let her head drop. It hit the metal lid. She slowly rolled it over to look at the doctor. He was several feet away from her, eyes extensive and scanning.

"Doris?" the Doc eventually said, his voice no more than a whisper. Doris let out a sigh of relief.

"I did it Doc." She began to cry, "I broke free!" The doctor jumped from his chair, springing to his feet with such force his chair stumbled over behind him. He rushed over to Doris,

"Doris!" He cried, "Doris, I'm so proud of you!" He shouted, patting the top of her head. I knew you could do it. The Doc then proceeded to unhook the latches that held Doris in the tub. He pulled off the lid releasing a plume of steam. It hit his face hard, and he covered himself with his hands. He could hear Doris laughing.

"Thank you, Doc, thank you…" While her voice was indeed her own, something sounded off. Twisted, and cunning. The doctor took a step back.

"Doris?" his voice only a low whisper. He took off his glasses and rubbed the lenses as best he could. When he returned them to his face she was standing there. Inches from him. Doris smiled, her eyes seemed to slowly manipulate themselves into slits, but went back to the way they were seconds later. The doctor could not be one hundred percent sure of what he saw. But something in his gut gnawed away at him. He was almost certain there was something more behind those eyes.

"Doc, can I please have a towel?" Doris's voice was back to her own. Back to her sweet-sounding self. Keeping an eye on her the Doc fumbled for the towel that had fallen onto the floor when he had flung his chair back. He handed it to her, looking away to give her some sense of privacy.

"I can't believe we did it, Doc. I can't believe I got out!" Doris smiled, wrapping the towel around herself. She began to cry, "Thank you." With tears streaming down her face, she lunged towards the doctor, catching him in a hug. He could see the steam still rolling off her pink body, but when she hugged him, her hands felt cold, and uninviting. The doctor pulled back at the touch, *just like the latches.* The Doc cleared his throat.

"Let's get you some water." He smiled, "And something to help with your skin. I'm sure it was a painful procedure. But he's all out?" the doctor asked skeptically. Hesitating over his question.

"I don't feel him in me. Nothing!" Doris smiled. She was beaming, her lips ear-to-ear. The doctor guided Doris to Dr. Freude, who treated her skin with a clear colored gel. Dr. Vernirelli then guided Doris back to her room. As he slowly closed her door a thought came to him. Something he had never once done or even thought of in the past, he turned to the guard and said,

"Keep an extra eye on her for tonight." The guard nodded. Turning back to face Doris's room, watching her through the small window. The Doc hoovered, as if to say something more, but shook it off, like a hound dog shaking off flies, he turned and retreated back to his office for the evening.

⟞⟋⟍⟋⟍⟋⟍⟞

The doctor sat in his office, looking over his notes. He eyed them carefully. But there was nothing helpful. He could not have Doris placed in sanctuary just because of something he thought he saw in the steam. No. Besides, sanctuary was a cruel word to use to define what it truly was. A dark room was placed in the farthest corner of the facilities for the soul purpose of being for the patients who were true dangers to everyone around them. The fact that Doris had not been immediately placed there hinted at just how bad it was. He would keep an eye on her for the next several weeks. And if nothing happened out of the ordinary, then everything would be fine. After all, if the creature he thought he saw was still a part of her he had his chance to kill him, didn't he? Well perhaps not kill him. For who knows what that would entail. Get rid of him? Banish him? Those seem more doable.

If Doris really was possessed in the tub, then wouldn't he have been dead, gonzo, caput, curtains? So, he had nothing to worry about. He paced about in his office. *Nothing to worry about. Trick of the steam. Just a trick of Oz the Great and powerful. Although, his tricks were just fakes. Just a trick of the steam and the man behind the curtain.* The Doc rubbed his temples.

Just watch her closely, Francis. Just watch.

The next few weeks moved slowly for Doris. She had fallen into a comfortable pattern at Tokema. Each day she lined up to go to the rec room. She stared out her window, watching the swirls of snow as they drifted down, encasing her and the other patients inside. Kansas did not snow very often, so Doris always found it to be a treat when it did. Doris would often go over to her friend Theresa's home when she was younger. Theresa's father had bought a TV and let the girls watch it when they were little. The two of them would sit side-by-side on the floor of the parlor, under a big blanket, and watch Scrooge, 1922 with cocoa drinks. Doris often looked back on that particular memory fondly when it was around this time of year.

Doris would also keep busy by playing cards with the other patients. The majority of them seemed to almost accept her as one of them now, although there were always a few who kept their distance. She did not mind though. They seemed to leave her alone to do her own thing, and she left them to theirs. No point in trying to make friends by stirring the pot.

But, then again, there was really no such thing as "friends" here. Everyone seemed to either float past each other, ignoring in a way. Caught up in their own world, unable to notice at times that there were other people around them. And for those that did acknowledge the others, they only did so in a fashion so they could play cards together, do a puzzle together, some danced together (not touching of course), some even whispered to each other in the corner. But no one ever represented a sense of "friendship" to Doris.

Today, however, Doris was particularly bored. She was not in the mood for cards. She did not see the point of dancing with the others. She did not want to watch anything on TV. And while there was something calming to her window, she did not feel like looking out that either. She longed for a book to keep her company instead. She had not been permitted to visit the library once while being here. Books were seen as a weapon, and she was still a high-profile patient. *Perhaps I could talk to the Doc about getting in there...* Her next meeting with him was tomorrow and she could wait one more day to ask. She had waited this long...

So, she sat there patiently. Waiting for lunch, which was assumed to be vegetable soup. It had been for the last few days. Doris guessed that the kitchen's vegetables were about to go bad and that was why they had been serving them so frequently recently. It would make sense, given that she had seen a garden a few times as she glanced out the windows. The garden was small, and while she was not certain of what kind of garden it was, it was safe to say there were some sort of vegetables inside. And given that the ground was no longer in season for crops, the vegetables soon too would be out of season for consumption if not consumed quickly. But there was no access to the kitchen. At least, not for her.

Doris had asked a few times to join the kitchen and cleaning staff but was denied each time. If Doris had not truly been insane before being at Tokema, she felt she nearly was now. The days were all blending together in the same dull routine. She had only been there since late Summer, early Fall. She would not be able to continue this weariness of nonliving for the rest of her life.

She always dreamt that one day she would get out of Kansas, her sleeping little town, her sleepy little life, and do something big and bold. She could imagine herself traveling to different countries. Drinking champagne in France, swimming in Greece, and maybe even seeing an elephant in India. But those thoughts and hopes were gone now. They faded away the second *he* had shown up in her life.

Doris remembered it clearly the day he came. She was at an estate sale looking at old knick-knacks, old toys, antiques more of. Some old woman had died and her children had thrown together an estate sale to try and get rid of the things none of them wanted. Doris had found a beautiful necklace. It was beaded with what appeared to be little pieces of turquoise. The beads swooped and swirled around each other, completely capturing Doris's eye. She slipped it around her neck, going to pay once she reached the front. She continued to walk around glancing at different objects, when she noticed a doll similar to one, she had as a child. It was an antique China doll that very much resembled the one her grandmother had given her.

Doris smiled at it. When she was younger, she took the doll with her everywhere. One day she was playing tea in her backyard when a neighbor boy accidently threw a ball over her fence, hitting the doll directly on the head and breaking it. Her mother had tried to find a replacement, but it was already an antique and very difficult to find. Doris turned, heading to the front to purchase the childhood memory when *he* was suddenly there.

A man stood in front of her, his skin a sickly gray color. He seemed ordinary enough, besides the color of his skin. But there was something about him. Doris still couldn't put her finger on it reflecting back. But something about that man had made her skeleton shiver. He simply stood there, watching her, not saying one word. Doris had looked behind her to see if he was not in fact looking at her, but over her shoulder at someone else. But there was no one there. He smiled at her. His smile made her feel sick, like he was looking at her like she was a new plaything for him to enjoy. And his smile looked hungry.

Doris tried her best to give a grin back, although she was never sure if she did or not. She thought she had, just to be polite. "Excuse me" she murmured as she attempted to walk past him, but he had caught hold of her arm. His grip was tight, and his hands were cold. She tried to pull away, but his fingers only held their position.

"What the hell do you think you're doing?" Doris said, trying to pull her arm away. But he just held her there. Doris struggled and then began to yell out for help. But no one seemed to notice her. No one even looked up from the items they were all sifting through. Everyone seemed to go about their business, as if agreeing not their pig, not their farm. A mutual understanding of silence and ignorance.

"Help! This man won't let me go!" Doris yelled out again, but still, no one even spared a passing glance in her direction, "What is wrong with all you people?" She wailed. Doris turned on her heels, trying to run the other way but it was no use. The man holding her arm turned her to face him.

It was then that she noticed his eyes were different. They looked sick, completely red, she could see a certain kind of desire in them. Something that made her begin to panic even more. It was not a desire of lust but of a kind of wanting. A cruel and evil want. A look of a predator finally grabbing hold of its prey.

He then grabbed her head with such force Doris thought that he would crack her skull like one does an egg if they squeezed it too tightly. She shrieked, reeling backward, but his grip did not loosen. It was then that she felt his teeth on her. As he shoveled her down, deep inside him. But then, it was just her. Doris stood dumbfounded.

She wasn't sure what had just happened. Was it perhaps an episode of some kind? Did she hallucinate? She looked around and she was still at the estate sale. She looked down at her arm where the man had grabbed her, but there was nothing there. Not even a scratch. Doris shook her head. Clearly, she had just experienced a miniature meltdown of some kind, although she was not sure what. She turned back to the table to retrieve the old doll, but it was not there. Maybe she had dropped it during whatever happened to her. She looked down, but again it was not there.

Doris spent some time looking for the doll when she overheard a young mother talking to her daughter, "Now be careful honey, that is made of China, so you need to play with it very carefully."

"I will mommy" Doris turned to see the pair walking away. Doris saw the girl was holding what she thought was her China doll. Doris probably dropped it on the grass and the girl must have picked it up when Doris was having her fit. She hoped to herself that the doll would bring the little girl as much joy as it brought her as a child. Doris went back to the sale, she found an old cookbook, a nice quilt, and silverware. There was nothing left at the sale that had piqued her interest however the same way that old China doll did. Doris returned to her home and her day continued as if she had never even had an encounter.

It would not be until months later when she would meet the man again.

———⟨○/○/○⟩———

Dr. Vernirelli laid in his bed. He knew he would need to start getting ready to make it to Tokema on time, but his body did not seem to want to move. He rolled his head lazily over his shoulder and read the glowing numbers, 5:45 AM. He signed. While he could have stayed in bed until 6 o'clock, he knew his routine would be thrown off if he did not force himself to his feet soon.

The Doc rolled his legs over the edge of the bed and steadily raised his body. He looked at himself in the mirror and decided a shower was just the thing to get rid of his bedhead today. Slipping into his moccasins and his robe, a gift from his sister, he made his way down the hallway. Flicked on the light and made his way to the mirror. He brushed his teeth; he would have to do something about that back left molar. While he was permitted to visit Dr. Tablani for free, and while he thought he was an excellent doctor overall, there was something that left him feeling unsettled about his co-workers. He did not like the way Tablani would get a glint in his eye before doing dental work.

Sliding out of his robe he stepped into the misty shower and began to clean himself. He rubbed the soap along his body, clearly scrubbing behind his ears when he heard soft music coming from outside the door. The Docs back stiffened. He slowly turned the nozzle, having the water lead to nothing but a small trickle. With soap still on his body he listened.

There was music playing from the hall. He was unsure of what to do. Someone else was clearly in his house. There were no windows in the bathroom. He could lock himself in the room, but then what? He would be a sitting duck.

The Doc scanned the room, looking for any items that could possibly be used as a weapon. He quickly decided his razer and a wooden-handled loofah were his best bet. Jumping into his robe and clenching both items tightly in his hand he approached the door. He pressed his ear against it and was able to hear the music more clearly this time, *anytime night or day, only trouble is, gee whiz I'm dreamin' my life away...I need you so that I could die, I love you so and that is why, whenever I want you, all I have to do is...* The Doc pulled his ear away from the door.

This was not an album in his collection. He was sure of it. Had someone really broken into his house, brought their own music, and turned on his record player just to scare him? The doctor drew in a quick breath. And slowly turned the handle.

The door *creaked* open in such an unsettling manner it made the Doc cringe. The noise of the door was loud, how could he have not noticed it before? He only hoped that the intruder did not hear it. He paused, waiting to see if there would be footsteps, if the music would stop, anything to indicate that he was given away; but there was nothing. The music played on, now louder in the hallway. And clearly not coming from his living room as he suspected.

There was only one record machine in his house, and it rested right next to the sofa. But this noise, this clearing came from back in his bedroom. The Doc could feel his hands sweating, his brow was hot and prickly as he stepped into the hall. His knuckles were white from clenching the loofah and razor with such force.

He stepped further into the hall. The corridor seemed to stretch further than he had ever noticed. It could have been that his steps were just smaller, but the walk to his room seemed to make him feel stuck in time. Yes, his feet were moving, but he seemed to be going nowhere. Trudging along as quietly as he could he finally reached his door. His back was against the wall, as he craned his head around the corner.

The music stopped. The doctor pulled himself back as quickly as he could. Holding his breath, eyes painted open, chest heaving up and down. The silence was more unsettling and disturbing than the music. For clearly someone had seen him and had used it as a ploy to get him to come to the room. He stood there, very still. He must have stayed this way for several minutes, he thought to himself before mustering the courage to once again look back into the room.

He turned once more and glanced into his bedroom. It was empty. The sheets were lazily thrown to the side of the bed, as he did every morning. His closet door opened, just the way he left it when he grabbed his robe. No clothes were out of place. He looked down to see if someone or something was perhaps hiding in them. But there were no feet. His nightstand was completely empty, except for his clock, 6:04 AM. He even looked out the window to see if someone had slipped out, but there was no indication that someone had even been there.

Warily glancing around the room, the doctor did a little walk around. Everything was in place as it should have been. The music was gone, and he seemed to be alone. He loosened his grip on the makeshift weapons in his hands. Just to be safe he would do another whole loop around the house.

He glided from room to room, careful whenever entering and always cautious. But there was no one to be found. The last vinyl on the record player was the Voice of Frank Sinatra, 1946 edition. The same one he was listening to last night before bed.

The doctor made his way back to the bathroom and determined everything was in the clear. Maybe a neighbor was blasting their music at full volume. Perhaps he just imagined it. As he stepped into the powder room and closed the door behind him, he once again stripped himself. He made his way over to the mirror. He looked in at himself, and standing there, over his shoulder was a demon-like man with flesh the same color as the bottom of an ashtray. Smiling down at him.

The Doc turned at such speed that he needed to catch himself on the lip of the sink. But there was no one there. No man in the bathroom. The doctor was once again alone. He turned back to the mirror and saw only his reflection. Only himself.

The Doc stood there for a few minutes. Holding his chest, attempting to control his breathing. *You are still shaken from the incident with Doris in the tub. She's been fine, therefore there is nothing to worry about. You are fine…* He whipped the sweat from his brow, and took one last glance over his shoulder, to truly make sure the man was no longer standing behind him. Just to put his mind at ease he would go about checking the other rooms in the house too. Looking for any signs that could possibly indicate someone else being there. He would listen for any sound, any at all.

Once the Doc determined again, for the half a dozenth time, that it would be safe to take a shower and get ready for his day, he would have to miss doing the daily crossword, making a pot of coffee, and taking the scenic route to work; he returned to finish his shower.

In the car, the doctor thought about what the man had looked like in the mirror. He had only seen him for a second, but he was certain that the man had black, slicked-back hair that seemed almost wet, a crooked mouth, a pointed nose, and teeth so sharp that they themselves could have been used as a shaving razor. He thought about how he could try and subtly pull out more descriptive clues for Doris to describe the man. Maybe if she really dove deep down into him visually, he could see if they were indeed the same person.

She really only discussed that his skin was a sickly gray, and had demon-like qualities to him, with his face being indeed human, but something twisted and sinister masked behind it. The Doc thought he finally understood now what she had meant, instead of what he initially imagined in his mind's eye.

While Doris's description was right on the money in a way, it was missing a few key details. Like, how the man's skin was pulled tight across his face, making his lips look like they were cracking from the sheer force of being bound so tightly. How his shoulders were twisted, and you could see bone poking through, even with clothes on. And there was a glimmer of something. The Doc wasn't sure what. Something glinted in the mirror as well when he first saw the man. It was subtle, but he was sure of it.

The Doc tried hard to think about what else he could remember of the man standing behind him, but the more he thought the more blurred the image seemed to become. As if he was losing it. He knew recalling a memory too many times tainted it. But this seemed different somehow. It seemed as if the incident was almost being erased.

He could no longer picture the details of the man's face. He knew what he thought he saw, but he could no longer draw on the specifics. Was he taller or shorter than him? What was the color of his hair? The Doc tried desperately to no longer think about what happened that morning. Perhaps if he did not think about it, the memory would stay preserved.

But by the time he pulled into his usual parking spot, locked up his car, and walked into his office, the memory was completely gone. The Doc could only recall that he had woken up late this morning, which is why he could not do his crossword, make his coffee, or take the scenic route to work today.

That darn alarm clock, buying a new one was definitely needed. After work, he would dash to the nearest store and get a brand-new one. Maybe one that he needed to wind and set himself. The same as he had when he was a boy. They were louder and more efficient anyway. You can never trust new technology.

———◦/◦/◦———

Doris lay in her bed. She was very still as she looked up and counted the ceiling tiles.

"114...115...116..." she murmured to herself. She already knew how many tiles were on the ceiling. She had counted them plenty of times before in her boredom. There were 346. But counting them had become a pass time. It came to be something to do while she was tired and unable to fall asleep. She would talk to the doctor tomorrow about going to the library and possibly finding new ways to entertain herself in this hell hole.

Doris could feel her eyes growing heavy. She could feel her lids starting to flutter. She closed her eyes. Humming to herself. Pretending that she was on a beach somewhere. Her toes were in the sand, the water spraying on her face. She could feel the warmth of the sand. It was relaxing. For the first time in a long time, she let out a content sigh. She reopened her eyes, only to discover that she was no longer lying on her bed, counting the ceiling tiles, nor was she outside on the sandy beach she had just seen so vividly. She knew where she was.

She was out amongst the trees, just outside of the facility. But it was not winter, instead, it was Fall. The leaves were changing color, some were even on the ground, and she could smell the crisp change in the air. Doris breathed in deeply. She looked around and there he was standing. The man in the oversized and disgustingly sloppy t-shirt. The holes were still a blaze, his skin still falling off the bone in certain parts. He seemed to be getting worse.

She was now becoming used to these dreams. Each time he would stand there, telling Doris to watch closely as he did his spasm dance, collapsing to the ground and then disappearing into no more than smoke. And while Doris knew what was going to happen next while dreaming, she could no longer remember once awake. All she was ever able to recall of the dream outside of itself was what the man looked like.

"Hello," Doris said to the man.

"Doris, watch…watch…" The man began to gag. Doris watched as the man requested. She stared closely as his eyes watered, his stomach pulsed, and he grasped at his neck in pain. Fear strangled his eyes as he continued on. He then stopped. It looked as if he were teetering on the edge of something. Slowly rocking back and forth on his heels just as a new mother would while cradling her child to sleep.

"Help me Doris" he seemed to say, although his mouth did not move.

Doris glided over to the back of the man, she began hitting his back with her palm, like he was a baby she was trying to make spit up. She struck his back harder, and harder until finally, the man collapsed forward. She stood there. Looking at the spot in which the man fell, he was no longer there. No crazy dance. Just vanished. She looked for dark marks, or indentations in the ground, but saw nothing. She looked back up, and standing in front of her there he was again.

Only this time, he floated slightly, transparent. She glared at him in awe. His skin no longer charred, and his clothes were no longer destroyed. In fact, he looked almost handsome. She seemed to be looking into his very essence, instead of the man himself. He nodded at her as if approving of her looking upon him in this form.

"Remember Doris, remember." He seemed to fade, and as he left, he hummed a familiar tune. One Doris recognized one that sat on the tip of her tongue, but as far as remembering which song the man hummed that was neither here nor there.

Doris closed her eyes. She tried to think of where she heard that music before. It seemed to float around her. It was comforting, and yet, it disturbed her to her bones. Her spine prickled, and she suddenly stood more erect than she had been before. *Dream...*

Doris jolted from her bed. Her brow was lined with sweat and there was a stain from where she was sleeping on the covers. She panted heavily, and just underneath her panting, barely even noticeable she heard soft music. It was coming from the hall.

Doris slowly swung her legs over the edge of her bed. She sat there listening, trying to control her breathing so it was not to distract from her ears. She held her breath. *Whenever I want you, all I have to do is dream, dream, dream...* Doris slowly crept out of her bed. Inching her way towards the window in her door. She peered outside. Standing there, was the burnt man.

Doris felt something rumble inside her, something dark and sinister, she reached for the handle. Wanting to fling the door open and pounce on him. She felt that he needed to be taught a lesson for medaling in her business. *I'll teach you to go around, interfering with business that's ain't fucking yours to interfere on.* He needed proper discipline, and she intended to give it to him. She grabbed at the handle, attempting to fling it open. But the door would not move. She screamed, this time throwing herself against the wood. The door shook but still did not make way. Something had taken over her body, she seemed to no longer be in control of her thoughts and actions.

As she attempted a third time the door swung open and onto her. She was pinned to the ground. One of the guards was holding her down,

"What's going on here?" He snapped. Doris looked around her. She tried to look towards the door, but her head was being held in place. She slowed her breathing and listened. The music was no longer playing. She no longer felt angry. In fact, she was not even sure why she was out of bed,

"What the hell is going on in here?" The guard repeated, banging her head on the floor as if to try to crack her head open and have the answer slip out and onto the floor.

"I'm - I'm not sure... I-I must have been sleeping walking sir." Doris said. She lay on the ground. Not daring to try and get up. The guard held her there for a few several seconds, then slowly got off of her. He huffed, as if saying, *Whatever.* As he got off, he gave Doris a swift kick to the side, and she groaned.

"Get back to sleep," he grumbled and turned. Closing the door and locking Doris back in. She crawled towards her bed, not wanting to attempt and stand, given the pain in her side. She once again crawled under her covers and eventually went back to sleep. Only this time she had no more dreams.

⚊⚊⊰⊱⚊⚊

When Doris awoke her side was a deep purple, with a pale-yellow undertone. There was also a deep gash from where the boot made direct contact. It had seemed to scab over in the night but was not completed. She tried her best to stand straight but crumpled like a rag doll being thrown to the side. She groaned and clung to her stomach where she received the kick last night. Her bruise was hot and as she clung to it little bits of pus oozed its way onto her fingertips.

Doris hobbled her way to the door as best she could. "Help... help!" she cried. She felt hot and dizzy as she made her way to the door. She could see someone peeking in looking down at her. It was a different guard from last night. This was the new guard with red hair who took her to the bathroom months ago. She thought his name was George.

George stared at Doris from outside the glass. *Why the heck is she lying on the ground like that?* George took out his keys and unlocked the door. He swung it open, being mindful not to hit Doris. She was groaning and her eyes remained shut.

"Doris?" he asked. *Maybe this is a trick. After all, she is a bloody psychopath.* George backed up slightly. His hand hovering above his stick that rested on his hip. Doris just continued to lay there. Her face was pale, and she seemed to be sweating profusely. She slowly turned her head and looked up at him. Her eyes were glazed, and she looked as if she was going to be sick.

George dropped his hand from his side. Gently and using his foot he rolled her over, so she was on her back, looking towards the ceiling. She screamed. George jumped back and instinctively went for his stick, before realizing he wasn't in any danger.

Fuck... she's looking real sick. Better call the infirmary. "Okay, Doris I'm going to get some help..." George turned on his heels without saying another word and closed the door behind him. He radioed in on his walkie-talkie.

"We have a situation in Doris Draker's room. She seems to be sick. Over."

"Copy that. Can she walk? Over."

"Not sure. I'll try and get her up. Over." George turned back to the room. "Doris, Doris stand up," he said. But she did not move. "I said stand up!" Doris simply laid there like a dead fish who had been pulled to the surface with no life. "She's unable to walk. Over"

"Understood. Sending a chair. Over and out." George stood there. Half in the doorway waiting for the nurses to come down the hall. He suspected they would be taking their time. While Doris had been here for a few months and didn't seem to cause trouble, she was still a killer he told himself. And ain't nobody's going to come rushing to the side of a killer. He knew the nurses felt the same way. He often overheard them chatting about the different patients over lunch.

'You can see it in her eyes' one of the nurses would say.

'She sticks to herself, but it's only because she's plotting.' another would go on.

'Wish she was in prison and not in this place… it's bad enough already. Filthy pigs' the first would retort. This would go on and on. At first, George liked to join in all the gossip. There was something fun about having control over a serial killer. When he first accepted this job, he imagined himself as the big man with the stick. *Speak softly and carry a big stick. That's exactly how I am going to be when I'm a guard,* he'd think to himself, *and if one of them gets outta line, BLAMMY! A good swift hit will teach them to mess with the likes of me.* Yes, these were the thoughts that George first had when he was hired by Tokema. However, after being here for a few months he found that the job was relatively boring.

Always standing around. Waiting for something to do. There was no real action besides following the patients around. Maybe walking them back to their corridors or to the bathroom if they woke up in the middle of the night. When he first started most of the patients would just go in their rooms. But George could not handle the smell, so anytime he saw one squatting down, ready to go, he'd rush in and drag them off to the facilities. By this time, most patients knew if they needed to go at night, and he was working, to just knock on their doors and he'd open right up.

Just as he suspected, the nurses rolled up with a wheelchair about 15 minutes later. A girl named Nora and the other one named Kitty. He smiled at them as they came strolling up in their clean, pressed, white dresses and little caps. Boy did they look mighty fine. At least that was one perk of the job.

"Morning ladies." He smiled, giving them a toothy grin. The ladies laughed.

"What's wrong with her?" Nora asked. Looking at Doris like she was a disgusting worm she wanted to squash beneath her shoe.

"Don't know. Just started screaming for help and she's been clinging to her side ever since."

The ladies strolled over to where Doris laid. They got on either side of her arms and tried lifting her. Doris let out a scream. Kitty shrieked and jumped back.

"She's guna snap, I just know it! Georgie, you handle it. You put her in the chair." George walked over to Doris and yanked her by the left arm. Doris once again screamed in pain as he placed her into the chair. He was no fan of Doris, obviously. But he did not want to toss her around either. What if she really was about to snap and a toss just triggered it? Doris once again crumpled to her side. Clinging to it for dear life.

"Wow she looks really sick…" Nora said, "Deserves her right." She laughed as she poked the side in which Doris clung. Again, making Doris cry out in pain.

As the ladies pushed her down the hall and to Dr. Freude, George watched as they left. Their hips swing from side to side. The little bounce in their step. He grinned, feeling his pants become tighter. He would have to follow up with those girls later, he thought to himself.

<hr />

Dr. Freude stood over Doris. He had her stretch on a table that was meant to serve as a medical bed. Doris no longer seemed to be responding. She was breathing heavily, and her eyes would flutter open from time to time, but never long enough for her to answer any questions. It was obvious that Doris was clinging to her side, perhaps a burst appendix? Freude tried to straighten Doris out best he could to the table, and to his surprise Doris obeyed. Laying flat as bored. Clearly not a burst appendix. *Überprüfen Sie besser zuerst Ihre Vitalwerte.*

Freude stretched Doris's eyelids open, flashing a light to check her pupils. He stared at them deeply. The pale blue of Doris's eye grew as the blackness of her pupil shrank. But then, if only for a moment, the pupil seemed to split. It seemed to elongate itself as if it were a cat or a snake's eye being examined instead of a humans. Dr. Freude shook his head and looked again. The pupil was back to the size of the head of a pin. Nothing unusual or out of the ordinary.

He checked her blood pressure, 128 over 79. It was indeed elevated. Freude checked her temperature, 99 degrees Fahrenheit. It was obvious that the temperature would be high from the get-go. Doris's face was looking flushed, and her breathing increased. Once all the basic vitals were checked Freude decided to strip Doris, looking at the spot in which she had been clinging to.

Doris's side was swollen and discolored. There was a large wound, crest moon shaped, like the tip of a boot. There appeared to be dirt and grime caked into the cut, although Dr. Freude was not completely sure. He could see yellow puss trickling out from the spot. The skin was a mix of yellows, purples, reds, and blacks. The flesh was elevated, and there appeared to be something almost sticking out. Something that was raised to the surface of the skin, but not quite making its way through yet.

Dr. Freude examined the area with great detail. "Vat is zat?" Freude murmured to himself. It looked almost like a string of beads underneath Doris's skin. Freude poked at it and Doris seemed to snap out of her dazed and confused phase.

Doris shrieked in pain and again tried to crumple her body to the side. Clinging to the spot that Freude poked. Freude shrugged; the screams did not turn him off. In fact, the opposite. He was determined to see what was lying beneath the skin. Even if it did seem to cause Doris pain. Curiosity in medicine always killed the cat.

"Nora, Kitty. Strahp un frau to zee table." Nora and Kitty did as they were told. Grabbing Doris's arms and legs. Forcing her to open up. Arms strapped tightly above her head. Legs spread wide and parallel.

Dr. Freude pulled open a drawer, revealing shiny tools and utensils. All for picking, poking, prodding, pulling, and his personal favorites, extracting! Freude carefully grazed his fingers above each tool. Giving each one special attention before moving onto the next. His fingers hovered above a small scalpel. It glittered in the light of the room. The handle was wooden. He had brought it with him when he first arrived off the boat from Germany.

The blade was slightly dulled from use over the years, but he did not care. The blade was clean, it just needed a little extra strength when inserting. That's all, and he did not mind one bit. Freude smiled at it. Then, he pulled a pair of scissor head curved clamp pliers, he nodded. As if agreeing with his choices of the instruments.

Dr. Freude turned back to Doris. Her eyes were closed, and she was breathing heavily still. Freude thought he heard some mutter from under her breath, but he could not be sure.

Dr. Freude walked over to the table and plunged the scalpel into Doris's side with one quick smooth motion, not even giving it a second thought that Doris had no topical to numb her pain.

Doris bellowed. Thrashing her body about, but the bands that held her wrists and ankles in place were strong. She did not move her position, only slightly raising her belly. But Dr. Freude did not mind. He was used to his patients wriggling like worms on hooks, and he loved being the fisherman.

Freude slid the scalpel slightly deeper, opening the wound to full exposure. There was indeed something in there amongst the blood and puss. Freude reached for his clamps, sliding them inside Doris and tugging on whatever it was he had seen. He tugged, but whatever was inside Doris seemed to be resisting. It seemed to be attached to something larger. Freude tugged hard this time. He heard what sounded like a slight tear, suddenly a string of beads fell to the ground from Doris's side. They were small and a brilliant turquoise blue. Freude eyed the beads that sprawled across the floor. Nora and kitty jumped back.

"What the hell just came out of her?" One of the girls gasped. But Dr. Freude ignored the question. Their questions seemed to blur, becoming murmurs behind him,

Baffled on how it even got inside Doris in the first place. *Ich glaub mein Schwein pfeift.* Freude thought to himself. He shoved the clamp back in, digging around for more. Ignoring Doris's cries in the background. Freude moved and blindly poked his way through Doris before deciding to give up. He could see glints of what he imagined to be the rest of the string of beads, however, it seemed to disappear, perhaps retreating further into the body, but it seemed as if it had never even been there in the first place. Freude sighed in defeat.

He threw the clamps down and grabbed a loaded syringe. He poked Doris a few times. It almost seemed pointless now, but if Doris was in a bit more or less pain it meant nothing to him. For pain was irrelevant. Even his pain was something to simply overcome. It was only a distraction which limited most people in their discovery for truth, especially in the medical field. He cleaned the cut how he saw fit and grabbed a straight needle and weaved it in and out of Doris. Closing up the enlarged wound he had created. He bandaged up his handy work nicely.

Doris's eyes still were closed, and she seemed to be silent. Dr. Freude was not sure if Doris had passed out due to the pain inflicted on her or if she was just resting from the ordeal. Either way, *Das ist mir Wurst.*

Doris awoke in the infirmary later that day. She had been given a proper bed and when she opened her eyes, she saw Dr. Vernirelli sitting next to her.

"Doc?" she whispered. Her throat was sore, and her neck felt strained. The doctor looked up from some papers he had been examining, he smiled at her.

"Hello Doris. How are you feeling?" Doris looked around the room. For an infirmary it sure was filthy she thought. But that seemed to be a repeating pattern in Tokema. Forever doomed to a life of unsanitary living. There were stains on her sheets. The walls seemed to have a grime on them, and on the floors, Doris could see more stains. One she was sure either came from other patients' vomit or blood or any other kind of fluid that leaked out of a person. Doris shrugged in response to the doctor's question. Her side stung. The doctor could see Doris glancing around at the filthy room.

"Yes, I know. Hardly the qualifications for a proper infirmary. But it is rather difficult to get things cleaned up around here when the big wigs don't seem to care. It was an ordeal getting your common room cleaned up." Doris nodded her head; she understood that the conditions of this place mattered to no one really besides the Doc. He was the only one who genuinely seemed to care about the people in this place.

Doris propped herself up as best she could. "I've been better," she muttered, answering his first question.

"Do you remember why you're here?"

"Yeah," she responded, "I think that guard kicked me a little too hard in my side. It was purple-ish when I saw it." Dr. Vernirelli raised an eyebrow and jotted something down. He knew the guards handled the patients roughly, but he never suspected they beat them so hard to cause a wound the size of Doris's.

"Do you remember which guard kicked you?" he asked, trying to sound nonchalant. Doris sat there for a bit, trying to remember what had happened last night. She recalled bits and fragments of her dream, seeing the man in the window of her door, and then the guard jumping on her. But she had not gotten a good look at his face, since he was on top of her so quickly.

Doris shook her head. "No."

"That is alright Doris. I will try and figure it ou-"

"No." Doris interpreted, "I don't want more trouble. I've had enough of it here." *But not nearly enough yet.* Doris shot her head up and looked around. It had been some time since she heard him talking in her head. *Push him out, Doris. Push him out like last time!* She thought to herself. She could hear snickering. *'Push him out, Doris. Push him out like last time!'* She could hear him mocking her from within.

"Doris?" The doctor asked, "Doris I promise there won't be any trouble. But I can understand why you might not want me to say anything." Doris nodded in understanding. She appreciated how the doctor listened to her, despite his wanting to intervene.

"Doc, I don't mean to sound rude, but is it alright that I take some time for myself? I'm really tired," Doris asked.

"Of course, Doris. I just know that you have been through something very traumatic, physically, and I thought it would be best if I was around when you woke up. But if you're sure I can go." But Doris wasn't sure. Part of her really wanted the Doc to stay. But another part. Somewhere deep down wanted him to leave. Did not want him anywhere near her.

"I'm sure," she said. And with that the doctor stood up, collected his things and left. He hesitated by the door, making sure there would be no, 'wait I changed my mind!' or any, 'On second thought I think you better stay.' But there were none.

Doris sat there quietly. She stared at her hands. Something she was not able to do for no more than a few seconds. But now, in this moment they seemed to be all she could look at. She studied her hands closely. Looking at every indent in her palm. Every line, every crack, every broken nail. Almost like she was trying to memorize what they looked like. As she examined the center line in her palms, she noticed a little red dot. She pulled her hand closer to her face to see. The dot seemed to be bubbling, oozing as it grew. Doris touched the dot with her other hand and a warm liquid slid its way between her fingers. *Blood.* Doris shook her head. She had not seen any cuts. She closed her eyes and reopened them. The blood was gone.

She looked at her other hand, there was nothing. Not even a stain. Perhaps she really was more tired than she thought. Perhaps her mind was under more stress from the incident to her side than she initially realized. Or maybe the infection on her side was causing her to see things that were not actually there. Whatever it was Doris sighed and closed her eyes. She would attempt to get some sleep. Just like she told the Doc.

———◦/◦/◦———

Doris breathed heavily as she scrubbed away at her hands. *Please come out, please. God what has he done now...* Up to her wrists was stained in a deep red. Doris could smell the iron and dirt in the air. She was sobbing over the sink, avoiding any eye contact at all with the mirror. She would have avoided her hands too but needed to make sure all the blood was rinsed away.

Once Doris was certain there was no blood or dirt underneath her fingers she turned to the shower. She was not sure if there was anything in her hair or on her face. She had made the mistake before of looking in the mirror the first time. Only to reveal the scratches, chunks of blood, and a bruised eye. Whoever he made into her first victim fought hard and tried to get away from her. But apparently, they did not fight strong enough. She could not remember her first victim. The details seemed fuzzy in her mind. Whoever it was clearly tried their best. Doris was sure if the man inside her did not control her every movement the stranger would have overpowered her.

She couldn't recall if the first victim was a boy or a girl. She remembered being in a field. She had packed herself a picnic and was set-up in a little meadow that led to the water. It was a quiet, secluded place that her mother used to take her to. She recalled her mother loving it so much because hardly any other people knew about that spot. And it was perfectly out of sight for some privacy.

Doris had taken a few of her dates down there. But today she came alone. She had just quit her job and received a new one as a secretary. No more cleaning houses for her. No more vacuuming carpets besides her own. No more scrubbing filth in other people's tubs pulling random clumps of hair from the drain; that were caked in a black, stinking, sludge of some sort. There would be no more!

That's when Doris heard the laughing. She remembered that she had turned around but could not recall what happened next. Doris did recall reading somewhere that the brain would block out truly traumatizing events. Perhaps this is what her brain had done the first time it happened. She wished for it to block out the rest, but apparently recurrences make events numb and ordinary at some point to the brain. Or maybe he stopped the brain from blocking out the memories. It was feasible after all that he wanted her to remember. Wanted her to see it happen.

Occasionally there had been times where she would indeed black out, like this instance, but something would always happen it seemed, triggering the event and making her remember...everything. She prayed that would not happen this time as she stripped off her clothes.

She noticed that her shirt was ripped and that there was mud covering her legs until a little above the knee. She could not recall where she was earlier that day or even what she had been doing. *I could have gone to the grocery store. No, that was yesterday. Maybe I went to the park to have a walk? No... Shoot Doris, what was it that you did today? Think girl, think!*

Doris tossed the rest of her clothes into the hamper by the toilet and stepped into the shower. Immediately crumpling down by the drain. Let the water pour itself over her face, down her back, between her buttocks, over her nipples, and eventually back down into the claw footed tub. Her eyes frosted over. As if they weren't even seeing the amount of filth that dripped off her just from the contact of the water.

It felt holy to her. Holy in the sense that the filth did not necessarily need a scrubbing, even though she was still going to deep clean every inch of herself, but it simply just needed the touch of something pure and translucent to be removed.

Translucent. Doris wished she could be this way. Wished she could turn herself in for everything that he was making her do. She tried to confess to people of what he was making her do, but she could never seem to get the words out. Already this had been her 3rd time being forced to kill. She did not wish to continue on such a path. But when she came close to admitting the demented truth he would be there. Standing behind the person she wished to confess to. He would be watching. And she knew, knew they would be the next casualties if she did not keep her mouth closed.

She laid there in the tub for a long time. Not one thought crossed her mind. She was numb inside. The water rippled and rolled off her body until, eventually, she reached for a bar of soap. Absent-mindedly she forced her arms to wipe the soap up and down her body. Gliding its way around her, taking the grime away with it.

She could see clots of what she assumed was blood dribbled off her body. The ivory-colored soap turned to light pink. It made her think of Pepto-Bismol. This thought made her stomach turn and flip inside, comparing the medication to this sickly color displayed on her soap. 'Drink your medicine Doris, you'll need it to calm your stomach,' she could hear her mother saying.

Doris closed her eyes and threw the soap. It smacked the clear curtain and slipped down outside of the tub. Great, now a new bar of soap will be needed now that that one is on the floor. Can't have dirty soap.

Doris groaned. She reached for her shampoo, lacing her fingers between her hair. She felt a sharp sting and winced her hands back. She looked down at her fingers. There was fresh blood streaming down her fingertips. Tentatively she reached her hand back and gently felt around. She felt the sting and lightly winced again. She blindly felt around her scalp. There seemed to be a cut, but nothing too deep. Thank goodness, no doctors will be needed.

Oh, but you need a doctor, Doris. You need one! You are sick after all. Very, very sick.

"I am not sick!" She screamed. Doris grabbed at her head and continued to scream, "I am not sick! I'm not! You are! You're disgusting and vile and, and, and..." She began to sob. She looked back down at her hands. They seemed to become dirty all over again.

———◦/◦/◦———

Doris jolted herself awake. She panted like a dog as she glanced around where she was. She was in the infirmary. She was still in Tokema. She attempted to raise her hand but realized she could not. Her wrists seemed to be held down by something, she looked.

There were thin leather straps across her wrists and ankles. She had not recalled them being there before. She supposed a nurse could have done it while she was sleeping. Doris pulled a little harder, but they were fastened tightly.

There was a click and Doris looked up. She could hear someone walking in, but the lights were now off and there were no windows in her room. Doris felt her heart begging to leap from her chest. She felt the hairs on her neck begin to prickle, under her pits begin to perspire. Then she saw a match light up. It lit the end of a cigarette. The light glowed revealed a face. The face of Dr. Freude.

"Hallo fraulein." He spoke. Doris wriggled in her straps. She could feel something disturbing hanging in the air. She felt it. She felt it like how animals can sense a storm hours before it erupts, or how a dog can sense the mailman coming up the drive.

"Dr. Freude " her voice shook, "Dr. Freude, what brings you here?" She tried to sound casual. She did not want him to know she was afraid of him. She tried to contain herself.

"I kame to examine. To get un closer look." He took a step towards Her. She could see he was inhaling as the light upon his face became slightly brighter.

"Don't, don't you need the light on?" Doris whispered, she tried to keep her voice from quivering. She was not sure why, but she would have felt much safer with the light on. Instead of it being pitch black with only the red glow of the cigarette. She knew the hallway was dark too. There was no light emerging from the hall. Even that would have been some comfort. But knowing there was no light, at all, knowing that he must have sneaked down the halls to where she was. Like a disgusting slug making its way through the dark dirt, that made her skin crawl.

"Nein." He said. And that was all he said. The smoke from his cigarette was clouding the room and making it harder to see than it was before. All she could make out now was the tiny glow from the butt end. She could see it making its way across the room. His face was no longer visible, hidden behind the smog. Only that tiny red glow made its way bobbing through the room. Then he was next to her. She could feel his hot breath on her face as he blew smoke at her, Doris coughed.

"Help!" Doris screamed. She began pulling at her restraints. Desperate to break free from at least one. She needed at least one arm or leg free to try and push him away, "Hel-" she began to scream again, but his hand was upon her.

His hand tasted like sweat and what she imagined embalming fluid would taste like. It made her feel sick, and she could feel vomit beginning to rise. Her stomach leapt with such force that a little had made its way to her throat, and back down again.

"Shh… fraulein, shh. Zis vill only huhrt iv you let it huhrt." He whispered. Doris bit down on his hand as hard as she could. But he did not seem to have a reaction. He didn't even flinch from the bite, even though she could now taste blood.

"Zen, I see, zis vill huhrt." He released his hand and Doris continued to scream. She screamed for anyone at all who might be walking down the hall. A nurse, a guard, anyone she prayed would come and save her from what was about to happen. She could hear the clicking of his belt buckle. And he smacked her across the face.

"Help!" Doris continued to cry out. He grabbed her head and twisted his belt around her mouth, tightening it to create a gag. Doris cried and tried to scream again but now only muffles were being made. She could hear Dr. Freude sigh with satisfaction.

"Now, I know vat you musp be zinkink. Vhy don't I knock you oud? Vell, I like vee schthruggle," he laughed, "Fügt etwas Besonderes hinzu."

There was a soft, *plop*, of what Doris assumed were his pants officially hitting the floor. Doris sobbed as she could feel him mounting the bed and eventually her.

Then, *click*, the door swung open. There was a guard standing there. The light behind him made him look almost like a dark angel.

"Dr. Freude?" The guard asked. He peered over Dr. Freude 's shoulder, seeing Doris sobbing on the bed. Dr. Freude turned quickly,

"Klus zee door sie dumm boy!" He barked. Doris sat up as best she could. Shaking her head for the boy not to close the door. Not to walk away. For him to instead come in and get her from this nightmare she was living.

But the guard just stood there. His face was still in shock and in clear contemplation about what was the right thing for him to do. The guard looked no more than 19, he must have been new to the facility. Doris had never seen him before, her eyes begged for him to stay.

"Bist du taub? Schließ die verdammte Tür!" Dr. Freude spat. Neither Doris nor the guard knew what Dr. Freude was shouting. But his body was shaking and the vein upon his forehead was swelling immensely. The scream seemed to trigger the guard back into reality of what he was seeing. He straightened himself up, nodded, and closed the door behind him. Just before the last glow of light was to be snuffed out by the door shutting, in the corner Doris saw *him*, a newfound hunger was upon his demon-like face. And as the door finally made its click, he was gone. Doris could hear the clacking of the guards' heels as he walked away. This was the one time she truly wished her personal demon would swallow her up. The one time she wished for him to stay and take her over, so she could fight back.

—⟨ၐ/ၐ/ၐ⟩—

"Doris? Doris!" Doris looked up to see Dr. Vernirelli. She was in his office sitting on his cream-colored couch, but she had not heard a word of what he said.

"What was that?" she mumbled. Her eyes were glued to the ash tray that sat next to Dr. Vernirelli. She stared at the lit cigarette hanging loosely in the bowl. The glow made her spine shiver.

"Doris, I'd like you to pick a subject to discuss today. Over the past weeks you have stayed eerily quiet. I noticed since your injury. Would you like to discuss? Should we continue to keep it simple? I need your help in leading these sessions. Without your participation they are useless."

"Yeah... that sounds great Doc." Doris whispered as she continued to keep her eyes down. The doctor sighed. He placed his pen and paper gently onto his side table.

"Doris, there is a relatively new therapy I think we should try. It is called cognitive behavioral therapy, and it might be worth giving a chance."

Doris just sat there. Another therapy, since the last one was such a great success in helping the demon-man emerge. Perhaps this one could get Doris to reopen up. Something must have happened since her injury. She now seemed like a lost puppy. Or rather a rescue pup. One that needed love and affection, due to their previous life. This eventually happened to all patients, they would slip back into some kind of depression. It usually occurred when the realization sunk in that they were committed here for life. However, Doris was making such strong strides before, what went wrong?

"This therapy is a newer therapy developed by Aaron Beck. I think we should use role playing to help face your fears."

Iv sie tell I vill hripp out dein schpleen unt make dein eat it, Dr. Freude 's voice rang in Doris's ear.

"No... Doc. I don't think that is a good idea." Doris said, bowing her head.

"Ah. Well at least you're responding to what I actually said this time. But Doris, we must do something if you want to make progr-"

"Maybe I won't make progress. Even if I play along, Doc, maybe it won't happen. I'm fucking insane, remember? Or, maybe, ha-! Maybe I am just evil. Maybe there is something about me that just attracts evil and it is going to keep on fucking happening. Ever think of that Doc? Sometimes people just pull in the evil." Doris huffed.

"Pull in the evil?" Dr. Vernirelli raised an eyebrow.

"Yeah." Doris threw herself further into the couch. Turning away from the Doc as so he would not see her cry. But she was sure he knew anyway despite her trying to shield herself. She felt a tap on her shoulder. She glanced as best she could without needing to do a full turn around. There was a tissue in the doctor's hand. She took it.

"Doris, my dear, not as my patient but as my friend please tell me what is going on. You were making such strides before. I could tell we were close to something. But these past few weeks you've changed."

Hripp out dein schpleen unt make dein eat it. Doris could once again feel the smoke in the air, she could see the cigarette butt hanging from his mouth. Doris closed her eyes and covered her face as best she could. Trying to block out the smoke that was not there. She could hear Dr. Vernirelli sigh.

"Please?" She heard him ask again. But she could not bring herself to do it. She could not bring to her mouth the words she needed to say. And while she desperately wanted to, despite Freude 's threat, there was something more. She could feel the words dancing on her tongue. She could feel them rumbling in her mind. And yet there they stayed. It was as if there was something blocking them from coming out. It reminded her of when *he* first came... But of course, that was a silly thing to compare it to.

Doris sat in the confessional booth. She was wearing a blue dress with a sailor's collar and a red ribbon wrapped around her waist. She played with the ends of her dress as she waited nervously to hear the priest come in. She heard the click.

"Hello my child. What confessions do you have to make?" Doris held her breath. She knew what it was, I've been forced to murder people at the hand of the devil or a demon. *But instead, all that came out was,*

"I'm starting to like Rock and Roll. I know it's the devil's music."

"Ah yes. Go on?"

I've chopped people up into tiny pieces at the hand of another. I need you to banish it out of me! *"I've had sex before marriage, and I liked it."*

"Oh, my dear, no... please continue."

Men, women, children. It does not seem to matter to my demon, who takes control of my body. He makes me do it all. *"And, of course, I am no stranger to taking the lord's name in vain on a few occasions."*

"Dear me... I see. My dear you must say three Hail Mary's, but not aloud. Say them inside your heart. Clearly and concisely, you must have it ring out from within you. Understand?"

No, I don't understand. And I don't care about the Hail Mary, get this demon out! *"Thank you, father. I will." And with that Doris stood, turned, and left the confessional. She felt a shudder at her back. She turned, sitting in the church's pew as she left the booth was her demon.*

We won't be confessing quite yet, but good try. *He smiled at her. Doris turned on her heels and ran out of the church as fast as she could. Stumbling her way past the line of awaiting others for the confessional. She could hear whispers behind her as she made her way to the door. She stopped at the statue of Jesus hanging over the door. She stood there. Watching him, a tear in his side, carved tears in his eyes, and nails in his hands and feet. Doris fell to the floor.* Why are you letting him take over me? She thought. Release him from me.

Doris felt a strong hand on her shoulder. It was the priest hovering over her. He helped her to her feet.

"It is alright my dear," he said, "While your sins were indeed sinful, they can and will be forgiven by God. It is not like you murdered someone." *He laughed. Doris could hear the man-like demon laughing too,* oh if only he knew, his voice mocked. If only he knew...

⟫⟫⟪⟪

The cigarette continued to burn in the ashtray. It rested on the side, still waiting for the Doc to finish it. But he never did. For every time the Doc seemed to take a long satisfying drag Doris seemed to freeze up, he noticed. He noticed she was staring at it. But not in a longing way, no. How she looked was the same way a small child looks at a growling dog. The same way one looks as the killer in a horror movie strikes again. The same look someone has as a doctor comes into the room with long awaited news. The look of fear.

This was a new look. He had never seen her look that way before. He almost always smoked during their sessions, and she never once seemed to bat an eye. Occasionally she would have the look of someone craving one herself, but never the look of complete and utter terror.

She was subtle about it too, he noticed as he later reviewed his notes. She would flinch a little each time he reached for it. And when he did inhale her pupils would shrink and she would nonchalantly reposition herself. She was careful about how she did it too. Like she was afraid to give something away. It was barely noticeable, and most doctors probably wouldn't even have thought twice about the movement. But working in Tokema as long as the Doc had he knew that nothing was subtle. Nothing nonchalant. Everything always seemed to be connected.

The Doc gathered up his things earlier than he usually did that evening. It was a rather dull day for the life of a therapist, especially one that worked in an insane asylum. He saw his usual amount of patients, a majority of them discussing the same routine things they had been discussing for years; how to keep anger under control, how to self-soothe without being inappropriate, avoiding the urge to fling one's waste, etc.

The Doc headed for the door and out to his VW beetle bug. He slid in the car and sat there for a moment. Thinking back to the instance at his home. While it had been weeks and no other instances happened, it had stopped him from returning to his house for the time being. He decided to spend that time with his sister. And while she was a lovely host, her husband thought it'd be a good time for the doctor to move back into his own home.

"His place is twice as big as ours!" His brother-in-law barked. "He doesn't need to stay here!"

"He's under a lot of stress from his job, Jerry. He needed a change of scenery to get away!"

"Get away my ass. We should be charging him 5 bucks a pop to spend the night here. God knows he's got the bread being a fancy-schmancy therapist for those looneys!" The Doc had walked in on that conversation yesterday and could still see his sister crying trying to choose between him and her husband, so he opted to leave. Causing his little sister's pain had been the last thing he wanted to do. And while she insisted that he stay he would not have it.

The Doc sat there still in the night. His car was the last in the lot. He lit a cigarette and slowly breathed in. He watched the red glow at the end. Mesmerized by the thought of what could have scared Doris by just looking at that little spark.

Could it have been her demon? She's never mentioned him smoking before but that doesn't mean that he doesn't. Maybe one of the guards said or did something to her and he happened to be smoking at the time. Maybe she developed a new fear from being cooped up around the smoke all day and night long in that common room, it could happen. Plenty of his past patients couldn't take the smoke around them and not be able to hit a drag of it themselves.

Heck, he even had one patient get so worked up a few years ago that she jumped a guard, bit his ear clean off, and then grabbed the thing while he was lying there clinging to his hanging lobe. She was a tiny thing too. No more than 5 feet. Resembling a child in such ways that she usually got off scot-free because no one wanted to punish someone who looked so childlike. Boy did that stop as soon as she took a chunk of Lou's ear right off. The Doc chuckled, reflecting back at the thought. It was amusing to think of such a small thing taking down such a big man, and all for what? A dumb cig. Heck if he knew it was going to go that far he would have let her take a drag from him every now and then.

He gripped his steering wheel and ran his hands up and down the circle a few times. *It's just your house. There is no boogie man waiting to grab you. 'Fear is the main source of superstition and one of the main sources of cruelty. To conquer fear is the beginning of wisdom.'* Ah yes. To be wise for himself and wise for Doris and his patients. And with that thought in his mind, he started the car.

The doctor's house was around a 30-minute drive from the facilities. His was the only car on the road at this hour, as it usually was. His headlights shined brightly and made the outstretched road look almost yellow. *Follow the yellow brick road. Follow it home Doc.*

The empty road, while normally calming, made him feel uneasy. As if he were driving into the unknown. With each mile approaching closer and closer to his home. The Doc turned on the radio,

"Dream a little dream of me…" Doris Day sang, Doris. She was not herself anymore and the Doc wasn't sure why. Perhaps she was still being tormented by the demon-like man, despite what she said about banishing him away. The Doc knew what he saw that day. He was almost positive that there was someone or something behind her eyes. The Docs' thoughts continued to drift to Doris as he drove on. Only 15 minutes away now. Come on Doc, keep following that yellow road, follow it home.

He continued on, singing each song as it came on the radio, then, "All I Have to Do is Dream" by the Everly Brothers came on. The Doc's back stiffened. His grip tightened on the steering wheel.

It is just a coincidence. It's just a song. A song and nothing more. Be wise ol' boy, be wise. The Doc's hand hovered over the radio. Tempted to change the song. *Avoiding danger is no safer in the long run than outright exposure. The fearful are caught as often as the bold. Be bold Doc.* He withdrew his hand back.

Gripping tight to the steering wheel the Doc began to sing aloud, "When I feel blue in the night And I need you to hold me tight, Whenever I want you, all I have to do is Dream!" The doctor sang louder, and louder, and louder until he was nearly shouting the song. "I need you so that I could die. I love you so and that is why Whenever I want you, all I have to do is *DREAM, DREAM, DREAM, DREAM, DREAM, DREAM, DREAM, DREAM!*" He bellowed.

That's when he saw it. There was a figure of some kind standing in the street. The Doc was unsure what he was seeing but slammed on his breaks, nonetheless. His car screeched loudly as it slid slightly across the road. In his yellow headlights, he stared out. It was a man, the doctor's heart leaped. The man was not in a suit, but a big, baggy gray shirt. There seemed to be a slight light glowing from his clothing.

"Hello?" The doctor called out, but the man simply stood in place, as if frozen. "Hello? Are you alright?" The doctor called again, only this time, louder. The man slowly started to turn so he could face the doctor, still safely tucked away in his car, or so he told himself. The man's face was odd, deformed, almost looked burned.

The man took one jarring step forward. The doctor quickly began to crank up his window, out of initial reaction and fear, but the man stopped. He stayed his distance, and the doctor eased his grip.

"Can I help you?" he called out, but again, the man said nothing. Dr. Vernirelli shuddered. He began to click his car into drive. He peered out his window one last time, but he saw nothing straight ahead. The man was gone. The Doc turned to roll up his window all the way up from its slightly ajar state, and there, inches from his face, if it weren't for the glass keeping the two of them apart, he stood. Dr. Vernirelli shrieked and started to press on the gas of his car in a warning for the man to back off. But he stood his ground, planted his feet firmly.

"Doc..." the man spoke, "Doc you have to help her break free." And with that, he was gone. Poof, vanished, nothing more than smoke. The doctor rubbed his eyes in disbelief. Where was the man at all? The doctor pressed his head against the glass without risking opening his window. He peered to the ground, to see if the man had somehow ducked under the car, but he saw nothing. He slowly inched his car forward. Expecting the man to jump out of the darkness somewhere and surprise him, but he did not. After sitting there for a few minutes, the doctor decided that it would be safe to continue his drive.

The doctor took the remainder of his car ride in silence. It wasn't a far way to go anyhow. He pulled in his drive and glanced up to his house. It looked like a normal house. One in which nothing goes on or happens, besides an old man doing his crossword, entertaining what family he had left, and listening to records.

The doctor slowly got out of his car. He hesitated at the door. Nervous that something or someone was waiting for him in the darkness of the foyer. Eagerly hoping for his arrival, and now he was finally here. He held his breath and turned the key. He could feel the hairs prickle up as he did so.

The door swung open, and he peeked his head inside. Nothing looked to be out of the ordinary. Everything seemed spick and span just as he left it. He wearily took his first step inside, nothing. He glided from room to room. Jumping at the smallest of noises, but with each room, he found there to be nothing.

After deeming it safe enough the doctor fully released his breath. He was glad to be home, despite his earlier scare. He was happy to be surrounded by the comfort of his things. He changed into his pajamas and slipped into bed. Met with a sleep not filled with demon men with sick, sinister clicking jaws smiling down at him, or strange men in the middle of streets with their faces or shirts on fire. He was instead met with a deep, much-needed, sleep.

———⟋ℴ⟍ⱺ⟋ℴ⟍———

Doris sat in her usual spot in the doctor's office. She had been silent for the past several minutes. All that could be heard in the room was the whipping of the winter wind as it slapped against the pains of the window. The doctor stared at her. As he did so he reached for his cigarettes and Doris flinched ever so slightly. If he had not been watching for something of the sort, he would have missed it.

"Doris…" he finally said. "…do you smoke?" She sat there for a few minutes and her back stiffened.

"Everyone smokes Doc."

"No, not everyone." he snickered, trying to make light of the conversation. "In fact, I have a brother who doesn't. Only person in the family who turns it down. I have six siblings, you know. Each and every one of us smokes, except Stephen. He's the oldest too. He's never even touched one. I don't know how he stands getting together with our family. It's like there's fog in the room when we all get together." Doris smiled politely at his story.

"We've never discussed if you have siblings too, Doris. We've talked about your father and mother. Mother mostly. Let's have a family discussion today."

"I thought I was meant to be leading the sessions?" Doris furrowed her brow.

"Well yes. But you have been unusually silent these past few weeks. We can discuss why if you prefer?" *He's egging you on.* Doris peered around the room.

"I have three siblings. I'm the oldest. None of them came to my trial or even rang me once they heard what happened. They cut me out. Who could blame them?"

"It's understandable given the mother you had."

"Yeah, I'm sure she got to all of them." Doris could see her mother pecking away in her mind's-eye. Claiming that she was not a bad mother, that Doris was simply a bag egg. The proof was in the pudding. Her brothers and sister turned out just fine. The good little chicks they were. Her mother had time to practice on Doris. The first child was always like the first pancake, a throwaway.

"We weren't close to begin with anyways. My brothers are twins and were born when I was 10. My sister a year later. Those three were close."

"That must have been hard being so much older." The doctor readjusted in his seat.

"Not as hard as you think."

"And why is that?"

Doris sighed and pulled herself up. She hadn't talked to her siblings in almost three years anyhow. She always felt awkward around them. Like she was their mother and simply skipped the actual birth giving part.

She was the one after all who fed them and changed them because her mother was too busy organizing the church bake sale or going over to Reverend Thompsons' house to plan the sermon for the upcoming week. Always nagged them about the rights and wrongs of life.

She even walked her siblings to school so her mother could clean the church's organ every morning. Her father was always working. He had 2 jobs to keep the family floating. 'No woman of mine is going to work if I can help it!' She recalled him saying to her mother.

"I helped raise them. My mother was busy with church and my father was always working. They didn't really see me as a sister, to begin with, I suppose. Are you and your siblings close Doc?"

"Why yes, I think so. In fact, I just stayed with my sister and her husband for a few days."

"Why'd you do that? A doctor like you. I assumed you had a big fancy house all to yourself." A flash on the man standing behind him in the mirror jumped across the doctor's eyes. That same feeling of numbness and his spine begging to chill washed over him again. But quickly he shut it out.

"Oh, I just wanted to see her for a bit. It's harder the older we get. We all have moved about through the years." Doris nodded. The Doc reached for his cigarettes absentmindedly. Pulling one from the box and sparkling a light. It was only when the flame reached the tip that he even realized he grabbed one. He looked at Doris. Her eyes once again fixated on the red end. He pulled it out from between his lips and handed it to her, she pulled away.

"Doris. I've noticed something rather interesting these past few weeks. You are afraid of my cigarettes. Why?" She shook her head.

"I don't know what you mean Doc." She said as she readjusted herself and reached for the cigarette. She took it between her fingers and held it to her lips. Hesitating to see if he would object to her taking a drag. When he said nothing, she inhaled.

It was her first cigarette in almost 7 months, and she let out a harsh cough, handing it back to the doctor. Even though she had coughed, the drag was still smooth and sweet as ever. It even seemed to float across her tongue the way she imagined angels floated across heaven.

"Thanks." She wheezed, handing it back. She paused, half hoping to keep it, and half wanting to throw it on the ground and light the whole damn building on fire. The doctor watched her for any indication she might give away. But he saw none. He took the cigarette back and leaned in his chair. He took in a long slow breath.

"Alright. If you say so Doris."

"I do." She sat back up in her chair. She began to chatter more about her siblings. As if the last few weeks of her strange behavior never happened the past few weeks.

She discussed how some days she would come home, and her siblings had pulled pranks on her. Nothing big that left her traumatized. Small things like leaving a frog in her bed. Or placing a tac on her desk chair. She usually noticed those kinds of things though and never did give her siblings the satisfaction of hearing a startled shriek or cry. They were terribly tacky tricksters. She could always hear one of them giggling from some hidden place.

It could be that she didn't do her siblings any favors, however. None of them were terribly clever or responsible. Doris did all that kind of stuff so they could have childhoods. And now that they had become all adults Doris found that she was always the one taking care of her mother and father, and then soon only to be her mother. None of the others would know how. She wondered how they were doing. How her mother was doing, did Liddy, her little sister step up? Or could John and Michael have? Doris doubted it.

As Doris chattered on, she soon got into her friends and the life they led together. Doris recalled when she was a girl, she was particularly close to the two little girls that lived next door, Holly and Hannah. One was a year older than Doris, one a year younger. Doris could not recall which was which. It had been years since she had last seen them. In fact, she had not seen them since they left when she was in the 9th grade.

✦✦✦

"I'm going to miss you girls, something awful!" Doris said. She was standing on the Hannigan's front porch. The moving truck was all packed behind her and Mr. Hannigan and the girl's older brother, Thomas, were loading it up along with some moving men he had hired. Doris could feel the tears swelling. The Hannigan family was moving to a different state, somewhere in New Jersey, or New York, New Mexico? One of the News. Doris could never quite keep them straight in her head. Mr. Hannigan's mother had gone ill, and he wanted them to move in with her since she was in no position to be moving herself. He had found a job as a salesman and was excited about their new upcoming life.

"Don't worry, we'll write to you, every day!" Holly said, hugging Dorris. This was true for a while. The girls did write Doris every day, for

a whole summer. And Doris, of course, always wrote back. This had kept up until the school year.

Apparently, Hannah, or was it, Holly? Had gone through an amazing growth spurt over the summer and all the boys had fallen head over heels. She had once written to Doris, explaining that she had a different date for every day of the week! And the boys never seemed to mind, they just thought of it as a competition, wanting to win her over. She wrote about how they would have silly competitions over her. Like arm wrestling and in one instance actual wrestling.

The other Hannigan sister kept writing to Doris for a while after the older one fell off. But she had found herself to be falling in love with sports of all things. And her time soon was taken over by that as well. Doris remembered reading something about her in the paper once. She had gone on to become a professional of some sort.

Doris would sit alone during lunch. Never really realizing how much she had depended on Hannah and Holly to be there for her. Doris soon found herself quite lonely. She tried to reach out to a few other girls she had classes with. They even went out a few times to get malts and watch movies. But no one seemed to last. They all would become distracted by other things, namely boys.

———◦❦◦———

"No one ever seems to last Doc. No one I want to anyways," she said. Listening to the wind as it continued to howl outside. "Probably for the best anyway. Considering, well, you know. *Him.*"

The doctor nodded his head. *Our demons do seem to follow us everywhere.* He thought to himself. *Because therein lies the issue, no matter how far we run, we're always there too.*

———◦❦◦———

Doris sat in the common room. The days seemed to drag on with the same old thing. There was something oddly comfortable in the maddening mindset that was repetition. She always knew what to expect.

She glanced outside at what she now thought of as *her* window. In fact, she had completely claimed it. People knew not to sit there. The woods were looking as bare as ever, the trees seemed like skeleton bones, dried up and brittle. They swayed their way back and forth. *Not the sturdiest of trees*, she thought. She imagined the wind picking up and the trees would snap with no resistance at all. Snap, crackle, pop! What would happen then? Power outage maybe. If that happened would anyone even care? The nurses might put up a fight, they always seemed to be wearing sweaters these days. A lot of patients took on wearing their bathrobes to keep warm. Doris did not mind the cold, it felt soothing almost.

Doris could hear the scratch of the record player from behind her. Perhaps the song had ended, she was not really paying attention. She had gotten to the point in which she blocked out the music. Since the facilities only seemed to have the same 5 records. Doris turned to see a nurse switching over the record. She was holding what looked to be a yellow-ish, green-ish record sleeve. Doris had not seen this record cover before. Slipping on the new record Doris waited with anticipation. Whatever it was was certainly a welcomed change.

Judy Garland soon filled the room. *When all the world is a hopeless jumble, and the raindrops tumble, all around…* Doris closed her eyes and thought back to when she was a girl singing this song. The Wizard of Oz was indeed her favorite movie, and she longed for Judy to continue on. *Heaven opens a magic lane. When all the clouds darkness up that skyway, there's a rainbow highway-*

FRRIP

Doris opened her eyes. A patient, one who was rather recently committed had rushed over to the record and ripped it from the player. Her hair was disheveled, and her gown was tucked into her underpants. She was, what Doris called, a crazy looney. One whose family had committed her because her sentences did not always make sense, easily triggered, and always having imaginary conversations.

"No!" she screamed. Throwing the record to the ground and breaking it. Doris jumped to her feet. "No! No! No!" the patient continued. "Not the devil's music! Upon us call him you will!" She shrieked. Quickly a guard ran over to her and struck her in the back. The woman went down like a sack of potatoes.

"Stupid bitch! We just bought that!" He yelled at her. Pulling her to her feet and dragging her towards the door. The woman continued to kick and scream, but also laughed as he dragged her away.

"You'll thank me!" She yelled, laughing hysterically. "Thank me when doesn't he come tonight. Doesn't come he won't!" *Clearly, this woman had been seeing demons of her own*, Doris thought. Were this woman's demons somehow attached to the Wizard of Oz? That didn't seem to make sense to Doris. How could such peaceful music draw out such a beast? Certainly, this woman was just against change.

Doris walked over to where the broken record lay. Suddenly, her heart felt heavy. She had longed to hear Judy sing and almost immediately it was taken from her. Was she not allowed even to have the simplest glee of loving music? Was she doomed to listen to the same, old, faded sounds of the same five damn records forever? Doris became flustered, hot even. She no longer felt the refreshing cool air in the common room, instead, she could feel the blood rush to her face.

Doris's chest rose and fell in a frustrated flutter. Her eyes began to water, and she could feel herself beginning to become enraged with the woman who had smashed the record. Doris took a sharp inhale, ready to scream when she saw *him* standing just outside the door window.

She held her breath. There was a smile on his face. Like he was waiting or anticipating for her to do something. He tilted his head forward and gave her a nod. Doris swallowed her breath. Feeling her anger subside and to be replaced with fear. She shook her head at him, she knew he was watching and was waiting for a reaction.

His smile faded and his eyes flashed to snakes. He continued to stare. His eyes fell into sunken sockets instead of flesh. He seemed to fade away, disappearing into a smoke and then nothing at all.

Doris let out her breath once she was sure he was gone. She looked around. No one else seemed to have seen the man. Of course, no one did. He was there for her and her alone. Why would anyone else have seen him?

A nurse pushed Doris aside, kneeling down and picking up at the splintered record pieces. Shaking her head and clearing her mind Doris kneeled down beside her, reaching for a piece when her hand was smacked away.

"Get away!" the nurse snapped, "You people have caused enough damage. We try to do something nice for ya'll and you had to go and fuck it up in less than 5 minutes! Animals..."

"But I didn't-"

"I said get away!" Doris coward away from the nurse. She retreated to her usual corner and looked out the window. She could see the wind biting at the trees.

⸺◦/◦/◦⸺

The Doc sat in his study. The night was coming to an end and soon he would need to be on his way. He looked around in his room, looking for anything that might give him an excuse to stay longer. Perhaps even be forced to spend the night due to an extremely large workload. He had already re-arranged his files, so they were now in alphabetical order, instead of arrival date order.

He had reviewed all his patient's notes and even written notes about what he would try suggesting or addressing in the next few sessions for each of his patients. He rearranged his room even. There seemed to be nothing more for him to do. He stood there, then slowly lowered himself to the middle of the floor.

Placing his hands behind the back of his neck he leaned forward and let out a low sigh. He rocked slowly back and forth on the heels of his feet. *Truly a ridiculous thing to be afraid of one's own home...* Perhaps he should talk to someone in his profession. He had learned from the first few years of being a psychiatrist that it was important at times to see one himself. Especially if things were becoming too heavy or serious with his patients. Over the years he had heard truly horrific things, and after a while, they began to take their toll on him. Sure, he loved his job and his patients, but how many times can one hear the same tales of insanity without feeling a little insane themselves? And recently, he felt as if he were Sisyphus, always rolling and pushing that same bolder, just to reach the top of the hill and have all his progress come crashing down. Take Doris for example, he felt that they were making so much progress. But then she flipped as easily as one would click a light switch. Something must have happened in those last few weeks, he knew that. He knew it involved cigarettes in some way, though she denied it.

The doctor breathed slowly in and out before rising to his feet again. *What are you doing, old boy* he half thought to himself. But his thought seemed from not only within, but from somewhere in the distance, like a resonance that drifted through the door. The doctor looked around the room and peaked into the hall. He saw no one and nothing from what was expected. He stood there as if waiting for something to happen. And in the back part of his mind, the one that was often kept boarded up with walls he heard it, *we're off to see the doctor, the doctor of Tokema home...* It sounded like Doris, but there was someone else singing with her, someone with sinister intentions.

The doctor jumped at his own thought. Springing to his feet as if he were young and spry again. Perhaps he should just walk by Doris's room before he leaves. He had access to visit his patients at any time after all. No, he wouldn't stop in for a visit, but a quick glance by. Just to make sure she was safe; she had not been herself as of late and she could use someone looking over her. At least, this is what he told himself, but deep down, he knew it was for him. To convince himself that there was nothing there lurking in the shadows. If he could just do a quick glance by and see that nothing was wrong it would help to put his mind at ease, even just a little.

As the Doc strolled down the dark and dimly lit hallways, and out the back door to Doris's ward he found himself to be absent-mindedly humming. It was a tune that he had not heard for a while, but one in which he instinctively knew.

"Oh, I… could tell you why, the oceans near the shore…" he mumbled under his breath. "…I could think of things I never thunk before…" And soon he realized which song he had been humming. *If I Only Had a Brain.* He paused in the winter air. Hesitant to continue his journey forward. Perhaps if he used his brain, he would not be walking into the thing he feared most. He could not help but feel, no, *know* that what happened in his home was connected to Doris. He knew it. There was a chance if he went to see her now that something might happen again, was he willing to risk it?

Don't be silly. She's your patient. You'll have to see her again no matter what. It does not matter if it is day or night. Do not be afraid of your work. And with that, he continued his march on, continuing his journey down the yellow paved pathway. Into the building slightly behind his own, in the back of it all.

———∘/∘/∘———

He pulled a ring of keys from his belt and examined them closely until he found a small, shiny silver one. He slid it into the keyhole and with a loud *CLUNK* the door swung open. He was careful to lock the door once more behind him.

The doctor glanced around the hall; it was surprisingly more lit than he thought it was going to be. There was a guard standing to his right, he gave a half-forced smile at the man, nodding his head, and continued walking forward. The guard did not ask him his name or what he was doing there. The Doc figured it was probably that he had a key and was well known throughout the facility that he was not questioned. People seemed to just know him, although he did not know them.

The doctor drifted down the corridor, peeping briefly into each room as he did. While he did have Doris's room number written somewhere in his notes, he had not thought to stop and look it up. "I could think of things I never thunk before..." he continued to murmur along his way.

What the doctor saw in each cell continued to disturb him more and more as he drifted from room to room. He had expected to see sleeping patients, and while there were some sleeping there were more of others who were not. Touching themselves in the corner, defecating in the middle, pacing back and forth, and some would even catch him walking by and charging at the door as if they were able to break it down with their skeleton-like bodies. A few times a patient would rush the door with such force that the doctor would jump back slightly.

The Doc knew the living conditions were not as he had hoped, but he never expected so unsanitary. Each wall was lined with a sluggish, yellow-looking grime. He wrinkled his nose slightly at the sight. Ever since Doris had pointed out how dirty everything was, he began noticing it more and more. Of course, his office was in the front building, and the front building was always kept neat and clean. But he tried his best to keep a calm face when the patients would notice him. He tried to keep moving forward, only taking half a second to look in, then he found her.

She was towards the end of the hall, adjacent to a clock that hung on the wall. A guard stood only a few feet from her now. The Doc took a look in. The Doc figured at least she would be asleep, unlike a majority of her peers. But when he glazed in, he was surprised, or rather not surprised at all, to find Doris was standing in the middle of her room. Her eyes rolled to the back of her head, and slack jawed. Her body twitched slightly.

Doris was escorted to her room that night, the same as she was every night. She heard the loud click on the door shut behind her and she crawled her way to the bed. She curled herself up, thinking of the demon-like man she had seen grinning at her, reflecting on those sunken holes where his eyes should have been. Doris shuttered. She turned and laid on her back. It was the only position she felt safe in now. If he tried creeping on her through the door, out of the walls, or from any direction she would be able to see it from the corner of her eye while lying on her back. The only place left vulnerable was under the bed.

She kept her ears perked in case she needed them. Listening for any sound that might trigger her at all. She stayed there for what felt like over an hour. Her back was stiff, and she longed to roll over onto her side, but refused to let her body move. Eventually, she was able to drift to sleep.

When Doris awoke, she was outside again. The cold air bit at her cheeks. Her feet felt frozen, and her head spun like a top. However, it was not winter, the season was Fall. There were several leaves on the ground and the trees were almost all bare. A few leaves still clung on, but Doris could tell it would not be for very much longer.

"Why do I keep having this dream?" She shouted from the top of her lungs. She could hear rustling and soon the same dirty, burned victim of a man emerged from the woods. Despite her knowing that he would eventually come, his presence never ceased to shock and disturb her.

"Hush!" He hissed as he ran toward her. Doris could feel herself wanting to run, but her feet remained planted. "Do not let him know you're here" the man urged. Holding a shaking hand up to her face. Doris began to open her mouth, but the man flung a finger over her lips. His finger smelled rotten and molded over. Doris curled her lips inward, not wanting to accidentally taste the finger.

She pulled away slightly, wrapping her arms around herself to try and keep warm. She nodded at the man, showing that she would not speak. The man stared at her with caution but soon relaxed a little when he saw that Doris would not be asking questions. He turned on his heels and gestured for Doris to follow him. Doris took a step forward and followed the man into the woods behind her building.

The wind howled and pushed Doris around like she was nothing, but a bug caught in the air. She stumbled forward, trying to keep an eye on the man who walked before her, but the breeze speeding by made it hard for her to keep her eyes open. With each gust, her lids would flutter, and her eyes would respond in turn by threatening to water. The man pushed on however, the cold seemed to do nothing to him. Occasionally he would check over his shoulder to make sure that Doris was indeed following behind.

He led her deep into the woods until they reached a clearing. The clearing made a circle and was surrounded by little stones. It almost gave the illusion of a fairy ring. But instead of a beautiful ring of soft, vibrant colored mushrooms, this ring was cold and hard made for sharp stone. Just before entering the clearing and stepping into the ring of stone, the man held his arm in front of Doris, catching her before she could take another step. Doris looked curiously at him, but the man said nothing. He just held a finger to his lips and slowly turned. He pointed forward with two fingers, indicating he wanted Doris to pay attention, and she did.

There before them stood a figure. The figure began to shapeshift into the exact same man standing beside her. Doris whipped her head to see if he had somehow moved, but he hadn't. The skin on the identical man standing before them seemed to be healing itself. The glowing embers on his shirt faded, his skin regrew, his hair came back in full. Doris gave out a small gasp. He looked completely reborn, he was sharper and more well-put together. Even his clothes began to change. He wore a flannel tucked into a pair of jeans. He appeared to be looking at something, with his fists hidden away in his jeans. He was staring at something with such focus. He then nodded his head and proceeded to make a motion as if he were opening an invisible door.

Doris watched closely. The man walked a few feet and then stopped. His hands looked like they were resting on a countertop, even though there was none. He was having a conversation with someone, although Doris did not know who. There was no one there. Doris strained her ears in an attempt to hear what was being said, but no sound came from the man's lips. He pointed in front of him. At a transparent object, Doris thought. The man seemed to grab whatever it was he was pointing and then he froze. His body became rigid, and his eyes widened, there was now a black shadow before him. The shadow didn't seem to hold a particular shape, but still, it seemed as if it were reaching for the young man. Grabbing him and forcing the man to enter it. Doris then understood.

She turned to the disheveled, rancid man standing next to her, he turned to face her and nodded. Doris could feel the tears welling up in her eyes. She knew she was no longer alone. The man placed a hand on Doris's shoulder, this time she did not recoil. In fact, she wanted to embrace him. To hug him and cry and fall to their knees together. But before she could find the strength to do so he turned back to the young vision of himself. The young man seemed to be catching his breath. Kneeling down, hand over his chest. Someone or something must have been trying to console him because he kept waving his free hand in the air indicating that he would be alright. Then the vision began to fade. It seemed to twist upon itself changing and rearranging. Doris watched, longing to know what happened next, and then she heard it.

"Doris!" A familiar voice was yelling. Doris's name seemed to echo throughout the woods. Almost, like someone was speaking into a microphone from overhead. She jumped and the man next to her coward,

"We can't let him hear us; he can't know we're here" the man whispered in a panic. But they heard it again,

"Doris, Doris wake up! Can you hear me?" *Doc...?* Doris thought to herself.

"Doris!" It was the Doc. But what was he doing here? He had never been in her dreams before.

"Shh!" Doris whispered loudly, wishing the Doc would be quiet. "Please, shh"

"What's she saying?" Another voice asked,

"I don't know, she's mumbling something. Doris!" Doris covered her ears. The man next to her was beginning to panic. His head darted around every which way. And there in the distance he could see it, a dark shadowy essence seemed to be leaking its way through the trees. The burned man reached for Doris's hand, grabbing it and forcing her to look at him.

"We must leave this place, he's coming. Do not follow me. Do not let him find you" he said as he sprinted off in the opposite direction from which they came. Doris, confused and frightened, began to run. She was not sure which direction she picked, but she did not care. She crashed through trees and bushes. Then she sensed it.

It was a cold sensation, not like the wind and the frozen ground beneath her feet, but one so deep down inside herself that it almost forced her to her knees. She knew he was coming for her and that he was close.

"Doris!" she heard the Doc yell again, but this time, she flung open her eyes and found herself lying on the floor. She was back inside her room, the lights were blinding, and the Doc stood over her with two guards and a nurse at his side.

⟢ ❦❦❦ ⟣

The Doc sighed with relief as Doris flung her eyes open. She looked confused and sweat poured down from her brow.

"Are you alright?" The doctor asked. Doris simply sat there. Confused and disoriented. She was absolutely dumbfounded to see all these people in her room. Of course, out of the four people who stood over her only Dr. Vernirelli looked scared and concerned for her. The nurse stood with her hands on her hips, looking annoyed that she was called in for a matter such as this. The guards both held no expressions at all. They hardly even seemed to process that she was there. Just another patient, another number, another burden to look after.

She tried to prop herself up off the floor. It was clear as day when she slid her elbow underneath herself and dragged her feet forward. There was dirt and some dried leaves clinging to her toes. Doris's chest fluttered and she tried to tuck her feet under her gown before anyone could notice, but it was too late and too obvious to hide. One of the guards was the first to react,

"How did you get out?" He raised his nightstick to strike her, but the doctor flew himself in between the bat and Doris. The guard lowered his hand.

"How did she get out? We saw her standing here the whole time!" Dr. Vernirelli snapped back. Doris tried her best to shelter herself behind the doctor. It is a feeble attempt to keep from getting beaten. But the guard did not seem to care. He reached around the doctor, grabbing Doris by her hair.

"Clearly, she snuck out and then had some sort of attack. Either way, she was out and she must be punished accordingly." He said forcing Doris to her feet.

"No please!" Doris cried. "I wasn't out, I wasn't." The Doc protested against the guard, but the guard did not seem to care for the doctor or his status and ordered the red-headed guard to his left to help him escort Doris to the "reconditioning room." The red-headed guard stood there for a moment. He was not sure who to follow. His eyes darted back and forth between the doctor and his superior. He wasn't even sure what the other guard was talking about. They had seen Doris there and there was no evidence that she was out and about.

"Why?" The redheaded asked tentatively.

"Why? Don't you see the grime on her feet? How could you miss it!" The redheaded guard looked at Doris's feet. They seemed clean as ever to him. The nurse looked down as well.

"What are you talking about Stew?" She asked. Doris's feet looked as clean as they could be to her.

"Are you two blind?" Snapped the first guard. "She's got dirt and leaves all over them. The doctor had indeed seen the dirt this time, but it appeared not everyone could see it. He decided it would be best to play along,

"There's nothing there! Now let her be." Stew looked around at the other three people in the room.

"I see what I see. It's not my fault you're all blind!" And with that, he hoisted Doris up. Doris began to scream, begging him to believe her, that she had not left her room. She kicked and wailed. The redheaded guard and the nurse stepped aside. Stew was much bigger than both of them and higher up. They did not want to argue. Dr. Vernirelli jumped to his feet. Placing himself in front of the guard and Doris. He took Doris by her shoulders,

"Calm down my dear!" Dr. Vernirelli snapped at her, "You are only making this situation worse for yourself. I will have a talk with some people and try to get this situation under control." Dr. Vernirelli turned to the guard, he eyed him up and down. Doris bit her lips, making them into a thin white line. She nodded; she knew Dr. Vernirelli would try his best to help her. She softly cried as Stew dragged her way.

—————

The nurse and the redheaded guard followed Stew out the door. Not willing to get involved, but definitely not willing to defy him. The doctor stood alone in Doris's room. He was not sure how he would go about handling the situation. He had seen Doris, simply standing in the middle of her room. Yes, he saw the dirt on her feet too. But there was no way he was going to admit that. If it was three against one in seeing the dirt that should let her off more easily. It looked as if she were in a trance of some kind. Like something was invading her mind. It could have been the demon-man. Doris had been uncharacteristically quiet as of late. Perhaps the man was visiting her? Perhaps the realization of being in Tokema for the rest of her life was setting in.

Usually when patients are here for about a year the full realization sets in and it is common to see breakdowns. Now Doris hadn't yet been here for a full year, but it could be possible that the breakdown was just happening early. But what of the dirt and leaves on her feet? There weren't even any leaves on the ground anymore. They had been racked up and burned days ago.

The doctor thought back. Trying to see if he could recall seeing the dirt on her feet earlier when he first burst through her door and started shaking her. But he had not noticed. His focus was too busy on Doris's face. Her eyes were like looking into a glass of already drunk milk. They were flickering back and forth, the same as an old film when it first began rolling. He thought back to the moment just before he opened her door...

...Before he unlocked the room there was a great moment of hesitation. A trader's thought drifted its way into his mind. He was not sure if she was being possessed and he recalled her file. And all the horrific, defiling, grotesque things that had become of her victims. One was found with bite marks all over his body, one was missing her eyes... His mind raced to the photographs he had seen when he was told that she would be his patient. Thoughts of shallow graves and dismembered bodies streaked their way across his memory, but before he allowed it to continue and have fear rule over him, he thought, *She is your patient and your duty is to help her, and help her I shall.*

And with that, he was able to yell for a guard, jam the key into the slot, and thrust open the door. When he approached her, he at first thought she was dead. A silly thought yes, since she was standing, and her eyes were somewhat moving. But her body seemed limp despite its upright posture. It felt cold. Her cheeks and nose were red as if she had indeed been outside. And he somehow recalled feeling the ripple of wind through her gown as he took hold of her shoulders. Again impossible.

The doctor felt unsure of himself just then. Unsure of what he saw, unsure if Doris did deserve to be in a place like this, and unsure if he would really be able to help her. But he was sure of one thing, Doris was not insane.

⸺◦◦◦⸻

Doris was unsure of where she was. She assumed the same reconditioning room as before, but the lights were off, she was in a straitjacket, and she had been thrown into the room with such force that she hit the floor and was unable to stand back up. How long she had been in the dark was unclear, but she did not care. She did not have the strength in her to be injected with poison and made to throw up again. She lay there, eventually finding a comfy enough position where she would allow herself to rest, until whatever torture that awaited her would come next.

In the silence and in the dark Doris thought of her family. Of her mother and father and siblings. She knew there were visiting hours at the facility. She had seen other patients being taken to the main building where visits were arranged. She heard them talk amongst themselves about a white room in which they were able to sit and interact with whoever was sitting across the table. Only the patients who checked themselves in seemed to be the ones to get visitors. Probably because their families saw there being hope for them. Doris thought it reminded her of a prison visit more, instead of a looney bin. She wasn't sure what she thought would be different about the two, after some light thought she figured there would be no difference at all. True, not all the patients in Tokema were dangerous, but there was always potential. After all, they were all thrown in here to rot for different reasons.

She wondered what it would be like if her family ever popped in unexpectedly one of these days. If her mother's head just happened around the corner. How would she look? What would she say? Would they be allowed to hug? Doris doubted that her mother would even stand for such a thing. She would probably slap her and burst out crying at the things her daughter had done, or rather, was made to do. Even though no one believed that, except, maybe the Doc. She wouldn't question if her daughter needed serious help or not. She probably would think that a prison for life or even the death penalty would be more suitable for Doris compared to Tokema. But little did her mother know, this place was far worse than either option, for here Doris was surrounded by the truly crazy and there was no relief from the demon-man still visiting her, despite her being able to crawl out of him that one time.

❦❦❦

It was unclear to Doris how long she actually had been lying on the floor. In fact, she only realized she must have been there for a good long while since she was woken up by a light flickering on. The light was harsh and too bright. It had an off-yellowish glow to it and flickered for a few seconds before settling on working properly. Doris looked up to see Dr. Tracy standing over her. She was reading some paper attached to a clipboard.

Dr. Tracy's eyes remained focused on the clipboard, never once moving them to Doris. She paced around the room, making disapproval-clicking sounds with her tongue, shaking her head back and forth as she did so.

"Tisk, tisk, tisk Doris my dear..." she muttered, "You know I'm surprised you pulled off a little stunt like this so soon into joining us. And so soon after our first visit together. Usually, I won't see patients for almost a year or so after the reconditioning. But I guess you just had to come back and see me. Missed me too much?" Dr. Tracy chuckled at this.

Doris just sat there. She had managed to prop herself upright and was resting her back on a chair in the corner. There was nothing for

Doris to say. She knew there was no right response to give Dr. Tracy. Anything she said could and would be held against her in a court of law, Tracy's law. For in this room, it was always Tracy's courthouse.

Doris continued to stare silently. Perhaps the best answer was no answer at all in a situation like this one. Perhaps if she just sat there and took whatever was coming to her, she would be left alone after that. Maybe even sent to her room, allowed to be alone with herself. But did she really want to go back to that room? After all, it was there where she was suddenly outside in the cold, confronted with fear and an overwhelming amount of uncertainty and insanity. She knew she was not insane when admitted, she was simply possessed. But here, she felt doubt in herself. For no one would believe a lick of what she said. But at least the guard saw the dirt and leaves on her feet. But what does that prove? Nothing clearly. To him, it seemed like she simply slipped outside for a midnight stroll for whatever reason. But why then would she possibly come back to her room? Why would she willingly re-enter this place? And re-entering with fully knowing a punishment would be waiting for her? *Now that would be true insanity*, she thought to herself.

"Well, Doris? Nothing to say." Dr. Tracy tapped her foot. And still, Doris remained silent. What was there to say? She was sure Dr. Tracy already knew the facts that were given to her. *Doris made an escape attempt and was caught in the act.* That had to have been the message relayed to the doctor, even if it was not true.

Was Doris allowed to ask for someone to be there with her? Could she request Dr. Vernirelli be with her? Possibly that would be too bold. But what worse could happen to her? She was already poisoned, raped, beaten. Doris was certain no worse could come from asking.

Doris cleared her throat, "I would like Dr. Vernirelli to sit in with us if you don't mind." She looked at Dr. Tracy as she continued to tap her foot. Trying to read the situation as to if it would be right for the doctor to join in. But Tracy's face did not change. It simply remained with her lips pursed like she had bitten down on a sour lemon with salt sprinkled on top. Then her lip quivered. It curled and twisted up into a crooked smile and she let out a roar of laughter.

"Of all things I was expecting, that was not what I thought would come out of your mouth. Awfully bold of you." Dr. Tracy wiped away tears streaming down her cheeks as she laughed harder. "No, no. Dr. V will not be joining this party."

Doris didn't think so. She bowed her head again and waited for Dr. Tracy to compose herself. She continued her sick laughter but was soon to be interrupted by the shrill ringing of a call.

"Hello?" Dr. Tracy asked, still wiping away her tears. "Oh, sir I was just about to call-" She was silent on the phone for a minute. "No, I-... I don't think-... Yes sir. Alright." She hung up the phone. She turned on her heels so quickly it made Doris jump back as best she could. Tracy glared at her. As if Doris was the person on the other end of the phone delivering news she did not want to hear. "Looks like an angel heard your wish for Dr. V to come and save you." she sneered.

⸻ ◈◈◈ ⸻

Dr. Vernirelli lit a cigarette between his teeth. He stood in his office, the phone clenched in his hands as he dialed for Dr. Turner, head of Tokema. Dr. Turner was not one often called. In fact, he rarely visited the asylum anymore. He was far too old and dated to still be in charge. His duties now rested more towards being a figurehead who would sign paychecks and attend board meetings. However, in this circus, he was the ringleader, and the ringleader runs the show. Turner would mostly show up a handful of times throughout the year, do his rounds, checking on each and every patient and then leaving to lock himself away in his office to either do paperwork, smoke a cigarette, or fuck his receptionist behind his wife's back. But Mipsy knew. It didn't bother her too much, for she got her kicks when the pool boy came on Tuesdays in the summer. And in the winter, she was blessed with the snowplow man whenever he'd come. She was also the one in David Turner's will, not that stupid whore that her husband kept close by, she made sure of it.

Turner had become bitter with age, working in a place like this would do that to anyone over time. Vernirelli wasn't all convinced that Dr. Turner was fully sound of mind to maintain his position anymore. He was often confused by small things, half blind from all the paperwork, and too frail to actually walk around the facilities, he would have his receptionist push him around in a wheelchair as he smoked and grunted. She didn't mind though, he reminded her of a small helpless baby. One that needed to be taken care of. Someone she loved, and who she hoped loved her in return. God, she hoped he loved her. Someone she could take care of. Someone who would leave her well off when he passed, someone who would make sure she was taken care of. If only she knew he only thought of her as a warm body to snuggle up with when his pills set in.

The phone rang. The likelihood of Turner picking up this late was a rare one, but still, the Doc needed to try. He didn't know how, but he was positive Doris did not leave her room and he was damn sure not going to let her get reconditioned over something like that.

BRIIINGG BRIIINGG BRIIINGG

The phone continued to ring when a woman suddenly picked up. Mipsy Turner was about 20 years too young for her husband, she was his third, or perhaps fourth wife at this point. She was awoken by the shrilling noise of the third party, demanding for her or her husband's attention. At first, she debated picking up the phone, only to immediately slam it down again. But she didn't do that, what if it was a sick family member? Maybe her father slipped and fell down the stairs again and she would once again need to rush off to Omaha to take care of him.

"Hel-low" she mumbled out, "Dad...?"

"No, this is Dr. Vernirelli from Tokema it' an-"

"David, David wake up" Mipsy snapped sharply as she slapped her husband to try and wake him. David Turner grunted a few times before comprehending that his presence was needed. Mispy gave him another slap across the stomach. Dr. Turner grunted and groaned as he rolled on his side.

"It's the asylum David, wake up!" she yipped as she threw the phone cord over her shoulder and onto her barely awakened husband's stomach.

Half sleeping David fumbled with the phone, trying not to catch his wife in the face with the cord.

"Who is this?" he asked, "What could possibly need my attention now?"

Dr. Vernirelli sighed as he began to explain what happened over the phone, he knew it was a long shot to get Turner involved, but something would need to be done. He presented his case that Doris was not guilty of trying to escape, and her reaction to what took place was totally understandable and the guards on duty were utterly out of line from what he could recall. As the Doc went on talking, he could hear Dr. Turner on the other end of the line.

He continued to make grunts and yawns and at one point he thought he heard a lighter being lit and a drag being had. After a while, it was only silence, and he thought the phone might have gotten disconnected.

"Sir, sir, are you still there? -"

"I'm here you big boob." Dr. Turner barked, "From what it sounds like we need to get that guard checked out. Make it subtle though, I don't want him to think we're trying to commit him. But if that's what it comes down to, we'll have to. Keep this to yourself too. We don't need word getting out that we have loonies watching loonies."

"Sir, I wouldn't call them loonies-"

"I'll give Tracy a call in the morning, in regard to the situation. Now goodnight Vernirelli. Don't call me this late again."

"But sir, please-"

"You got what you wanted. I suggest you quit talking while you're ahead. Goodnight!" and with that the phone was slammed down with a mighty click.

"What did the hospital need?" Mipsy asked as she pulled out a smoke from her nightstand. She lit the cigarette and puffed. The smoke floated across the room, only adding to the yellow-stained walls.

"Nothing that required a phone call in the middle of the damn night" David replied. He went to kiss his wife on the cheek, but she recoiled, hesitated, and then let him kiss her after all. She took in another deep inhale.

"If someone felt the need to call you, I'd say it seemed pretty important. When did we ever get a call in the middle of the night-"

"I said it wasn't worth the call dear so let us leave it at that." David spat, getting more aggressive than necessary. This was something Mipsy was used to. David never had been an entirely pleasant man before, but he was old and rich, and he smoked cigs like his life depended on it. So, it wouldn't be much longer Mispy ol' gal. *Not much longer until he is out of the picture and the funds will be dropping into your account.* She thought to herself. Mipsy smiled to herself at the thought of such things. She could finally be with the pool boy, a silly fantasy she knew, but boy did he know how to please her. Yes, the plowman was nice, but nothing compared to her little thong-wearing pool boy. Mipsy grinned at the thought. She almost giggled to herself.

"Now that we're up, why don't you and I have a little fun miss missy," David said, sliding himself closer to her, making an attempt to mount her. She gave him the slide eye he was so used to seeing and sighed. She had half a mind to shove him off, but then felt bad for her husband. He'd be on his way out soon enough.

"Make it quick," she said, smushing out her cigarette.

Dr. Vernirelli stood in his office silently, still holding the phone in his hands. He could go to Dr. Tracy's office himself, but that would lead to trouble if she relayed anything back to Turner. *It's always better to ask for forgiveness than permission*, he thought to himself. *Besides, I got what I wanted. Why do I still feel the need to intervene? Patients, wait for the morning.* Still squeezing the phone as he slowly put it back into its cradle. Resistant at first to let it go.

He rocked back and forth on his heels as he thought of what to do. He lifted the phone up again and then smashed it back down, the phone gave a loud ring and then a defeated cracking noise. The Doc screamed as he flung the neatly stacked papers from his desk to the ground. He grabbed his plant and flung it to the ground with such force that the pot shattered and laid broken across the ground. Dirt now caked into the carpet and shards everywhere.

"Fuck it!" he yelled as he stormed out the door, flinging it open with such force that the handle left a dent in the wall. He lumbered out of his office and down the hallway to Dr. Tracy's reconditioning room. He knew he would not be able to get to Doris tonight. The best solution would just be to go home. But he needed to see her at least one more time before he left for the night. Just to simply make sure that she was okay.

The halls seemed to stretch on longer than they usually were. Where Amelia's reconditioning room was not too much further down than his, but it was on a separate floor. Dr. Vernirelli mounted the stairs and seemed to climb what felt to be Mount Everest. Even though it was a mere floor above his own. As he made his way to the door he paused, looking around. There were no guards, which was rather unusual. Doris would have been thrown in the reconditioning room until morning.

He approached the door slowly. The door was made of solid wood. There were no windows for him to peek through to catch a glimpse of Doris. He jiggled the handle in hopes that it would be open, but the handle did not move.

"Doris?" the Doc whispered as he knocked gently on the door. "Doris, are you in there?" But there was no response to be had. The doctor waited for a few minutes and then decided to knock again, this time a little louder. "Doris?" he called out in his usual talking voice. "Doris, if you're in there please answer me. I got you some help." But again, no answer.

The doctor moaned. He was not surprised that there was no answer. For there was a real chance that Doris had been taken to another room. Or, maybe she had fallen asleep. Although he imagined that would be terribly uncomfortable given that she was put into a straitjacket.

There would truly be nothing he could do at this hour besides comfort Doris. Telling her that it would be okay and not to worry because the head of the facilities said she did not need reconditioning. The next time he was to see Doris he would start that new cognitive behavioral therapy. He nodded to himself. Indeed, that would be the best move. But now how to handle that guard? Dr. Turner wanted him tested to see if he was insane too, but Dr. Vernirelli saw the dirt on Doris's feet as well. So, he knew the guard was not crazy. And it was a guarantee that Doris saw it. But the other two, nothing.

The doctor turned his back to the door behind him, he leaned against its wooden frame and sunk to the floor. He placed his head between his knees and thought to himself. *I could think of things I never thunk before...* he could lie to the guard saying it was simply routine and do an "evaluation" on not only him but a group of guards, to make things seem less suspicious. Or he could be upfront and say that it was requested from Dr. Turner, but no that wouldn't do. Turner asked him to evaluate this man subtly. He did not want him exploding now.

Dr. Vernirelli sat there for a long time before raising his head again. He felt almost dizzy. He did not realize how long he was actually sitting there for until he sat himself fully back up. Alright, time to get your thoughts straight Doc. *You have to evaluate Stew. Stew is big, Stew is irrational. Stew will take offense and could possibly become dangerous if he feels threatened. You want to avoid that no matter what. You could try having a conversation with him, but that would come off as strange given you've never even had contact with him before last night and he knows you're defensive over your patients. I could ask another doctor to do it, but that wouldn't be subtle... think man think. But I saw the leaves too... I know he's not crazy. Only a certain group of people must see them.*

Dr. Vernirelli finally stood himself up after having a long thought on the matter at hand. He straightened himself up, brushing off his pants. He turned and headed out of the facility. There was nothing he could do in the moment; the best beat was to now actually head home. He would revisit Ameila Tracy in the morning, collecting Doris and getting back to matters at hand.

His eyes were heavy as he continued to make his way down and to his car. He had not realized just how late it was, past 1 am at this point. The doctor glanced at his watch and groaned. He would need to be up sooner than later. Perhaps at this point it was best to just stay the night here. Although he did not have a change of clothes, people would definitely notice that kind of thing.

Once he made it to his car, he slowly shut the door and placed his head on the wheel. *Please don't see anything tonight...* he thought to himself. *Please.* And with that final thought he turned his key and headed off into the night.

❦❦❦

Dr. Tracy woke that morning eager to begin her day. She always loved doing what she did. Reconditioning people was like cleaning off the stains of the world. And the people at Tokema were the toughest stains of all. But of course, it is most satisfying when those tough stains come out.

Her morning went about as usual. Fixing her hair and makeup to be perfect. A well-balanced breakfast, only half a grapefruit! Anything more would affect a woman's figure. And she was sure her husband would thank her for being so mindful about such things. Just before leaving, as she always did, she kissed the picture of her nephew on the fridge. A handsome, strong young man. He would always be 18 to her.

As Dr. Tracy drove to work, she hoped to see a patient today. There were often days when she would not see anyone at all. Weeks even, in the worst-case scenarios. Yes, reconditioning was fun, but what good is it if there is no one who needs it? Oftentimes she would sit at her desk, reviewing old case files about which method she took to help her patients. Or sometimes she would doodle at her desk. She kept a pad and pen in the top left drawer just for that. She wasn't talented by any means, but it was something to do and keep busy with.

Pulling in Dr. Tracy could feel it in the air, the feeling that someone was waiting for her, and she was excited. She skipped from her car, through the double doors, waving hi to Angela who was already in her chair, and straight to her work mailbox. Resting in her mailbox she found a sealed up manila folder. She tore it open with such gusto that shreds of little paper fell to the floor. As she read the incident report in the folder her eyes glittered with delight.

"So, Doris tried to leave last night… oh dear" she smiled. She was hoping to have Doris again. She felt a strong urge that reconditioning would not be nearly enough. This was not due to the fact that Dr. Tracy seemed to have a certain enFreude ment about harming her patients, oh no. This was far too personal for that. When Doris was first admitted to the facilities all the staff were asked if they bore any personal relationship to Doris's victims, because if that were to be the case Doris and that worker were meant to keep a strict distance from one another. And while Dr. Tracy had marked no on that paper, she should have marked yes.

Dr. Tracy continued to examine the incident report as she made her way down the hall. She sipped on her coffee as she pranced her way down the hall. How to deal with Doris? Clearly the vomiting did not work. Maybe Metrazol therapy? But how would she justify the means of that? Bloodletting is good, although again, how to properly justify the means? Complete and total insolation would be better. Completely isolate her for a week, in one of the basement cells. Sure, they hadn't been used for years, but she knew where the key was. Doris would not be allowed any contact with the outside world, not even her doctors. *Ugh, Dr. Vernirelli, he thinks so great, that he's better than the rest of us.* Amelia was certain she could do this, yes, she knew Vernirelli would fight back, but if she just called Dr. Turner, she was sure he'd sign off on it.

Dr. Tracy swung her door open, and there lying in the corner was Doris. She knew from the chart that she would be waiting there for her. Clicking on the light Dr. Tracy continued to study the clipboard. Of course, she already had in mind what she was going to do to Doris, but she wouldn't be giving it away so easily. Making her squirm a little would be best.

———◦/◦/◦———

"Hello?" Dr. Tracy asked, still wiping away her tears from her previous laughter at Doris's remark of wanting Dr. Vernirelli in the room.

"Amelia, it's David."

"Oh, sir I was just about to call-"

"Amelia, listen. I got a call from Dr. Vernirelli last night. He explained the situation to me. Since only one guard saw the dirt and things on the girl's feet, we're not going to have her be reconditioned, right?"

"No, I-"

"Don't interrupt me. I told you we're not reconditioning."

"I don't think-"

"I said don't interrupt me damn it! What is it with you people? Dr. Vernirelli is on his way to pick up Doris and bring her back to her normal schedule. I want that guard evaluated. I told Vernirelli this last night. You should assist him if you can. The guard was Stew Walker. Got it?"

"Yes sir. Alright."

"Good. Goodbye." and with that David Turner hung up the phone. Dr. Tracy stood there for a moment, clinging to her phone. She was not expecting a call like that. How dare Dr. Vernirelli go behind her back and call Turner, how dare he! It was clear that Dr. V was getting too closely attached to his patients. He was putting personal feelings above the rest. That kind of behavior would not do. Would not do at all. Amelia slowly hung up the phone. Inching her body to take a step back. She stood there for a moment. Pondering the situation and how to handle it. How to make Dr. Turner see things *her* way.

Amelia turned on her heels so quickly it made Doris jump. She lunged at Doris in a way that made her body quiver. "Looks like an angel heard your wish for Dr. V to come and save you." She let out half a laugh. "Figures..." she muttered. Doris sat there quietly. She was afraid one wrong move would make Dr. Tracy snap, and recondition her anyways, despite Dr. Vernirelli coming. And what was to stop her? *Nothing really*, Doris thought. For she still was in her jacket. Arms unmoving and stiff. Best not to re-adjust. Just sit as quietly as possible. Try not to even blink. One move could change everything.

Dr. Tracy moved about her office. She muttered, pushing papers around and throwing different manila envelopes into various filing cabinets. Her heels clicked and clacked away as she did so. After several minutes there was a knock on the door.

"Come in!" Dr. Tracy sang out. Doris was surprised to hear such a sweet sound coming from out of her voice. Despite the huffing and puffing that just took place.

Slowly, Dr. Vernirelli swung open the door. He was accompanied by one of the security guards behind him.

"Hello Amelia, I'm sure David rang you to tell you I was coming." Dr. Vernirelli made his way over to Doris, helping her up, and out of her jacket. Doris rubbed her arms in gratitude.

"Yes, he called." Dr. Tracy replied without even looking up from her papers. She seemed to be busying herself with things that could have waited. She looked over papers, scribbling something down. She glanced over her shoulder, now fully acknowledging her colleague. "You're still here?" she asked, one lip curling over her teeth. Without a word Dr. Vernirelli took Doris by her shoulder, turning her towards the door, and the two of them walked out side by side.

Once in the hallway, away from Dr. Tracy's ears Dr. Vernirelli asked,

"How are you fairing my dear?"

"I'm alright. A little shaken, but much better than the alternative." Dr. Vernirelli smiled at her.

"Let's get you to the dining room for breakfast, shall we?" Doris nodded. She walked with the doctor down the hall. The guard is not too far behind.

It had been a few months since Doris's last encounter with the ashed skinned demon-man. Although, that did not stop her from jumping and glancing over her shoulder. She still felt as if she could feel him, like a sly whisper of wind as it slowly made its way through an Autumn Day. Never quite detectable, but definitely hung in the air. The feeling would creep up on her every so often. And when it did, she would look about, but never saw.

Her routine continued on more or less the same. However, with one special exception, she was now permitted to go into the library. Ever since Dr. Turner deemed her well enough to not be reconditioned, Dr. Vernirelli seemed to pull some strings for her that would not have normally been permitted.

True, books were still going to be thought of as a weapon for her, so she needed to be followed by a guard and was only permitted on days when Dr. Vernirelli was willing to have their sessions there. *But a win is a win,* Doris would think as she was escorted down the halls. She actually enjoyed having sessions in those hallowed halls. Well, hallowed halls that were covered in grim, dust, and occasionally a found piece of shit shoved in between the pages of the books. This happened to Dr. V on their first trip to the library together. The more time he spent with Doris around the facilities that went outside his main building, the more discovered how truly awful the grounds were kept.

Each new and disgusting encounter would result in an immediate phone call to Dr. Turner. Who was becoming quite sick of Dr. Vernirelli at this point. The floors need constant mopping, and shit on the walls needed to be constantly cleaned. How was Dr. Turner meant to respond? He only came for mandatory board meetings and that's where it ended! He hated visiting the facilities and frankly could care less about the condition those loonies were in. However, Dr. Vernirelli was an insistent man and if actions typically weren't taken within a week there would be several more calls. At this point, he was really pushing his luck, Dr. Turner would often think to himself after hanging up the phone.

Doris traced her fingers along the backbone of the books laid out before her. She had a fondness for fairytales. Often picking out fables and other short stories to flip through. She was not allowed to take the books out of those small four walls in which they were held. So, she would gravitate towards the one's she knew she could finish within the hour sessions. She had always had a fondness for reading and she knew if she selected one that was too long, she would grow inpatient waiting a whole week to continue where she left off.

And who knows what kind of condition the book would be in at that point. There were several incidents, even with her short stories, in which she would get to the end of a book only to find the last few pages ripped clean out. She had her suspicions that it was the patient who was given the informal title of "librarian". A patient named Lori who was admitted in at the age of 15 for disobeying her parents and was now 30 years into her joining the Tokema family. Lori had locked herself in the library when she first arrived, refusing to leave. And when she was finally either coaxed out, or rather beaten out, Lori turned into a machine of pure destruction and chaos. Apparently, the only place in which she was peaceful is amongst the princesses, elves, noblemen, and historians.

Doris suspected she was simply a headstrong child, whose parents did not want to waste time on training her. And merely threw her in here as a way for them to continue their lives without being inconvenienced with a child. Now, Doris did not actually know if this was Lori's background or not. The only thing she was certain of was how long Lori had been in Tokema. However, Doris was bored for so many days that she would find small ways of entertaining herself. And one of those ways was to make up fake stories about her fellow patients. Although, she would never tell them such things. And would continue to keep it her private game. Even from Dr. Vernirelli. Afterall, she still needed some things for herself.

Doris eyed each book carefully. Dr. Vernirelli next to her. Both of their eyes fixated on the gold, blue, red, and black lettering on the spines. Doris turned her head to read better, squinting her eyes to focus in on the golden letters which caught her eye, *Native American*

Folklore Stories. Seemed interesting enough, but she was not in the mood for such tales. She turned and examined the other books nearby. Suddenly, she heard a soft *thud.* Doris turned to find a book that had fallen.

Doris plucked the book from the ground. It was the *Native American Folklore Stories. Now how did this fall?* Doris asked herself. She went to put it back in its comfortable resting place in between *The Grapes of Wrath* and *Valperga* by Mary Wollstonecraft. A terrible filing system. Doris wasn't sure how Lori arranged the books, but every time she had been there Lori would wander the small isles grabbing books, shuffling them around, and placing them in peculiar and specific ways. Doris did not question it too much, however. She was just happy to be there. Just before letting the book go Doris felt something almost like a tug at her sleeve. Something was pulling the book back in. Doris looked down at it once more.

The book clearly had not been open for some time. The pages were stiff and stuck together, slowly resisting being peeled apart. But giving into that satisfying, rustle as Doris shuffled through the pages. The papers were yellowed with age, and the book smelled sour. But there was something intriguing and eye-catching about the font of the letters. They seemed almost nostalgic to Doris. As if she had seen them long ago in an old picture book.

No, the letters were not childish. But rather structured and inviting. Coaxing the reader into wanting to continue on. One word was not satisfying enough to decipher, all must be read. To miss even one seemed to bring about guilt.

Flipping open the book, Doris examined it carefully. There seemed to be a total of eleven tales. The Adventures of Wolf-Marked, The Boy Who Was Saved by Thoughts, The Dead Wife, The Fate of the Boy Witch, The Girl Who Always Cried, How the Man Found His Mate, In the Land of Souls, The Little Spirit or Boy-Man, The Man-Eater, The Origin of Stories, and The Wendigo. Doris glanced at each story casually. None were particularly long from what she could tell. On some pages there were pictures of the stories. She stopped on one of the images. It appeared to be a young girl, placed in a woven basket amongst frogs and toads. She wailed as a giant owl looking man carried her away. The image made Doris's backbone quiver, triggering what came next.

Doris felt a sudden chill within the air. Not quite like the one in which sent her back tingling, but a literal gust of wind rolling past the back of her neck. Instinctively, she reached for her nape. Feeling the hairs stand one by one. She peered up, turning her head frantically from side to side, like a rabbit sensing a dog. She could feel something near but did not know what. It was then that she heard it. Not from within the halls or amongst the people and walls, but in her skull, it rattled back and forth. Follow *the yellow brick road, follow the yellow brick road, follow, follow, follow, follow the yellow brick road*. Doris slammed the book shut with such force it made the doctor jump.

"Doris, are you alright?" The color from her face had flushed away and her breaths were sharp and short. She nodded her head.

"Yes... yes, I'm sorry. I thought I heard something." Dr. Vernirelli was quiet for a moment, listening as best as he could. But the only noise his ears were met with was the soft flipping and turning of pages as Lori shuffled her way through books. Larry, the guard teetering on the balls of his feet back and forth while looking at novels of his own. And a third-party patient who he did not know the name of was sucking on his thumb while hugging a book tightly to his chest.

"I'm sorry I don't hear anything out of the ordinary. Would you like me to read that to you? It might help calm you down." Dr. Vernirelli gestured to the book in Doris's hand. She still held an iron grip on it as she drummed her fingers against its hard cover.

She looked down at the book, shocked to see that it was still in her hands and that she had not dropped it due to fear. Doris loosened her grip and handed it over to the Doc. Nodding her head in agreement and motioning to a set of chairs set-up by the window.

Doris, Doc, and Larry took their seats. Doris knew that Larry secretly liked being assigned to her on days when she was permitted to come to the library. He often sat with her and the doctor as they read stories back and forth. He would claim it was only part of his job, but she could see the look on his face when one of them was reading a story aloud to the other. He would lean in at parts. Showing a deep interest and desire in wanting to hear more. He even groaned on a day in which they were unable to finish a tale and could not find the same book a week later. The disappointment on his face was clear, and Doris even went to give him a sympathetic pat. But when she reached for his hand he pulled back, reaching for his stick, and barking at her to know her place. There were moments like this when Doris would be pulled back into the reality of where she was. She was not in some place temporarily, she was not going to make friends, she would never be seen as a person again.

Doris settled into her seat. Getting as comfortable as she could. Which would not say much given the beaten and bruised conditions of the chairs. If only they could check books out like a normal library. Then they could take them back to the Docs office and read comfortably on his couch. Doris liked to entertain this thought from time to time. It would bring up old memories of her father reading to her as she sat snuggled next to him on the couch. Her father often read to her when she was little. He had more time on his hands before her siblings came. A family of six was not a thing to take lightly. And with her mother not working her father spent the rest of her childhood away doing labor somewhere.

"Is there a particular story in which you'd like me to start?" the Doc asked as he thumbed through the first pages of acknowledgements, credit, publishers, and citations.

"Why don't you close your eyes, run your finger along the stories, stop when I tell you, and we read that?" Doris suggested, giving a soft smile.

"I like that idea," the doctor agreed. He turned to the page that listed the folktales, placed his finger at the top of the page, closed his eyes and slowly began to trace up and down. Doris closed her eyes as well. Not wanting to peek and see which story he was hovering over. She counted in her head, *1...2...3...*

"And... stop," she said. Opening her eyes to see which of the eleven tails they would be reading today. The doctor glanced down at the paper, 'The Wendigo' it read. The doctor looked at the words for a longer time than he meant.

"What are we reading Doc?" Doris asked, looking over the cover to get a glance at where his finger had landed. "The Wendigo?" and again Doris felt it. That cool snippet of airbrush past her nape. And for the first time in months, she heard the soft melody, *Whenever I want you, all I have to do is Dream, dream, dream, dream...* Doris grabbed the back of her neck, tugging on her braid. She could feel something was close. Something was keeping in her. Was it the demon-man with the ash-colored skin? No. She was certain she would see him if it was. This was something more. Something important, and sinister.

The doctor flipped to the last story in the book. Adjusting his glasses upon his nose and no longer on his head. He cleared his throat...

Deep in the forest there once stood a mighty village. The village was known to be prosperous and fruitful. The men of the village were strong, mighty hunters, always well stocked and prepared. However, the most skilled hunter of them all was Dakota. Dakota was as strong as the most powerful bear. He was clever like the fox. Had an eye keen as any hawk. And moved just as light and as fast on his feet as the wind. His glory had earned him the hand of the most beautiful woman in the village, the chief's daughter. To show his undying love for her, he made her a brilliant necklace of turquoise blue. The intertwining beads represented their souls as one, the color of the beads showing health, protection, and life.

As the years went on Dakota's strength and pride only grew. Due to his many talents and great hunting skills, Dakota soon became vain with power. Dakota would go about the village boasting about his latest accomplishments in the woods. Always bringing back bucks, moose, mighty caribou, and bears. One day he asked his wife to make him a cloak, a cloak made from the skin and fur of each of the mighty animals he killed. This cloak he would wear proudly, showing that he indeed was the best hunter. His wife warned him about the consequences of pride and gloating, but he did not care.

So, his wife made the cloak. A gorgeous sight to see. The shiny fur and length caught everyone's eyes who gazed upon it. Dakota was pleased. He wore his cloak everywhere he went.

Soon winter came. The gusts of wind were stronger than any other. Snow piled higher than the trees. The ice was as thick as trucks, and soon everyone was forced into their homes. Dakota and his wife were trapped inside, just like the rest of the village. Dakota began to eat the dried meats his wife had saved up for the winter.

"Husband, do not eat so much," she warned him, "For we are stuck inside and will not be able to go out and gather more." At this Dakota laughed.

"I am the most skilled hunter in this land. I fear no harsh winds. We are far better stocked than anyone else in our village." And with that, he continued to eat.

Weeks went by without being able to leave their home. It was not long before Dakota had eaten every scrap of meat in the cabin. Dakota tried to leave the cabin to hunt, but the winds and snow were too strong, even for him. Soon, Dakota and his wife grew famished. Their eyes sunk into their sockets, leaving deep black circles, their bellies extended, and their ribs pressed so tightly against their skin it looked as if it was transparent.

'*I cannot starve. I am the greatest hunter in the land. How would others see me?*' Dakota thought. '*Think… there is always something to hunt…*' And with that, Dakota turned to his wife. '*There is always something to hunt…*' Dakota approached his wife, beckoning her to come closer to him. But she could see in his eyes that he no longer was the man he once was. There was a darkness behind his smile now. A dirty lust in his eyes.

Dakota took out his hunting knife and stabbed her directly in the heart. He cut it out and ate it. When it touched his lips, he realized it was the most delicious thing he had ever eaten. He wanted more, and soon. He devoured all of her. Taking her skin and hair he added them to his cloak. He wanted the world to know what kind of hunter he was. One who could conquer any beast, animal, or man. He took her necklace and slipped it upon his own neck. As a way if still keeping her with him.

Not long after this, the snow began to melt. It peeled away, revealing the beauty of Spring hidden underneath its icy grip. One by one the villagers drifted outside, back amongst their neighbors and friends. But Dakota did not leave.

Soon the village began to worry. A group of his fellow hunters went to his lodge to check on him and his wife. Upon entering they saw Dakota, in his cloak, still hunched over her remains, trying to suck whatever juices and flesh that might have still clung to her bones. Seeing his fellow man Dakota felt something in him snap. He needed more. His wife was not enough to keep him satisfied. He must have more. Dakota sprang to his feet, attacking one of the hunters. Ripping his throat out with his teeth. The other hunters managed to pull him off and banished him from their village.

Wandering the woods alone Dakota would hunt and kill different animals, but none were as tasty as the man's flesh. It soon became his every thought, consuming his very being. A sickness it was. One that festered and infected his mind, and his heart. His skin soon became gray as ash, his lips tattered and bloodied. His bones pulled so tightly around his flesh that they poked through. Dakota knew what he must hunt next. The only thing that would satisfy him, man. He waited in the woods, picking off hunters one by one. But no matter how many he seemed to take; it never made him feel full.

Word of the missing hunters did not take long to reach back to the village. The group of men who had seen Dakota over his wife and rip out the throat of another with his teeth, knew that it had to be him. The group went out on their own hunt. Looking for their once long-ago friend.

It did not take long for the other hunters to find him. For they found and followed a trail of bones leading to a cave. There the hunters stabbed, beat, and fought their former friend. But nothing seemed to kill him. Terrified and defeated, the remaining men ran back to their village.

They prayed to the spirits, asking for wisdom on how to defeat the monster. And in their dreams that night their prayers were answered. Each of the men had a vision. A vision of returning to Dakota's cave and setting him on fire. It was only then that the monster would be defeated.

The next day the men took off. Preparing themselves for the upcoming battle. Reaching the cave, they began to taunt Dakota, calling him out of his stone fortress. And soon he came. He ran at the men, faster than ever. He seemed to have grown, despite his malnourishment. His limbs were now long, extended, and distorted. His stature now towered over seven feet. Reaching for all those around him to swallow them whole. But soon, bright sparks began to emerge from within the forest, and the man that Dakota once could feel his flesh being torn. Fire was the devil's only friend and it was this that was calling him back down into hell. The men threw torches at Dakota, and they watched as he burned to nothingness.

Soon the fire died, but something still remained in the ash. A brilliant blue peered through. One of the men approached, a stick in hand, he pulled from the ash the necklace of Dakota's wife. The men brought the relic back to the village, encased it in wood, and buried it deep within the forest. Never to be dug up again.

The men, warning anyone and everyone of what had happened and how to kill the beast. The people of the village decided to strip Dakota of his former name, giving him a new one, one that meant cannibal and monster. A name only fitting for such a beast, Wendigo.

———◦/◦/◦———

Doris sat frozen in her chair as the Doc slowly closed the book. He let out a heavy sigh. This story he knew was too much for Doris. He could feel it while reading. He had wanted to stop, but something in him persuaded him to continue until the story was completed. To leave the tale unfinished would-be blasphemy. The air between them had shifted, it was now stiff and heavy. Unlike before, which brought promise and lightheartedness given the pleasure of reading. The Doc was not sure if the shift was for the better or worse. Yes, the mood had changed to a darker presence, but something about it seemed important and transformative.

The Doc looked down at the page, it was the last story in the book and the story said, "The End." So, it must have been over. But there seemed to be one more page. The doctor flipped it over and there he saw the picture. A wendigo burning in flame. The skin was ash gray, eyes sunken so deep they seemed to only be black circles. However, the pupils were still clear, pin-prick blood shots. The lips curled over its sharp teeth; blood dripped. The bones were so tightly pressed to the skin that they seemed to poke through. The creature's jaw seemed to be open wide as if it were screaming. From pain or pleasure, the doctor could not tell. Then it all came flooding upon him as if a dam were broken, it was the man Doc saw in the mirror that one night... He slammed the book with such force it caused not only Doris to jump, but Larry too.

"Are you okay Dr. Vernirelli?" Larry asked, picking up the book and placing it on a table nearby. Doris looked stunned, but not surprised. The doctor was certain she had not seen the image. It would be no good for her. The doctor stared at Doris, to see if there was any indication of fear on her face. And while she looked startled, there was no real fear. Not like he had seen before.

"Yes, yes, I'm alright. Just a- a body spasm. That's all," the Doc rubbed his neck, "That's what happens when you get old. Your muscles start having a mind of their own." Larry nodded, seeming to accept this answer. But Doris knew the doctor well enough at this point to know he did not have body spasms. She knew better. He saw something amongst those pages. Something he did not want her to see.

"Doris, I'm sorry but looking at the time our session is up." The doctor motioned to the clock on the wall behind her. Doris turned to see that indeed the hour was up. "I think it would be best if Larry escorted you back."

"You're not coming?" Doris asked. It was strange for the doctor to not at least walk her back part of the way. He usually drifted apart when they walked past his office.

"Not today. I have something to do that won't take me back the way you're going." Doris stared at the Doc puzzled. She could tell he was not being honest with her. What had he seen within those pages? Doris slowly stood, nodded, and turned. Larry walked briskly behind her. He motioned her toward the door with his extended arm.

The Doc sat in his chair watching the two of them walk away. As soon as the wooden door to the library shut and Doris was out of sight the doctor scrambled to his feet. He lunged at the book, scooping it up before Lori could grab it and move it to a new location, one where it might be lost to the sea of unkempt books.

He flipped quickly to the page that made him drop the book. There it was, clear in black and white ink. The monster in which he had seen in his mirror. He was positive. It held the face of such evil it would not be forgotten, no matter how much one tried to push it aside. The monster burned in fire, and while it seemed to be in pain there was a look of satisfaction on its face. Like it was glad to be descending back into the depths of hell.

The doctor was not sure how long he sat there observing the image. There was something deeply disturbing about it. In a way that made someone want to tear out their eyes, but always one that held your sight. One not letting you look away. Its eyes held yours with such possession that the doctor truly struggled to close the book again. Doris had been his last patient for the day, so he had nothing to rush back to. And even if he did, he was unsure he'd be able to. The hold those eyes held, even in a picture, seemed to hypnotize and taunt.

"Library closing," a small voice said over the doctor's shoulder. And with that invisible hold, the trance seemed to weaken.

"Wha-what?" The doctor asked, shaking his head and looking back to see who was speaking to him. There stood Lori. She looked smaller somehow even up close. Her oversized nightgown and baggy slippers did nothing to help this appearance.

"Library closing!" Lori barked again. Her voice was high-pitched and irritated.

"Oh… right. Sorry Lori, good evening." The doctor said as he stood. Still holding the book in his hands. He went to walk past her, but she held out her arm blocking his path.

"Book please" Lori squeaked. Extending her hand to take it from him. But the doctor could not let it go. He needed it. He needed to examine the book. He needed to do some research.

"I'm sorry Lori, but I am going to be checking it out. Can you help me with that?" Lori started. Deciding what she should do. After a few moments, she shook her head and held her hand back out.

"The book please, now!" She yelled, her voice rising to almost a scream.

"No Lori, I'm sorry but I need this. Please may I check it out?" The doctor asked again, this time sweeter. Hoping that his niceness would persuade her into letting him take the book with her permission, instead of just taking it because he could. Lori looked puzzled again. She examined him. Looking at his slacks, button-down shirt, and sweater vest. He was not sure what Lori was looking at. Perhaps she was sizing him up to see if she could get the book by force. Or maybe she was seeing if he was a patient or not. He was not sure of Lori's mind, given that she was not one of his patients.

Skeptically Lori nodded. "You may take the book," Lori eventually said. She clearly was not happy to give it up, but it was clear that she knew he did not need to ask her, and he simply did it to be polite.

"Thank you, Lori," the Doc said, tipping an imaginary hat in her direction, "I'll remember your kindness." He smiled and went for the door.

"Kindness…" he could hear Lori mutter and she retreated back into her books. The doctor was not sure if she actually stayed there during the night or if she had a room. It would not surprise him if it was just easier to leave her there. There was a bathroom in the library and Lori never hurt a book. She never even ripped the pages by accident. They were her children, and it was clear to everyone.

———◦/◦/◦———

As the doctor made his way down the hall to his office, he thought he could hear the light tapping of shoes from someone behind him. He turned to see that the halls were bare. The image in the book was beginning to frighten him, that's all. His mind was playing simple tricks on him. He continued to walk. This time picking up his pace. But the transparent follower seemed to increase their pace as well. Keeping in time with him.

The Doc glanced over his shoulder again, and again he was met with nothing but hallway. *Get a hold of yourself ol' boy.* The doctor slowed his pacing, once again walking at normal speed. And so did the follower. He stopped. The follower stopped. It was silly, he knew this, but despite logic he called out,

"Who's there?" But not to his surprise no one answered. He called again, this time louder, "I said who is there?" And again, he fell upon nothing. The doctor turned. He was close to his office now. He could just get in and shut the door, lock it. As he reached for the door he hesitated. And then what? Go back home. After seeing the vision clear as day in this book. He could be waiting there, and not in a mirror this time. What if he were to be sitting in his lazy boy? Laying in his bed? Or would he greet him at the door? The Doc could try his sister's place again, and while she would welcome his unexpected drop in, his brother-in-law would not. But spending the night in his office was not ideal. He would need a change of clothes, a toothbrush, and what if whoever was following him could slip through doors.

Home seemed to be the only option. Who knows, perhaps the Wendigo would not be there waiting for him at all. *And if it was, bring it on!* The doctor thought. For now, I know it's one weakness, if the tale in this book is true, fire!

⟞ⰔⰔⰔⰑⰔⰔ⟝

As the Doc approached his front door, he could feel his stomach filling up with dread. He stayed with his key in the keyhole for a long time. Not daring to turn it. He breathed in deeply. The winter air nipped at his cheeks and despite the cold he could not feel it. His body was numb with the anticipation of *it* being behind the door frame.

For *it* knew his fear. He was certain of that. He counted, *1...2...3...* and pushed the door open. But he found nothing strange or out of place. His seemingly ordinary house was just that, ordinary. The Doc stepped one foot inside and glanced around. It was absolutely silly to be afraid of one's own home. This was meant to be his safe place, his sanctuary. He stepped both feet inside now. And to his surprise he was not over washed with gloom and doom. In fact, he felt only the comfort that his home could provide. Puzzled, he hung up his winter coat.

Yes, everything was just as he left it. No records out of place, the shag had not been disturbed, and even his cup of tea still rested comfortably on the side table where he left it this morning because he was running late.

The doctor peered in his bathroom. Everything there seemed to be in order as well. His razor and toothbrush both hung neatly in their holsters. He gave the shower curtain a quick tap before flinging it open to find that nothing was there. And lastly, with a deep breath, he looked in his mirror. Only to find his own, tired reflection looking back at him. He left out a sigh of relief.

With this he deemed his home to be monster free. He retired to his bedroom in which he undressed, crawled into bed hoping to softly drift off to a dreamless sleep. He took the book out for one last time. To glance at the demon amongst those pages or perhaps to not glance at the demon among those pages. That was indeed the question.

Something in him longed to see the image again, but he knew better. He knew if he were to flip it open again and gaze upon those sunken eyes of death he would be in a trance once more. And this time there was no Lori to pull him out of it. How long would he be stuck like that? For only a moment? All night? Or would the night creep into day, forever holding him in place? This was something he did not want to find out.

He placed the book on his nightstand. He would re-examine it in the morning. But he would not, however, look at the last page. Perhaps starting his own research about the tribes in which the book originated. *That would be a good place to start*, he thought. *Yes, tomorrow I will call in sick and that is exactly where I will start.*

Doris laid in bed. Her eyes wide open. She knew the doctor had seen something in that book. Something that he did not want her to see or know about. She stared at the ceiling. Straining her thought on what it was. Was there more to the story? Perhaps a picture was included? Whatever it was she was determined to find out. During their next session she would request to go to the library again. Hopefully with luck she would be able to find the book again and get a sneak peek before the doctor can snatch it away. That is if Lori has not filed the book away somewhere. Doris was not sure of Lori's methods of filing, but she knew that planning made no sense. No sense at all.

For the first time, in a long time, Doris turned on her side in bed. Normally she avoided doing this at all costs, thinking that her personal boogeyman would snatch her when she was not looking, but tonight Doris left another presence in the air. Not necessarily one of danger. But one that made her not want to fall asleep, nonetheless. True, she had not experienced a nightmare since she was almost subjected to reconditioning, but she knew that she would have one tonight. She could feel it.

Laying in bed Doris counted her fingers, toes, the titles, strands of her hair; anything to keep her from drifting off. She tried doing jumping jacks, running circles, and at one point even attempted standing on her head. But as the night went on, she could feel herself growing weak and tired. She glanced at the clock outside of her door. It read 12:34, and then she heard it. That all too familiar sound.

Whenever I want you, all I have to do is dream…

dream…

dream…

Doris stood outside. She knew exactly where she was amongst those trees. Standing in the bitter cold. She wrapped her arms around herself in a small attempt to keep warm. Standing next to her was the disheveled burned man she had seen so many times before.

"What do you want from me?" Doris cried out.

"He knows you know Doris."

"Who does? Know what? What are you talking about?"

"Think Doris. Think back to today." The man placed a finger to her heart. And with a flush Doris thought about her time in the library. The book with the gold lettering, it flying itself off the shelf, her wanting to put it back but feeling a tug at her arm not to.

"It was you! You wanted me to read that book." The man nodded,

"You now know Doris." And Doris did know. She knew then what the doctor had seen. And she knew why he flung the book closed too quickly. She let out a puff of air. But how could it be possible? Wendigos are not real. It was only a story. One made up to scare people into not eating one another no matter how hard the times would get. And besides, she was not consumed by the thoughts of man flesh. Even when she was taken over, she did not have those thoughts. It wasn't possible.

It seemed to Doris that the man standing next to her could see what she was thinking,

"We are not Doris. We are simply vessels. Vessels that are used and abused to satisfy his hunger when he most needs it." Doris could feel the wind beginning to pick up and bite at her cheeks. She could no longer feel her feet and her eyes were beginning to well up. Not from sadness, but from the night air snatching at her hair and skin.

"Before you go Doris you must know I will not be back to guide you. But I will show you how to escape." And with that he took her hands and placed his head upon hers. Doris closed her eyes. There she saw.

⎯⎯◦∕◦∕◦⎯⎯

Simon stood looking at the ring. He had been saving up to buy it for some time now. He was ready. He knew Sarah-Lynn was the one for him. He knew it the second he laid eyes on her, just like he knew this ring was the one for her the second he laid eyes on it.

Someone had brought it to the antique store in which he worked about 6 months ago. He prayed that no one else would purchase it at that time, and no one had. He was 6 dollars short, but my god he was going to get those six dollars even if it killed him.

The ring was a beautiful circle cut, it had a silver lining that twisted in amongst itself, and little bits of onyx on either side of the head stone. Yes sir, that was the ring for him and her. He looked in the glass, admiring it as it sparkled.

"Shoot Simon, if you love that ol' ring so much I reckon you shoulda just put it in the back so no one else takes it." Richard said as he passed by, carrying a big old box of new antiques to be placed out.

"Nah, I can't do that. It's the honest thing to leave it out as is. Act as if it were in any other place. I'd need to be patient all the same." Simon shrugged.

"Well, it aint in any other place. It's here and you work here, so you get the first call," Rich remarked back. Simon shrugged again and went back to his admiring. "Alright lover boy, we gotta cut it out. Come 'er and help me unload this box." Simon drifted over to where Rich stood. He reached for his box cutter and with a quick flick from his wrist the tape gave way and the box gilded open.

There were several items inside, an old doll, a necklace, some shoes, silverware, a jewelry box, books, cups, plates, some clothes, and at the bottom of it all there was a clay pot. Richard and Simon took turns unpacking each item. Until finally only one of the necklaces remained. Simon plucked it from the bottom of the box. He held it up, admiring the turquoise as it gleamed in the light. It was then he felt a sudden chill. He heard the ding of the antique door swing open, and there he saw him. The ashed skinned man.

Doris closed her eyes, for she knew what was to come next, and did not wish to witness it again. She felt a gentle touch on her hands and the man in the burned t-shirt and chard skin slowly removed her hands from where they were.

"It's okay, I won't show. Just listen." he said, Doris nodded.

"He possessed me, he did. Turned me into his puppet. At first, he just used my body to flop around in. I was terrified. Not knowing why or what he was going to do to me. He'd come when nobody was around. It seemed like he just wanted to use me as something to play with. And although I did not like it, I grew to accept it. He didn't seem to want to hurt anybody. And that was all I could ask for. But that soon would change.

I did manage to save up and buy that ring for Sarah-Lynn. Shoot, how her face lit up when I gave it to her. There was no hesitation in her voice at all when she said yes. And I couldn't have asked for a better response. It was that night, while laying in bed I felt him over me. He seemed to crawl on our bed. He grabbed me and forced me down as he had so many times. I did not want to scream. I was afraid I'd wake Sarah-Lynn and I would scare her with my disjointed movements. Looking back now I wish I had screamed. I would have yelled, 'Get out! Run! Leave me behind and forget me!' but I didn't do that. Oh, I wish I had.

She was the first he made me eat. I remember crying so hard inside him I thought I would suffocate myself from the huffs and puffs. But I didn't. I kept on going. Living, but no life was living without Sarah-Lynn. I couldn't face myself for what he made me do.

I retreated. Left town without a word or a trace. Soon people noticed that Sarah-Lynn and I were gone. I reckon someone went to the house and found her remains. Because it wasn't too long until I heard a rumor about myself. They called me, 'the killing crazed fiancé' and I saw my face plastered on every milk carton, wall, and billboard. I panicked. Grew my hair out real long, became kind of like a hermit. I would drift from place to place. Sure, he'd snatch me up and stuff me down and use me to eat again along the way. But I was a hollow man now. Without Sarah-Lynn I put up no fight. I know I should have, but I didn't, and he liked it that way.

One day during my travels, in an old train cart. I was hoping to make my way to the west coast when there was this red engine man.

He told us a story of a man eater. One he called, 'a wendigo' and I knew I needed to talk to him. I knew he'd know how to release me.

I didn't tell him I thought I had one attached to me, but I could tell from the look on his face he knew. One of pity, fright, and doom. When I asked how one could free themselves of a Wendigo he began to weep. He said the only way was to set oneself on fire. Destroy the vessel and the Wendigo would be destroyed as well.

Later that night I went out of town, as far as I could. I found an old junk yard. It was late at night, and they were burning the trash. I knew what I had to do then. And I threw myself in. I was pronounced dead at 12:34. Do you see now, Doris? How to free yourself?" The charred man looked at her with sympathy in his eyes.

Doris jumped back, "No!" she shrieked. "You don't understand, I got rid of him. I fought my way out, we-we did this hot bath thing and I got rid of him!"

"No Doris, you didn't. He's just laying in wait. There is no other way. It can only be destroyed in the fire for which it was made."

"No! I did! He's gone! I will not!" Doris screamed.

"Shh!" The man tried to put his hand over Doris's mouth, but she pulled away from him, "He will hear you! Doris, please, you are still in grave danger and so is everyone else around you. He's playing you." Doris stepped back. They listened. She could hear the trees moving, they seemed to be towering over her, moving closer and closer. And the ground started to shake and rumble. She felt hot and flushed,

"I-I will not… I will not…He's gone, he is! Wake up! Doris wake up! You have to wake up Doris! It's only a bad dream…" Doris stood there, her hands bawled into fists, her eyes squeezed so tightly shut they were beginning to ache, "Wake up!"

—————

Doris flung her eyes open. She sprang up from her bed. She was back in her room. She breathed heavily, sharp, and tight breathes.

She looked at her feet and with astonishment they were not covered in dirt. Her toes were red and ached, but there was no dirt to be seen this time. She could feel the sweat running down her forehead and back. She wiped it away as best she could. It hurt to breathe, it felt to her as if her lungs had been on fire already. She felt her skin, making sure there were no charred marks. No wounds, no gashes, or sores. And there was nothing. Doris sighed and sat up in bed. Slowly getting out she made her way to the door. Peeking out, she looked at the clock, 12:35.

"Dumb clock…" she murmured.

———⌀⌀⌀———

Doris sat in her usual window, observing the world around her. There were no animals playing, no birds in the sky, and even no wind in the air. It felt as if the whole world on the outside had gone still. Regardless of the world on the outside, the world on the inside still seemed to buzz and move about around her. She could hear the patients talking, the nurses complaining, the guards flirting, and the tv humming. These noises that once were a nuisance to Doris now seemed to comfort her. They helped to drown out the inner thoughts of becoming the next Joan of Arc, burning at the stake.

Doris was not sure if she should tell Dr. Vernirelli of her dream last night. She first wanted to find the old book and confirm what she thought he had seen amongst those pages. Only then would she decide what to do next. If only she could go to the library on her own. That way she could slink and snoop her way through those novels, searching, and hopefully eventually finding the book.

Doris sighed and continued to gaze out amongst the world.

———⌀⌀⌀———

Dr. Vernirelli did not go into work that day. No one seemed to question why he wasn't there. Yes, he did call in sick and that seemed to be that. He had only called out twice before, both personal days for when his parents died. So, when he made this simple statement of being sick no one batted an eye.

Dr. Vernirelli loaded himself into his car. He was off to the library to find whatever information he could about the Native American tribes in which this story came. However, he was at a loss. There were over 500 Native American tribes, and he did not know which ones this legend came from. Where to start? The Doc contemplated this as he drove. His mind drifted, completely driving only on autopilot. It was a miracle he did not run someone over so occupied with his beehive of thoughts.

Pulling into the library he parked his car, walked up the leading steps, past the lions that protected the holy knowledge, and into the front door. He figured the first place he ought to go to was the information desk. They would at least be able to point him in the direction of Native American books if they did not know any information about the Wendigo off hand.

Strolling up he noticed the woman at the front desk. A young thing, he guessed her to be right out of college, or perhaps on an internship. She was wearing a plaid dress and his lipstick smeared on her upper lip, but somehow missed the bottom one entirely.

"Hello young lady," he said. The girl looked up over her dark pointed frames and smiled at him.

"Hello sir, what may I do for you?"

"I was wondering if you knew anything about Wendigos, and where I might find them." The girl looked puzzled for a moment; he could see the cogs spinning in her mind only to come up empty.

"I'm sorry I don't know anything about this, how did you say it? Wind-ee-gos? But I would be more than happy to get the head librarian for you. She has a better knowledge of information like that than I do." The Doc grinned at her,

"If you don't mind."

"No, not at all." And with that she disappeared through the door behind her. The Doc traced his fingers along the desk, he guessed it was real mahogany. The dark polished wood was nice and cool against his fingertips, which were blistering hot from his gloves and the heat from his car. He realized then that he was still wearing his hat and coat. Just as he was shedding his layers another woman walked out from behind the door, followed by the same girl as before.

This woman was much taller, and more slender. She did not wear any makeup like that last girl, nor did she have glasses. She eyed the doctor up and down and he shook the snow from his pant leg.

"Hello ma'am," he said, giving her the warmest smile, he could muster. "I was asking this nice young lady here if you had any information on the Wendigos? And if so, where might I find it?"

"Wendigos are thought to come from Ojibwe, Saulteaux, and the Cree tribes. They can be found in our Native American section, second floor to the right" The doctor's eyes beamed with this information.

"Thank you kindly," and with that he made his way up to the second floor.

It was clear that the second floor was the least visited part of the library. It was significantly smaller than the bottom level. It had large marble columns that shot all the way up from the ground floor and to the skylight up above. It was truly a beautiful sight. Especially one in the middle of the day when the sun was at its wintertime peak and no one was around. For they were all either in grade school, college lectures, or work.

It did not take the Doc long to find the Native American section. It was indeed to the right like the woman had said, but it was tucked away in a far back corner, one that could easily be passed by, unless you knew what you were looking for.

Luckily for him there were not too many books to sift through. The library seemed to hold a very small collection of these books.

And to his disappointment the books pertaining to the Ojibwe, Saulteaux, and the Cree tribes were in one large book titled, "The Great North Native American tribes." The Ojibwe must have been the largest of these tribes for it took up a good section of the book, while the other two only seemed to take up a few pages each.

Scanning the book for some kind of sign about Wendigos he was surprised to see very little. The books only seemed to talk about the tribe's nationality, culture, and everyday ways of life. There were no legends or stories outside of pure informational facts.

Frustrated, the doctor placed the book back on the shelf. He decided to scan for the more specific answers he was looking for, books about Wendigos. But again, to his disappointment there seemed to be no books strictly dedicated to the beast.

Ready to give up, the doctor noticed a book from the corner of his eye; a small book, with a spine covered in familiar writing. It was the same book he had taken from his own work library the day before, *Native American Folklore Stories.* The doctor plucked the book from its resting place. Longingly he eyed the cover. Did he dare to turn to the last page and see the beast? There almost seemed to be an invisible force beckoning his hand to flip the book open and he gazed upon the forbidden page. Almost eagerly he turned, but there was nothing there. No illustration of half man half beast burning in the flames. Only a plain white page, simply put in for the sake of being put in.

The doctor began to frantically flip through the pages, each one fluttering by faster and faster, but there was nothing. Just from a quick scan alone the doctor could tell the story was the same, but where was the picture? In his frustration he flopped the book down on a table, and nearly threw his body into the chair beside it. Pinching his eyes, he let out a low breath and looked down into the lower parts of the library, and there, for a split second, he thought he saw him. The demon with its ashed-skin.

The doctor sprung to his feet, nearly flinging himself off of the railing to get a better look. But he was gone. The Doc turned his head side to side, looking behind him, and even above through the skylight, but there was no one there.

It's simply your imagination playing tricks ol' boy. You thought you'd see the picture and it wasn't there, so your mind made it up...nothing more... And with that the doctor gathered what little belongings he brought with him and headed back down the stairs. Passing by the two women who directed him he lifted his hat in slight gratitude and went out the door into the bite of the winter air.

Suddenly, out in the cold, the doctor felt an overwhelming urge to get back to the book he had taken from Tokema. He could not put his finger upon it. Was the book in danger? No, that wasn't quite it. But something was wrong, he could feel it. It seemed to bubble inside him, consuming his thoughts.

And without another second to lose the doctor bounded down the steps, skipping two at a time. He probably looked like a mad man at the pace he was running, in his loafers and for his age. But he did not care. He knew something was wrong. And without that book he would have nothing. He needed it to help him know more about Doris. The two clearly were connected. The ashed-skin demon-man? It seemed to be too much of a coincidence to ignore.

Flinging his car door open he threw his hat to the passenger seat beside him and sped down the road back to his home. He had left the book on his nightstand; he was certain of that. He had not touched it that morning. Strange, now that he thought about it, he didn't seem to think of it all that much this morning. Yes, he went to the library in search of finding more information about the Wendigos but the book itself hardly seemed to matter to him at the time. Why was that? Now, it was all he could think about.

Pulling into his driveway he did not bother to park the car in the garage, that seemed as if it would take up too much time. And this was something he was short on, time. Something big was coming.

Not quite in reach yet, but still lingering its way high above. Like a storm does days before it hits.

It starts small. A dark, foggy cloud every now and then. Then the next day it seems to call more of its friends in and more. By the late afternoon the sky is full of dark clouds. But they don't let their rainfall go, not just yet. First, they hold it, storing it, only showing what could potentially happen, but has not come to pass yet. And then, the third day, at the most inconvenient time, they slowly begin to release. And another one, and another one, and soon the winds are wailing, the rain is so heavy it seems to come up from under you, sideways, and somehow makes it down your back. And just when you think things can't get any worse, the thunder booms and the lighting sparks.

Yes, that is what is happening now. Ever so clearly to the Doc. Flinging his front door open he darted for the bedroom. In a mad scramble he jiggled the latch open. And there sat the book. Just like how he remembered, on the nightstand. The Doc slowly approached the thing. Picking it up ever so gently. It almost seemed more delicate now. Like one wrong move or turn of the page would send the whole thing into a pile of ash…

Lifting the book with the greatest of care the doctor flipped to the last page, but there was nothing there. Only a blank white page.

❧❧❧

"Doc, can we return to the library again today? I want to find that book again." Doris asked.

"Of course," said the doctor, "but whatever for? You want to subject yourself to that story again? When it seemed to strike so close to home?" Doris breathed in sharply,

"Yes, I do."

"It is a brave thing to face one's fear like how you do every day, Doris. You should be proud of that." But Doris was not proud. How could she feel anything of herself other than hatred and pity? There was nothing more to feel about herself. But she did not say that. All Doris could muster was half a smile, this at least showed she appreciated the Docs attempts in trying to make her feel better.

As the two walked to the library, with Larry trailing behind, the Doc could not help but feel guilty. He knew Doris had every right to that book, probably more of a right than he ever would, but he would not bring himself to tell her it was not there. *Could not* bring himself to tell her it was not there. While Doris thought the book would help her, he knew it wouldn't. They both knew how that book ended. They needed to find another way to free her from her demon. One that did not involve fire.

However, after his visit to the library the other day and the utter lack of information found the Doc was not hopeful. Not hopeful at all. He planned to go to another library, one town over. While it was smaller it was known to have a wonderful and insightful collection of books from all over the world. There would be more promising.

Approaching the library door, the Doc held it open for Doris, extending out his arm, ushering her in. He gave a little bow and Doris chuckled. She thanked her and drifted her way in.

"You know," Larry whispered to the Doc, "You should be more careful when showing favoritism towards her, compared to your other patients. People are starting to talk. I like you, which is why I'm saying something." And with that Larry passed by and through the doors next.

The doctor paused. Had people been talking about his and Doris's relationship? Were people offended by it? Sure, they were close but was it really to the point where others were beginning to notice? Perhaps pulling back from Doris would be a wise option. It's a thin line to ride. That line between being a professional and creating a personal bound. One that could easily be stumbled over.

"Sir, they are too close. I think you really should reconsider having him reassigned as her therapist."

"We've been over this Amelia; I need more reason to pull her as his patient. And you just saying that he would not allow her to be reconditioned is not enough. No one else saw the mud on her feet. That guard clearly was not well. Speaking of which, have you kept an eye on him like I asked?" Dr. Turner asked. This was not the first time Dr. Tracy had requested Doris to be reassigned to a new therapist. And he knew it would not be her last. And honestly at this point he was tired. He was tired of dealing with this petty drama. He knew Amelia hated Dr. Vernirelli, or perhaps she hated Doris... either way he knew she did not like them as a pairing.

"Well, he seems fine. Perhaps he was just tired that night. He hasn't shown any other usual behavior." Dr. Tracy answered.

"How is his temper?"

"Well, he's a bit more on edge than the others-"

"Well, that's it then!" Dr. Turner interrupted, "He's a guard with a short fuse. He probably lied about seeing the mud to see her get punished. They do that you know! Let's be honest Amelia, our guards are not perfect. And some get in this profession to hurt others. Don't deny it. It happens all the time." Dr. Tracy knew that Dr. Turner was right. So many guards did get in this profession just to have the false sense of power over people who were much weaker and far too ill to really fight back. But some people deserved to be hurt. Doris deserved to be hurt. Afterall, what she did to her nephew was beyond the pale.

"Okay, I'm sorry Dr. Turner. I won't call again unless I have more concrete reasons to." Dr. Turner sighed.

"That is what you always say Amelia. You better mean it this time. My job is not meant to handle childish qualms. It's to run an asylum." But it wasn't childish. Not to her anyways, but she couldn't tell him that. He wouldn't understand. And Doris could possibly be relocated if that information came out. No, it was far better to stay quiet. Not say a word and just lay in wait.

"Yes. I understand." And with that Dr. Amelia Tracy hung the phone back in its cradle.

———❧❧❧———

Doris hurried to where she remembered finding the book last time. She nearly threw herself into the walls looking for it. Some books were the same with their blue and red writing, but most were different. Lori had clearly been through here. Moving things in one particular order. Doris scanned the room looking for her, listening for her. Surely, she was around here.

"Lori?" Doris cried out. "Lori?" There was a slight shuffling and then Lori seemed to appear from thin air. Standing before Doris as if she was summoned.

"Yes?" Doris jumped back and gave a slight squeak.

"Lori," she sighed, "There was a book for her last time. Very old, gold lettering on the spine-"

"Books... books books books" Lori interjected. Doris pinched her eyes,

"Lori please, it was about Native American folk stories. I really want to read it again. Can you please help me find it?" Lori nodded her head, as if she knew to which book Doris was referring to. But after showing a suggestion of which Lori pointed behind Doris.

"He took it." Doris turned to see whom Lori was referring to, Dr. Vernirelli. Lori walked up to him with her hand extended out. "Book?" she asked, eagerly waiting for its return. The Doc stared at her hand, and he shook his head,

"No, Lori. I don't have the book." Lori's face became red, her body trembled, giving out a horrible and high-pitched shriek.

"Book! You took the book! Give it back!" Lori seemed to lunge at the doctor, but before she was able to reach him Larry grabbed her by the arm. He held her down. Some other patients had been in the library that day as well. They all began to scream, some taking cover under tables. Others covered their ears and shook in the corner of the room. One even tried to make for the door, but Larry stuck out his foot tripping him.

"Back-up!" Larry cried, "Back-up! Back-up!" A few guards from the hall must have heard him and came crashing through the library books. Some other ones emerged from somewhere amongst the books and isles. A guard ran over to help Larry, while the others attended to the screaming patients. They managed to get her in restraints.

"Doris," Dr. Vernirelli motioned for her to come to him, and she did. "I think it best if we leave and simply have our session in my office today." Doris nodded and the two of them headed for the door.

⸺⳩⳩⳩⸺

Back in the familiarity and comfort of the Docs office, away from the screaming patients and chaos Doris sat on the cream-colored couch. She traced her fingers back and forth over its lining. The doctor eyed her. He knew she obviously had heard what Lori asked him. And he had never kept the truth from Doris thus far. So why should this time be any different? Why didn't he want her to know he had taken the book and brought it home? Tomorrow he would need to do something about that. He would need to sneak it back in amongst the others. Would Lori be there tomorrow? It would be best if she didn't know, she would throw a fit all over again.

Doris continued to play with the lining of the couch. Pulling at its loose strings, but never hard enough to pull them out of their place or make them longer. After a little while she smoothed them out. She sighed and turned to the Doc.

"Doc?" He nodded in acknowledgment, "Did you take it?" The Doc hesitated.

"Yes."

"Why didn't you say something earlier?"

"Doris, I know you know that I saw something in those pages. And with what I saw, I think it is wise that you do not see. I didn't want all your hard work and progress to back slide. I also wanted it so I could research what we read more." Doris sat there. The look on her face was a rare one for Dr. Vernirelli. See, he had gotten into his profession because he was uncannily talented at reading other people. It was a rare thing not to be able to know one's thoughts at a glance. And even if he could not pin down exactly what they were thinking he could always at least get the emotion. But now, on Doris's face there seemed to be none.

"So, then, why would you agree to go to the library Doc?" She finally asked. He sighed again,

"I was not ready to tell you yet that I had taken the book. I wanted to gain some more insight first." Doris seemed to listen. She gave her head a slight nod. Now, was that in agreement or understanding? This the Doc did not know. "Doris," he said, "I certainly hope you do not think less of me." Doris jerked her head up at this response,

"No Doc. Never. I don't like that you were willing to put up a front, but you always seem to have my best interest at heart. And I couldn't be upset at you for that. Especially with all that you've done for me! Don't be crazy. Come on, that's my job." The doctor gave a small laugh.

———◦◡◦———

Doris had no more dreams of the charred and ember skinned man, or rather Simon, once he had told her the truth about who the Wendigo that haunted her. Now that she knew the creature's real name it seemed cruel to herself to refer to it as anything but a Wendigo...

How did the Wendigo get that way? It couldn't have been the same way as in the book. No. That would be too much of a coincidence... unless... unless Simon knew more than he was leading on. He was the one who guided me towards that book after all. He must know something is going to

happen soon. Why else would he tell me the truth? But needing to end it all in fire? There has to be another way other than self-mutilation and setting one aflame. There must be other answers. And surely the library could have books on Wendigos.

Doris sat up in her bed. She made her way to the door and glanced out, 11:45 pm. Obviously the library would not be open at a time like that. And there would be no way to sneak out and get there. And, to make matters worse, she would not be seeing Dr. Vernirelli tomorrow. It was one of his odd days away from her.

Doris groaned loudly and made her way back to the bed. It was odd not hearing music, seeing things from the corner of her eye, or even dreaming about Simon. There was something a little too quiet about it all.

But why are you surprised Doris? You banished the ashed skin, I mean Wendigo. The tub, remember? You crawled out of him, it, whatever! You managed to escape. He won't come back. So, no more worries about needing to set yourself on fire. Simon doesn't know what he's talking about. It's not haunting you anymore, using you. You're okay. You're okay. You are okay.

Doris closed her eyes and sat on her bed, curling her knees up to her chest and rocking herself back and forth. She began to hum. A comforting tune from her favorite movie. *Somewhere over the rainbow, skies are blue and the dreams that you dare to dream really do come true...*

Just then Doris stopped, her spine stiffened, and she held her breath. The humming continued. She could hear it in the room. First quiet, but it slowly began to build, like thunder rolling up and over the hills. She knew who was humming it. She knew it was *him*. But it couldn't be. She knew he was gone.

"You're gone!" she shrieked, breaking the silence with such force that she even made herself jump. "You are gone! I crawled out of you!" The humming continued. It neither grew nor faded, but stayed in the air, lingering. *He* wanted her to know that *he* was there, and that *he* was not going anywhere. Or rather, *had* not gone anywhere.

Doris threw her hands over her ears. She did not want to believe it. She rocked herself back and forth.

——◦◦◦——

Dr. Vernirelli pulled into his drive. This was not the day he had been expecting. He felt almost silly for trying to hide the fact about taking the book home from Doris. Well not almost, he did feel silly. He was an utter fool. Why hide something from her?

He had taken the book for more research and that was that. Yes, he wanted to protect her too and that wasn't wrong. He loved her. She was his patient and he loved her. He could feel a bond closer to Doris then he had with any other patients during his time as a professional.

He tried not to get too close to them, what good would it do? He saw too many minds slowly get consumed in that place and he did not want her to become just another dead face. Alive, but not truly living. Just another reason to get another plant. He moaned and banged his head against his steering wheel.

The wheel gave out a slight squeak noise. He jumped at its sound and laid his head against the back of his seat, then slowly got out of the car. He turned to lock his door, and there down the street, underneath one of the lampposts he saw someone standing. Perfectly still. He could tell it was a man, but the black figure was all he could make out.

How peculiar, the man did not seem to be looking at anything in particular from what the doctor could tell. But then again, he was not close enough to see the man's face at all. The Doc thought it was best to leave the stranger be. There was no point meddling in other affairs, especially when he had so many of his own to take care of, not to mention his patients as well.

The Doc headed for his front door and turned the key. He hung his jacket up in the front hall closet and locked the door behind him. He headed for the bathroom, brushing and flossing away at his teeth.

Once they felt clean enough, he hung his brush back up in its little cradle. He washed his face and made his way to the bedroom.

Still, unmoving on the nightstand was the book. *I really need to take that back. Not just for Doris to look at it if she wishes, but for poor Lori who I lied to.* The Doc grabbed the book. He held it in his hands. Just watching the cover. He did not know what he expected to see, or what he expected to happen. It was, after all, a normal book.

He flipped it open to the last page; it was still white. Maybe he was the one going crazy. He thought he saw that burning image, but there had not been one at the public library, nor was there one now. Has his imagination gotten the best of him? Could he have just been tired that day and his mind played a cruel trick on him? It was possible. He had been having many late nights at the office and the lack of sleep had done him no help whatsoever.

He walked the book back out into the living room. He placed it in his bag so he would not forget to take it with him to work tomorrow. Before retiring to the bedroom, he stopped at his living room window. He pulled back the curtain and gazed out into the night. The mysterious man who stood under the lamppost was no longer there. He must have been looking at something and then went back on his way once he found it. Nothing out of the ordinary or to be scared about.

⌁⌁⌁

"I brought something for you" the doctor said, reaching into his satchel, pulling the book out, and handing it to Doris. The two of them sat in his office. They had been making small talk, but he could tell Doris wanted to know if he had brought the book back.

Eagerly Doris reached for the book, then she lauded, hand just hovering over. "Are you sure?" she asked. "I trust your judgment about my, for lack of a better word, condition." The doctor nodded.

"It was wrong of me to take it," he said. Doris took the book from him. She did not immediately throw open the pages like he thought she would. Instead, she just held it close to her chest, breathing in and out. She closed her eyes and swallowed hard. She clearly was trying to muster the strength to talk to him about something.

"Doc, you know how I was able to break free of *him*?" The doctor bent his head in understanding. "Well," Doris began, and then she saw *him,* the Wendigo. The Wendigo standing there with his ashed colored skin. *Him* with his unwavering eyes. *Him*, the very being in which made her spine crawl. Doris froze, eyes wide like a deer in headlights. Her lips quivered; she had not seen *him* in so long. It made her feel sick, and her toes began to curl in such a way she thought they might break off one by one from aching so hard.

The Doc could see the fear sprawled out among Doris's face; she had not had a look like that since the day she was confronted by her demon in the tub. The Doc turned over his shoulder, it seemed to be perfectly normal, at first glance. But the Doc knew something more was there. He could feel it in the room. And there, in the far-right corner, was a black spot, a shadow.

"Doris!" The Doc turned back to face her, "Doris he's here, isn't he?" Doris could barely move, she felt utterly frozen in place. The Wendigo did not move at all. He did not nod, grin, or even hold his fingertips up to what was left of his battered, bloody lips. Doris could feel a tear rolling down her cheek. She did not know she was even crying, or able to move until she felt the touch of her own hand catching the drop.

"Doris," the doctor repeated, "Doris, try and tell me what you see."

"Th-there… there." She slowly lifted her hand, pointing in the direction of the Wendigo. The doctor followed her finger, although he already knew where it was going. The doctor turned, now fully facing the dark spot.

"Get out of here!" The doctor yelled. That had caught the demon's attention, he turned his head so quickly in the direction of the Doc that it made Doris leap back. Her back pressed against the wall; she stood on the cream-colored couch. Arms outstretched and reaching behind her for whatever she could grab. But she was met with only a wall.

The Wendigo ogled in the doctor's direction. Doris was unsure whether or not he would make a move. Doris needed help, and yes, while the Doc was her biggest ally, she was afraid that *he* would take over her, possess her, and make her hurt the Doc. If the guards were around there would be less of a chance of something happening.

Doris squeaked. The Doc looked in her direction, taking his eyes off of the black spot. He could see her face of disapproval. Her stern look of fear. Her eyes had not yet moved from the black spot, but he could see her fingers beginning to move ever so slightly. He looked in the direction that her left hand was now pointing. It was pointing to the desk.

Was there something on his desk? Had the man moved positions? Clearly not, her eyes were still on the dark patch. The Doc continued to follow her finger, scanning over his desk when he saw what she was pointing at. The red button. She wanted him to press it.

The Doc slowly turned his head back to the black spot in the corner of his office. To his relief, it had not moved. Which he was sure meant that *he* had not moved. Slowly, the Doc shifted in his chair. Trying to make a subtle attempt at moving closer to his desk.

Doris watched as the Wendigo remained unmoving. His head and eyes were still glued onto the doctor. Doris was afraid that if Wendigo saw the Doc moving toward the desk, he would abandon his resting place either onto her or the Doc. And she could not let that happen.

"G-get out of here" Doris mumbled. The Doc and Wendigo both turned to face her. "I said, get out of here!" She shrieked. Pointing in the direction of the Wendigo. Now, now was the doctor's chance, quickly, while the Wendigo was distracted.

The Wendigo's lips started to coil, leering at Doris. She prayed the doctor would recognize her distraction and take the opportunity of the moment. She was too afraid to tear her eyes away from the demon. For if she did, he might know it was a ruse. She stared him in the eyes, determined to not move.

The Doc eyed Doris, he could tell she wanted the beast's attention. She was buying him time. He could see the black spot had shifted ever so slightly. It now seemed to be facing in Doris's direction. True, he could not tell before where it was facing, but somehow, he knew this time. He needed to act fast.

The doctor slowly moved his right hand, sliding it against the cushions as best he could to stay subtle. He could see the black spot edging its way closer to Doris. Was the beast approaching her? It was now or never. The Doc lunged himself forward and slammed his hand down on the button.

The Wendigo turned in the Docs direction. Doris could see it begin to fill with rage. A flash of anger crossed its eyes and before it could move closer to her a guard had entered the room.

"What's the issue?" He asked, but Doris and the Doc both just sat there dumbfounded. Both eyes glued in the direction of the Wendigo. The demon looked to Doris, and slowly his body began to fade away, only leaving a small wisp of smoke where it once was.

The doctor watched the floor, the black spot almost seemed to be growing smaller, and smaller, until it was completely gone. He let out a sigh. He knew it was not over yet, but at least it was done for now.

"We," paused the doctor, "We just felt more comfortable with you sitting in with us today," he said. The guard nodded. This was not that uncommon of a request. The Doc would often make these requests if he could tell a patient was on the tightrope end of having a breakdown. Just a precaution.

The guard took a seat on the couch, next to Doris. This way if she tried anything, anything at all, he would be able to grab her. But Dori did not try anything, there was nothing for her to do except slowly lower herself from her upright position. Doris had not realized that she was holding her breath that entire time until she released it. She sunk back into the couch, the way she was sitting before. Looking down she noticed the book was on the floor, she must have dropped it in her panic. Doris scooped it up. Now she was terrified, utterly struck with horror at the thought of opening the book. But clearly, there must be something important within it. She knew there had to be if *he* showed up.

The Doc could see Doris eyeing the book. Her gaze did not waver from it and still held strong. He did not say anything though. It was Doris's decision if she wanted to open it or not. She knew what she was up against better than he could ever understand.

Doris's grip tightened as she ping-ponged back in her head what to do. On one hand, she could bring the book back to the library, return it to its proper resting place, and to Lori, who Doris was sure was still having a breakdown over one of her precious relics being out of place. On the other hand, the book must be important. She was guided to it. It showed her what she was facing, a Wendigo. And clearly, it was important enough for *it* to show up. And for what? To scare Doris not into opening it? To try and turn her away from the truth? No. No. Doris must face her fear and open it.

And Doris did. Letting out one last breath Doris flung the book open, scanning for the last chapter. The last story in the book. Finding it she flipped through each page, searching and scanning for answers in every line. The letters almost seemed to blur together, but she knew none of them were what she was looking for. She was looking for what made the Doc slam the book with such force that it made him and her jump.

Doris continued flipping frantically until she had just about reached the last page. The Doc could see her growing closer and closer with every flip. Soon, he was the one holding his breath. He prayed that the image would not be there. That he made the whole thing up. He had checked it twice before and it did not rear its ugly head. Why should this time be any different? *Because she's here,* he thought. And before Doris even made that final flip he knew; he knew the portrayal of a fiery death would be there.

Doris turned to the last page. Her spine stiffened, it seemed to cut off all the nerves to the rest of her body. She was frozen in place. Eyes glued to the image. She now understood why the doctor had flung the book shut. It was *him*, her demon so clear as day engulfed in flame. Every detail in the illustration made Doris question if it really was an illustration or not. It was so realistic that Doris swore she could even feel the heat from the flames on the page.

Doris looked up and nodded at the doctor. She did not need to say it. It was clear that it was the same person, demon, creature, *Wendigo*. The Doc nodded back in understanding. No words needed to be spoken at a time like this. The guard sitting next to Doris leaned over her and looked down,

"That's disturbing," he muttered. Doris broke from her trance of silent communication with the doctor and looked to the guard. With her eyes off the image, she was able to close the book.

"Yes," Doris agreed, "Yes, it is."

⸺⧼⧽⸺

Doris sat in her room. The only thing burning in her mind's eye was the demon set ablaze. How that was the same fate Simon had met. How maybe there was no escaping it. But that could not be the only way. Wendigo's must have other weaknesses besides fire. The Doc said he did some research but was unable to find anything at the first library he went to. He promised Doris that he would go to another, one with a larger set of knowledge.

But the asylum was filled with strange and clearly informative things. Given that it had the book of Native American Folklore. It had the answer to Doris's troubles all along. There could be more books to help guide her with what to do.

They had agreed after tomorrow Doris would return to the library with Dr. Vernirelli. She was sure that with a determined mind and with both of them searching they could find something. Although Doris was not so sure if the Doc would return to the library with her. And no, it was nothing against Doris, but Lori!

Lori attacked the Doc once, who's to say she wouldn't do it again? Or she might not even be there given her incident. However, Doris needed Lori to be there. No one knew those books better. No one else would know how to navigate Lori's crazy system of arranging the books. Lori would certainly know something.

And if the Doc was to apologize for lying maybe Lori would help. It's worth a shot. Worst case scenario Lori attacks the Doc, but then she would be dragged away again, right? Not too bad. Actually, the worst-case scenario is that Lori no longer wanders amongst the books and never comes back, and the answers are all lost somewhere in that mess. Doris shuttered to herself.

The library was not that large. In fact, it was roughly the size of Doris's high school library. A library in which most of her days were spent since Hannah and Holly left. She found herself thinking more and more of them during her time here. Well, more than she had during her time on the outside.

⸺⁘⸺

No more dreams of being in the woods. No more music drifting in from nowhere. Had Doris become so accustomed to these strange and disturbing happenings that it almost seemed wrong when something did not occur? True, when they were happening all, she wanted was for them to go away, to cease. But ever since seeing Simon come to her and speak to her and share his story, she longed for him to come back.

By no means was he a friend, or even in the category of a peer, but he was a strange and unusual comfort. He had shown her so much. He had been subtly guiding her towards knowing the truth. He made her feel as if she were not so alone.

Doris wanted to ask questions, to know more. And if he was unable to provide her with those things at least she could have talked to him and related. She could not relate to the Doc, no matter how much she talked to him and confided in him. He would never understand what it is like having the Wendigo breathing down your back. Feeling him slurp you inside and then using you as a pawn or a hostage in getting what he wanted.

And what he wanted was flesh. He always seemed to want more. It explained why Doris was eventually caught in the end. True, she wanted to be caught. But it became so much more evident, *he* was becoming cocky. Presenting himself in moments that were not as hair splitting as others. She tried not to think about the day she got caught. It was a day of relief and of terror. Everyone knew of that day. Hence, she wondered why the doctor never asked her about it.

No one really knew what had been happening up until that point, until they started making connections. Putting the pieces together. It took them longer than she thought it would. Especially given that she had been to confession so many times. And had reached out for an exorcism. And while she never actually was able to get the words of details out, she did however say she was possessed.

Strange, how the Wendigo never kept her from telling others that part. There were times when *he* would appear and almost seem to block her from expressing what had happened. But never once did he try to silence her on being overcome with a demon. Most thought that she would make this confession too and took it as meaning she had sinned a lot. Never fathoming that she truly *was* possessed. Or rather, still is.

Doris wondered if those priests that she confessed to ever felt regret. Regret not taking her seriously enough. Regret for not outing her to the rest of the public eye. And what about the doctors she'd seen as well? She went to therapy. She told them she was possessed by something. Yes, they all probably thought she was crazy, but not to the extent of being institutionalized. And here she was. How funny that they never truly listened.

Did they also feel regret? Guilt? If time travel were possible, would they go back, throw her in sooner than later? She hoped so. And true, it had crossed her mind to try and commit herself. But *he* always stopped her. Swallowing her up before she could really make her move.

Doris was becoming lazy. She made no more attempts to hide the bones. She almost wanted to get caught. No one believed her, it was that simple. True, she did not want the punishment of being caught. She knew what would happen if she was straight to the electric chair. She'd fry. And while she did not want that, she could not keep living like this. He had been coming more and more frequently she felt like, ever since John. *He* had come to her twice since that. Sometimes *he'd* go months without seeing her. But John and that teenage frat boy were only a week or so apart.

Doris sluggishly threw the bones aside. She had been on a nature walk when *he* came. She was walking by herself amongst the woods and trees to get some alone time. She had been walking at Wyandotte County Lake, admiring the water as it sparkled. Smelling the trees at the beginning of Spring when the snow had all melted away. The ground was muddy, and she could feel her feet sinking ever so slightly into the mud, but she didn't mind at all.

She was completely on her own. She had not seen anyone since her hike, and she liked it that way. She needed peace and quiet. Away from the voice in her head. Away from anyone who might threaten to have that voice coo its awful song in her ear.

She had walked to the edge of the dock on the water. She stared out into the vastness that was Wyandotte County Lake. She tried to strain her eyes to see if she could find any fish in the water, but it was too deep of a blue to tell. She stayed on that dock for a while.

Looking out at nothing in particular. She seemed almost frozen in place. Not wanting to return back home. She could just stay here, in this spot, unmoving, forever. If only the universe worked that way.

Doris took a deep breath. She reached for the pack of cigarettes in her pocket. She lit one and felt the hot air burn her lungs. *What a glorious feeling*, she thought, *not needing anyone's company except my own.*

After Doris finished her cigarette, she put the ash out on the side of the dock and flicked the butt end into the water. She wiped her hands on her jacket and slipped them back into her gloves once they were clean enough. She turned and there standing at the end of the dock he was, blocking her path back to the trail.

At this point, Doris was not completely surprised. Although his appearance never ceased to make her spine crawl and her skin shiver. And while his appearance alone was enough to drive one to the nut house, it was knowing that if *he* was near, surely someone else was too. And that meant it was time to feed.

Doris took a step back, hitting her back gently on the railing. She opened her mouth, ready to scream, ready to warn off whoever was coming her way for she was about to be gobbled up. Doris opened her mouth wide, the words on the tip of her lips, almost rolling their way out, "Run-" but before she could get out the words she needed, *he* was already there. Head in mouth, body in stomach, possessed.

At this point, this being the ninth time he had taken over her he knew how to move her. How to manipulate every vein, every muscle in her body. *He* knew how to make her seem perfectly, for lack of better words, normal.

He did not move her, however. He simply turned her and made her wait, continuing to look longingly out into the water. A good hunter knows his prey, and being the best hunter there was, *he* knew it would come to *him*. There was no doubt about that. It was a natural talent. Something inherited, not practiced or honed. Simply put it was second nature, always had been for *him*. Since the very beginning.

Doris's body continued to gaze out into the water. Watching the light as it shimmered and shined its way across the ripples. Waiting peacefully. After what seemed like a very long time to Doris, she heard it. She could feel her ears twitch, perking up behind her. Someone was approaching. The body did not turn. Staying perfectly still, frozen in its place. The footsteps came closer and closer.

"Such a beautiful view, don't you think?" A woman nestled in next to Doris at the end of the dock. She was a thin woman, around Doris's height. Her lips were painted red, an unusual thing to do one's makeup, just for a nature hike. Her hair was blonde and cascaded over her shoulders, making her facial structures appear strong and healthy. The woman smiled at Doris.

"Yes." Doris answered. While the demon within her could talk in her voice perfectly, he often chose to use as little as possible. Doris could feel the hunger rolling in her stomach. She could tell *he* wanted to drool but kept it together. Patiently waiting for the best moment to strike. Doris could not tell, however, if *he* would simply suck this woman dry and then devour her flesh quickly, or, if he was going to play with her first. Like how a cat bats around a mouse, torturing it by making it think it stands a chance of survival before it takes a final claw to the throat.

The woman remained in place. Just as unmoving as Doris. She breathed in deeply and let out one slow breath. "Do you mind?" She asked, holding up a cigarette. Doris shook her head, showing she did not mind at all. "Great!" The woman lit the stick between her teeth. "I promised myself not to smoke anymore. Nasty habit really. But it's just so darn satisfying. Plus, it keeps you skinny. Wish they could do something about the smell though." The woman flicked her ash into the lake. Doris did not say anything. She simply was made to smile as best she could.

"Sorry, I'm talking your ear off," the woman said. "You probably came out here to get some alone time and here I am blabbing it up. Don't worry, I'll finish my drag and be on my way." She smiled at Doris again, inhaling once more.

"No, I don't mind" Doris was made to respond, "Stay with me." The lady looked up again and beamed. It was obvious that this woman was the chatty type. She may have started this walk with the intention of finding herself, bettering herself, or doing whatever to improve herself. But it was obvious the second she saw Doris that itch to strike up a conversation hit her. And how could she possibly say no when Doris was inviting her to stay? It would be rude not to.

"Thanks. So, why'd you come out here?" The woman asked. Doris stood there for a moment. Her inner, true self, was screaming as loudly as she could for the woman to run, but the demon using her did not let this phase him.

"I just needed to get something." Doris eventually answered, sounding like an old windup toy. The woman raised her eyebrow,

"Oh?" she asked, "What's that?" Doris could feel her body loosen. She knew it was about to happen soon. She knew this woman was done for.

"Flesh." Doris's body flung forward. She tackled the woman pinning her down under her. The woman shrieked. Usually, the demon would have made her kill the victim first, then devour it. However, the creature controlling Doris seemed to be growing more and more comfortable with each kill *he* did not even seem to care anymore.

Doris turned the woman's face and sunk her teeth into the woman's neck. Once again, the woman screeched in pain. Calling out for someone, anyone, to come and help her. Doris's body turned the woman's face, so she was forced to look into her eyes once more. She began to suck out her soul. Slurping her down, she could feel the energy moving within her. Spreading out through each vein, muscle, and blood vessel. And it was still not enough. The flesh was needed too. Doris's teeth took chunk after chuck of the woman's flesh.

"Oh my God, oh my God!" Doris's body jolted up, turning behind her to see two men standing at the very end of the dock looking at her. Both ran forward to the blonde woman's aid. Although it would not matter. She laid dead and half eaten.

The demon inside Doris did not stay. Quickly, he regurgitated her, and Doris fell forward. She could see the tattered and torn ashed skill colored man watch as the other two charged forward. Doris was relieved and terrified. She was finally caught. *It's finally over*, she thought to herself.

As the men reached Doris and the woman, they both seemed to unknowingly take a step back, absorbing what they were seeing. The first man to reach her seemed to snap out of it more quickly than his friend. He turned to Doris, forcing her to the ground. He seized her hands and forced them behind her back. She did not even resist.

"Oh fuck, oh God!" The second man tried in vain to cover his eyes from the incident but ended up vomiting through his fingers.

Doris did not remember much after that. She knew the two men must have dragged her back up the trail and found a phone to call the police, because what Doris did remember next was being inside a gray room. Sitting in a metal chair, a bright light shined in her face, and three men all yelled at her, questioning her.

She answered everything as honestly as she could. She admitted to nine murders altogether. She told them of the possessions, not that they bought any of that. She told them where to find the bones. Turns out those police and detectives had been looking for her.

They apparently talked about the cannibal killer in the news and in the papers. Somehow, she had not seemed to notice. She was never one for the news anyway. She occupied her time with books and getting out and about. Not that she would be able to do that anymore.

Doris remembered very distinctly being offered a call. She assumed they wanted her to call her lawyer, she informed them she did not have one and would not be able to afford one anyways. One would need to be provided. Something odd struck Doris. One of the men, the shortest one, black hair and blue eyes, told her, "You don't have to call a lawyer." But Doris refused. Who would she call? Her family? Of course not. There was nothing to say to them. *'Hi mom... So, I'm going to prison. Or getting the death penalty. Why? Oh, you know, murder and cannibalism.'* Absolutely not.

Doris just shook her head. The last thing she clearly remembered of that night was saying, "Can I just be taken to a cell so I can go to bed now? I want to escape this nightmare." She did not know why she said that last remark. She did not realize it, but up until that point she found the only way to escape her demon was by going to sleep. He was not one to visit her in her dreams. Her dreamless sleep was the only sanctuary she seemed to find in those days.

The cops and detectives did let her go to sleep to her surprise. It could have been because of her compliance and confession; she was not sure. They obviously did not handle her with care. But she was no use if she was falling asleep at the table either. And she certainly opened the doors to several missing person cases.

The detective eyed her as the police took Doris out of the room. She was not big at all, some of those confessions she made were for killing fully grown men, twice her size. It was clear she had to have been working with someone or using some kind of poisoning over time to weaken those victims. But only one victim was actually related to her in some kind of way. John Hammer, she had been seeing him for a few weeks. She admitted to this. They weren't serious, she never met any of his friends and as the detective went to confirm this later with them it was true, they weren't serious. None of them even knew he was seeing someone. So why did she choose her victims?

The only thing that was in common with all the victims was that Doris was alone with them. Alone with her first case that was brought to his attention, the woman at the YMCA. He had been working on that case over the last several months, Tina Baker. The second case was Sam Hatter, a young man who was killed on his way home from work. Then Laura Kidnip was killed during her lunch break. John Hammer was killed while having dinner with Doris. Johnny Dutchman is on his way to a frat party. Camilia Zimmer, walking her dog at night. Steven Shusher, a jogger in the park. And the woman who happened to be on a nature walk, Katy Rind. It would be months later when the detective would uncover Doris's actual first victim, Jonah Usher. It turned out that the high schooler liked to read in a more secluded part of a park near his home. Apparently, from what was pieced together, was that he ran into Doris in the spot where he usually read. It was there that the boy met his demise.

None of them were connected to each other the detective would later find out. None of them even seemed to cross paths. All at random times, all happened to be alone when Doris Draker found them. One would never have guessed it, looking at Doris. She even looked sickly the detective would often think to himself. Guess that's what eating human flesh would do to someone.

The detective would go on analyzing Doris, poking and prodding at her to confess to another person who was really the muscle that would assist in the killings. But Doris never fumbled, she never lied to satisfy the detective. She continued to tell him she was possessed. She would not admit another to be at fault simply because the detective could not accept the truth about her possession.

—————◦/◦/◦—————

Dr. Vernirelli sat in his office. He had been reviewing case files. He was trying his best to not only focus on Doris but to pay attention to his other patients as well. But how could he when at their last session *he* appeared? The Doc had seen the dark spot move across the room. He saw the look on Doris's face. One could not fake that kind of horror, not even a professional actor of any generation was that talented. Doris looked as if she were peering into the gates of hell themselves.

The Doc rubbed his brow. He could not focus on anything, except for that incident. Just then he realized Doris had given him back the book. It was still in his office. He had taken it from her and placed it in a drawer, leaving it there until the two of them could return it to its proper home. They would have to take it the day after tomorrow, given that he would not be seeing her tomorrow.

The Doc suddenly felt a cold shiver down his spine, knowing that the book still remained in his office made him feel uneasy. His flesh crawled as if covered with maggots. He did not know whether he should take the book with him when he left or leave it. The library would be closed now, and he did not have a key to that particular room. Besides, something told him he needed to wait for Doris, for the two of them to return it together.

Perhaps just a peak in his drawer, to make sure it really was still there. He eyes the handle. He slowly lifted his hand, hovering above the black-painted knob. To pull the drawer open left like spinning a jack-in-the-box. To spin it slowly and precisely one could prepare themselves for the popping out of a puppet. But to become overly eager one risked surprising themselves at the sudden pop.

Slowly and using the greatest of care the Doc gripped the handle. He let out a loud sigh and gently pulled the drawer open. There, sitting on top of his papers was the book. Just the way he left it. He had not noticed before, but the back of the book was completely empty. There was no description, nor author note.

How odd, he thought to himself. Part of him wanted to open the book, to try and see who the author was. More importantly, who the illustrator was. But to open the book meant to eagerly spin the handle and he could not bring himself to do it. He would wait for

Doris. The two of them would look together to see if they could find a name. Something about waiting for her and doing it together gave him great comfort. And with that thought he closed the drawer.

Cleaning up his things the Doc decided it was time for him to head home. Late nights long after hours seemed to have become the norm for him. Opening the door, the doctor stepped out into the hallway, turning to lock up his office. Then, from the corner of his eye, he saw someone standing in the hall. The doctor turned his head as if it were on a swivel, no one seemed to stay this late, and he never saw any guards on duty when he locked up before.

The figure barely stood in sight. Just enough for the Doc to see its ashed colored skin and tattered smile. The Doc jumped back. Instinctually he slammed his eyes shut, but soon realized to have them closed was to be too vulnerable. Just as quickly as he had shut them, he opened them again. Only to find no one there.

The Doc turned frantically from side to side. But again, no one. He even called out into the hall. No response. *Just on edge from today, that's all.* He told himself. A comforting lie.

————◦/◦/◦————

"Doris, how do you feel from our last session?" The doctor asked. Doris sat in her usual spot on the cream-colored couch. Her legs were curled up to her chest and she had her head turned to the side. She rocked gently on her heels.

"I feel alright. Luckily, he did not visit me that night or yesterday. Although I keep flinching at every corner." The Doc knew how she felt, he could not confirm what he'd been seeing lately, but with the library, the streetlamp, and the hallway he had certainly been seeing something. But he would not be admitting this to Doris, he did not need her worrying about him.

"Shall we go to the library today and return the book?" Dr. Vernirelli asked. He was hoping she would say yes. He felt wrong returning it without her and uneasy having it in his office. His office felt sinister knowing that it was held in his drawer. He had been able to persuade his other patients to have their sessions in other places instead of there. It did not take a lot to convince them to change rooms. Most of his patients enFreude ed a change of setting and offering it during their sessions made most of them feel a more personal connection to the Doc.

"Yes, I think that is best. There is something about it not being in its proper home that makes the Wendigo seem closer..." Doris's voice trailed off. She had felt uneasy knowing it was on the doctor's desk as well. The book that had brought them to knowledge and therefore confirmed knowing what she was facing, also brought on a weight that seemed too heavy for her to want to continue carrying.

Pulling open the drawer the doctor plucked the book from its place. He was relieved to see it was still there. He could not explain it, but he was half expecting to find the book missing.

The two of them walked side by side while Larry followed a few feet behind. While walking the two of them hardly spoke. No words seemed to be necessary at a time like this. Words would come once they were able to put the book back. Until then, silence felt like the only way to communicate.

Approaching the library door, the doctor found himself to be hesitating. He had not seen Lori since her backdown, and he was nervous to confront her again. He would need to admit that he lied to her. He would need to apologize. And while apologizing was not the issue, he still felt a pit in his stomach. Throwing open the library doors the doctor looked around. He did not see Lori.

"That's strange," said Doris, "No Lori."

"My thoughts exactly" replied the doctor. The two of them walked back to the shelf in which they originally found the book on. Placing it gently in the spot she had first laid eyes on it Doris let out what was almost a sigh of relief.

"I'm glad it's back where it belongs." Doris smiled. She gave off a facade that almost seemed like everything was going to be alright.

But the Doc knew better, he knew that returning the book was not the simple solution to Doris's demon. There was no simple solution. The only way to end it is to cast it out, throw her into the fire, like the hunters did with Dakota.

The Doc shook his head. Of course, he would not throw her into a fire like what happened to Dakota. An awful thought to pop in, awful. *No, here's what we need to do,* the doctor thought to himself. *We need to create a fire, pretend to throw Doris in, trick the demon into revealing himself, and then ambush him and throw him into the fire.*

"I'm glad it's back where it belongs. My office felt menacing with it there."

"Now you know how I feel all the time." Doris let out a small chuckle. One not out of real humor, but out of dark humor.

"Did you wish to stay and look around?" the Doc asked.

"No," Doris responded, "now that it's back the library feels…"

"Menacing?" the doctor chimed in giving a small self-pitying chuckle.

"Exactly," Doris half smiled, "Let's return back to your office." And with that the two of them walked out the doors and back down the hall. But before banishing the library completely out of sight the Doc turned around to the guard who had been escorting them.

"Larry, where's Lori?"

"She passed away two nights ago. Surprised you didn't hear about it." Larry mumbled.

"Oh…no…" the doctor trailed off, "…she's not my patient and we were not close." Doris shook her head. No words were needed to be spoken; the body language alone was enough to show her remorse about the situation. Lori was not old enough to die from old age. Which only meant there needed to be another factor. Whatever it was took her before her time.

Back in his office Dr. Vernirelli and Doris settled in. The energy in the room had shifted. It no longer felt as heavy. However, there still was the memory about what had happened only a few days before. Doris found her eyes to continuously circle back to the same corner in which the Wendigo stood. Having a name to put to the demon now made Doris not as afraid. Knowing what you're facing is far less terrifying than not.

"So, Doc, what now?" Doris asked, she slid her body forward. Elbows resting comfortably on her knees, her back slightly hunched and she leaned in as if she were the one examining him, not the other way around.

"What do you mean?" the Doc asked.

"What do we do now? We put the book back. But the Wendigo is still here. How do we get rid of it?" The Doc hesitated. Had he not been thinking about this less than 10 minutes ago? The two of their wavelengths constantly crossing one another was one that truly astonished him. Most therapists longed to have this kind of connection with their patients, but now that he actually achieved it, he wasn't so sure he wanted it. Being this close to someone who was struggling and going through so much made it far more difficult to bear. He never knew how much he needed that professional separation until her.

"Well… We know it needs to be cast into fire-"

"No!" Doris cut him off, "I am not throwing myself into a fire!" Doris had not told the doctor about the dream in which Simon had sacrificed himself. It was one she'd rather forget than discuss.

"What?" The doctor was shocked at such a statement. How could she think he would do such a thing to her? "No, Doris, of course not. We should use it to coax him out. We'll create a fire, and he will come. It'll be up to you to push him in." Doris sat there, frozen. Her responsibility is to push him in. She did not want to get that close to him. The only time in which she had ever been close enough to touch him he consumed her. It was risky. What if he ate her the second, she got close enough for the two of them to touch? She could risk accidentally throwing herself in. But then again, if she didn't, she was doomed to a lifetime of always being haunted.

"Alright Doc. I can do it." The doctor smiled at her,

"I know you can." Of course, the doctor would keep the part about pretending to throw Doris into the fire to himself. He knew if he told her this, she would be too resistant to his plan. He needed to make it seem as real to the Wendigo as possible. There would be no room for error. If they failed to do this the demon would surely come back and kill him or drive Doris to the point of true insanity. There is no room for error.

"Now," the doctor began, "How to actually get outside and start a fire. That will be the tricky part. The flames need to be large enough to burn him. But, obviously, Tokema will not let us go on starting huge fires in the middle of their property. We'll need to be sneaky and calculated." Doris nodded her head.

"But Doc... someone will surely find out. To create a fire that big there will be smoke. And people will see it. And when we're inevitably caught, you'll lose your job, or worse!" He knew exactly what she meant by worse. He might become a patient at Tokema. Starting a huge fire at his work facility, sneaking a patient out, basically witchcraft to summon a demon. No one would understand. He knew he wouldn't be fired. He knew those were grounds to get him thrown in the nuthouse as well. The Doc hesitated. Carefully calculating his next set of words.

"It's a price I am willing to pay." Doris felt the tears pierce her eyes. Never, in her whole life, was someone ever willing to give up and potentially sacrifice so much for her. But would she allow him to throw away his life like that for her? She was touched at his willingness.

"No Doc." She eventually said, "If we see or hear guards coming, I want you to run. I want you to disappear. I will take full responsibility, reconditioning or not. You have to promise me."

"Doris-"

"Promise me Doc. You've already done so much and have believed me more than anyone else has. Promise?"

"I promise Doris."

<hr />

Ideally, they would do the fire in the Fall. When the leaves were dry, they would easily burn, the ground would be dry, and the smell would be covered from far off neighboring properties burning their own leaves. But, unfortunately for Doris and the Doc, time was limited. The Wendigo had made himself present to Doris in front of the Doc, twice, technically, now. And the doctor feared that if there were to be a third time before the fire the Wendigo would not leave without causing harm to someone.

They had spent the rest of their session plotting and planning. They eventually decided that the best time to have the fire would be in about a month. The worst of Winter would surely be over by then. They had not had snow for several weeks. The ground, while damp, would be dry enough to start a fire. The Doc would need to bring things to burn of course. Regular old wood and leaves would not be enough. He could purchase some firewood and starters from the store and hold them in the trunk of his car. That would be the easy part. He always worked later than everyone else in the facility these days. Each night before leaving he could bring a bundle of logs deep into the woods, set them up, and have everything prepared for when it was time. He would of course need to bring a tarp to make sure the wood would be safe from the elements.

The tricky part would be to sneak Doris out of her room. This would be no light task either. Given the guards outside of her room every night. He would need to create a distraction of some kind. Luring them away long enough for him to bring her out. He would figure out these details later.

<hr />

Doris was looking up at her ceiling. She was thinking about the risk the Doc would be taking. How could he be willing to risk something like that? He saw the conditions she was living in. And while the doctor had improved her way of life here, for what little he could there still was so much unseen.

The Doc had no idea what Dr. Freude did to Doris. And while she doubted Dr. Freude would do something like that to Dr. Vernirelli he could be in for his own form of torture and punishment. He knew what went down in the reconditioning room, but he had not experienced it himself.

And yes, he promised to run away if it looked like the two of them were going to be caught. But what if they weren't? She'd still be forced to live the rest of her life in Tokema, was that really the life she wanted? Of course, it wasn't. Longing to be free of the Wendigo but forced to live out the rest of her days surrounded by filth and madness; that was no future she wanted.

Doris considered this for a long time. She had not thought about what would happen to her once the Wendigo was gone. Would the Doc help her run away? She knew they were close, but would be willing to help her out that much? Or, perhaps, she could keep that part secret. She could run away into the woods while the fire was raging and while the Doc was distracted. She could just disappear into the smoke. Never to be seen again.

Of course, her running away would also put the Doc at risk. People knew they were close. There was no denying that. Would people assume he helped her slip away into the night? What would happen to the Doc then? He could go to jail, become a patient, he could go to trial…

Thoughts like these continued to echo in Doris's head all night. She could not find true comfort in their plan anyway she looked at it. But the freedom of her soul felt so close. She was so close to having her full self-back again. She craved it. She needed it. After what Doris felt to be several hours, she sat up straight in bed. For too long she had suffered, too long kept a prisoner, it was her time to be a little selfish. The Doc knows the risk and yet he is still willing to help her. *The Doc is a grown man and can do what he wishes.* After all, Doris had already suffered so much. This was her final thought of the night, before returning to laying on her back and drifting off to a dreamless sleep.

—⟂⟂⟂—

The next day the doctor found himself at the store. He must have looked like a madman buying that much wood, a tarp, and fire starters. The young man working behind the counter didn't seem to be bothered or suspicious of him, however.

"Ya building a bonfire?" The pimpled-skinned kid asked.

"Something like that," the Doc replied.

"Groovy must be a big party." The Doc nodded. He did not mean to be rude or come off as disinterested, but he had more important things on his mind than making small talk with a teenager most likely working his first job. The kid reached into his pocket and took out a smoke. The doctor eyed him suspiciously. To lit a cigarette around all this fire-starting equipment made him uneasy.

"Oh," the kid laughed, putting the cigarette into the ashtray, being careful enough not to put out its spark. "Sorry man. Should use the ol' noggin next time." The young man chuckled as he continued to ring-up each item.

All in all, the doctor had purchased 15 bundles of wood (10 logs in each bundle), 15 fire starters, and a 15-foot by 15-foot tarp. The pimpled-face boy helped him carry the materials to his car. It took up all the trunk space, his back seats, and the passenger seat. Luckily, he never used his back seat for anything except casually throwing his coat and briefcase back there. With a click of his trunk and a turn of the key in the ignition, he was off.

It was a good thing that Doc and Doris decided to set their plan in motion for a month away. It would take him several trips to carry all the items deep into the woods. And without being able to get help from anyone else it would take twice if not three times as long given his age. True, he was in wonderful health, but seventy-four was no spring chicken. His bones ached every night and he could feel his skin grow saggy on his skull as the years went on. Someone his age should have retired years ago, he could afford to. But there was something that always kept him from doing so. A feeling in his gut that stopped him.

Driving his way home the Doc turned on the radio, he flipped it over to the religious station. Normally he was not one for bible thumpers, but something in him flipped to the station almost naturally. He could not explain it, but his fingers seemed to have a mind of their own as they fiddled through the dials. He had never listened to the station before; he did not even know he was absent-mindedly listening to it until he looked through his mirror. There, sitting amongst the wood in the back seat was the Wendigo. The doctor screamed. He laid on his brakes with such force that he did not have time to stop and check for anyone behind him. His forehead whipped forward, and it just grazed his steering wheel. He turned, only to find the wood that he had purchased sitting there. He turned back to his mirror but still was only greeted with wood.

Only a trick of the light, the doctor thought. *Just jitters about the plan taking place, nothing to be concerned about.* The doctor turned up the radio. Something about hearing those men preaching seemed to make him feel a bit more at ease. The words did not stick though. He just kept seeing that image of that creature in the back seat burning through his mind. His smile was one that was pulled too tightly around his head. He lusted and longed in hunger.

The thought of that *thing* getting closer to him was more than he could bear. He did not know how Doris was forced to manage for so long. Then again, she really didn't have a choice, now did she. It was then that it hit him. The man he had been seeing at a distance, in the library, under the lamp post, down the hall, he was getting closer. Next time *he* would be close enough to touch the Doc.

The doctor felt his skin crawl and his spine tingle. He needed to pull his car over and get some fresh air. His head was spinning, and he grew weak. The ground beneath his feet whirled about sending him into the side of his car. He clutched it, fearing if he were to let go his whole world around him would crumble into the madness, he faced every day at work.

He's getting closer. He's going to take me next. He's going to somehow leave Doris to latch himself onto me! I'll be the new Draker... only this time they'll say Vernirelli. They'll call me Vernirelli the vile. Vernirelli the vulture. The Doc could not silence the thoughts in his mind. Each one spinning, jumping, and crashing into the next. His breathing quickened, and his hands shook through his gloves. His body was vibrating with such force he was afraid he'd leap right out of his coat, shed it like skin. Like a snake taking on a whole new form. And while it was technically the same snake, was it? Was it really? Or did it rather change into its true form, its true identity? Each time peeling away its old self to reveal the snake it was always deep down.

It was unclear how long the Doc had been hunched over the side of his car. The sun was beginning to set. But that did not really mean anything. It was late afternoon when he went to get the wood. He slowly stood himself up, holding his right arm to his temple. The spinning had finally stopped. He knew what he was facing now. He thought it was just Doris facing this battle, he never imagined he'd be pulled in this way. Sure, he thought the Wendigo might possess Doris and try to kill or eat him, but he never expected the threat of being drawn in as prey to become the next vessel!

The Doc now knew what he had to do. He knew what he must overcome and how to do it. He grinned; he finally had an answer. With that final thought the Doc pulled up the door of his car, slid into his seat, and drove home.

Two days went by until the Doc was able to see Doris again. The two of them sat in their usual spots.

"I picked up some things to help with our plan," he told her. Doris nodded.

"I hope it wasn't too expensive," she remarked, "I feel bad that you're going through all this trouble on my behalf." The doctor waved his hand as if it was no trouble at all.

"Money isn't everything Doris. Besides, we have to get rid of *him* at all costs." Doris nodded again. The time would be approaching sooner than she probably could ever be ready for, but she was ready for it to be over and done with.

"I've been thinking a lot about my life after we've finished the job. I'll no longer be crazy, but I can't get released from here. I'm here for life! How am I to go on?" The Doc hesitated. If Doris ran away, he would immediately be blamed for her disappearance. They were so close that guards, nurses, and other staff alike took note. He knew that his occupational peers did, especially after saving Doris from a second trial of reconditioning. He would need to be careful about what he said next to her.

"What would you want to do Doris?" She waited there. She knew that he knew what she was about to suggest. Should she tell him? He would probably oppose the idea. After all, he would be risking far more than she would be.

"I'm not sure…" she eventually managed. "I just think living the rest of one's life out in a place like this, especially when there is no real reason to at all, would be an awfully sad life, don't you? As you once said, 'not truly living'." The doctor nodded.

"Yes, I agree, no one should have to suffer that fate. Especially when they're already being through hell and risked so much, like you." They both knew the words the other person really meant to say. Doris's eyes shouted them all at once, and so did the doctors.

Doris had already made up her mind about running away after the fire. She could escape through the smoke. He would never be able to catch her, he was too old. There was nothing that could change her mind. She was truly grateful for all the Doc had done for her; she was. He would just need to do one more thing.

The Doc had no trouble reading her face. He knew her plan, and he would have none of it. The wheels in his head had been turning ever since he saw that picture. And since then, they had only seemed to grow faster and more efficient. The Doc was set on his plan, just as Doris was set on hers.

⊷◦◦◦⊶

The doctor cleaned around his office. He would need to stay late if he was going to sneak the wood, traps, etc. into the woods each night. He knew Doris was unable to help him, but he wished someone would. His bones were already aching at the thought of lugging the materials deep enough into the facility's woods where no one else would look or find them.

The Doc had scoped it out a few days before buying the materials, he knew exactly where to bring everything. He had found a mini clearing in the woods where the trees seemed to circle around each other. It was the perfect spot of enough tree cover, open space, and far enough from the main buildings. It almost like it was set-up for this event exactly.

Making his way to his car the doctor glanced down each hallway. He had seen no one for almost an hour and assumed it was a safe bet that no one was in the area. He walked out into the cold, the wind bit at his cheeks and he could already feel his hands beginning to cramp. How he longed for someone else to help him.

Grabbing a small bundle of the wood the doctor marched on for the clearing. He walked at a steady pace, trying not to make too much sound. True, he was far enough away where if he stepped on a twig or a branch it would not alarm anyone, but he did not want to take the risk. As he pressed on, he heard a *snap*.

The Doc turned so quickly, he almost set himself falling on the ground. He looked around frantically, but could not see anyone there, still he could sense it. Was it the Wendigo? Was this it? Was this the moment at which it could thrust itself upon him, choking him down now to become the new Doris? The doctor began to panic. His eyes continued darting left to right, he could feel his heart in his throat, his pulse seemed to quicken so much it was now the only sound he could make out.

No one stepped forward, nothing else in the forest seemed to make a sound. Not even the wind dared to rustle the branches overhead or turn the leaves over on the ground. After a few minutes the doctor regained his composure and continued on his way.

It was not long into his march that he heard it again, another snap of a twig and this time a stumble. The Doc turned around once again, this time more sure it was not the Wendigo. He was sure such a monster would not be tripped up by upturned roots.

"Who's there?" The doctor called out, "I know you're here, so might as well step forward now." There was a hesitation. But then, from behind a tree, a few yards back, Dr. Tracy emerged from the shadows.

——◦/◦/◦——

"Amelia!" The Doc gasped, "What are you doing?"

"What- What am I doing?" Dr. Tracy pointed to herself and laughed. It was the kind of laughter that was forced out through one's belly, a deep rumble that set the body to shake all over. Her eyes rolled in her head as she threw it back in exasperation. "Look at yourself!" she eventually yelled out as she lunged in the Doc's direction. "What are you doing Dr. Vernirelli?"

The Doc took a step back. His mind began racing, searching for any excuse he could give at all to his whereabouts that did not immediately raise suspicion. He stood there for a moment, shifting uncomfortably on his feet. Dr. Tracy continued to eye him, she had him cornered. He was as lost as an experimental mouse in a maze for the first time.

"I knew it," she snorted out eventually, "I knew this had something to do with Doris. Sneaking about at night. Wait until Turner hears about this. You'll be out so fast you old-"

"You don't even know what you're talking about Amelia! You have no idea what is even happening." Dr. Vernirelli snapped. He threw down the logs and marched in Amelia's direction. "You have no idea at all. It's real! It's all real! I've seen it!"

This time it was Amelia's turn to take a step back. She had never seen such determination, fear, and anger in a person before and it frightened her. She began to shiver in her boots. She could tell that the doctor meant business, and with whatever it was he was doing he was going to get it done no matter what. She could see that crazed look in his eyes. She knew that look all too well in her profession. She had seen it on so many others before, but never in her years at Tokema did she expect to see it on a colleague, especially him.

"What's real?" She asked. Dr. Tracy's throat was suddenly very dry. There seemed to be a low buzzing in her ears, and she feared for what she was about to hear.

"Everything Doris said is true. You saw her trial; you know her claims and case reports. I'm finishing it. This nightmare must come to an end. And I know what to do. Now, if you turn me over to Dr. Turner, I guarantee no matter how many of your new, 'methods' you try, it will not fix or cure anything. You'll be trapped like I am if you take her on. Now, if you choose to accept that, that's your fate. It will not be mine. However, if you do not choose that fate then pick up some logs and help me carry them." And with that the doctor turned away from her, bending over, and picking up the slabs of wood he had thrown to the side with such vigor before.

Dr. Tracy stood dumbfounded. She was not expecting the doctor to share any information with her about what he was doing. In fact, he shared very little with the average Joe. But to her, Dr. Ameila Tracy, he seemed almost to confess.

"He was my nephew you know." She eventually said. Dr. Vernirelli paused,

"Who was?"

"One of her victims. I know we were supposed to come forward if we had connections with any of her victims. But I never did. I was hoping she'd be sent here. I needed to cause her some pain myself." Dr. Vernirelli hesitated. Pondering her words in his head. While he did not want Doris hurt, he could not carry the cross of the Wendigo. He turned slightly back towards her,

"Pick up the logs Amelia, we need to talk."

Not saying another word, she walked over to the doctor and grabbed some wood. The two of them walked quietly through the forest for a while. As they reached the clearing, far into the heart of the woods, Dr. Amelia Tracy finally decided to break the silence that hung in the air.

"So, what's going on exactly?"

———◈◈◈———

Doris paced nervously in her room. Today was not one of her days to visit the doctor and she felt uneasy. She knew he would have started carrying the things he bought into the woods last night. She hoped it wouldn't be too much for him. He was, after all, so old. Despite his age, however, he proved to be strong as an ox and that thought at least put Doris's mind at ease. She nibbled at her fingertips as the minutes ticked by.

Time seemed to move slower that day. Doris drifted about, just an outline of who she was. Her mind on bigger, more serious matters than the soup once again returning to its cold offering and the sandwiches being taken away. She wasn't sure when the food went back to being cold or when the facilities went back to their original state of green-gray sludge and fecal matter. Those issues hardly seemed to bother her now. The days were soon to be, if not already, fast approaching as to when she would have to face her greatest fear.

Soon she would be given no choice, her freedom was so close she could almost reach out and grab it. And grab it she shall. This thought is what made her want to continue on, although it was a thought that brought with it shame and tactless greed. She was about to betray the Doc. She needed to, she had to. Once she was to be free of the Wendigo what other choice did, she have? None! Escaping into the dead of night, changing her identity and running off was her only chance of any normality again.

For where you have envy and selfish ambition, there you find disorder and every evil practice, James 3:16. No! Doris thought, *No! I am not evil; I am not wicked. I have suffered far greater than most and I need this. If James had understood or had been inflicted that way, I have been he surely would understand. Jesus will understand. Yes, I'll still get in. I'll be forgiven for this act. God will understand.*

Doris's fingers began to twitch, her eyes soon to follow. Her hair fell long below her waist, she grabbed at it and plaited it into a braid. As she stroked her hair she began to prey, she was not sure how much longer she could wait. While waiting there was comfort in knowing there was no need to confront her demon head on just yet. But in the same breath with waiting came unease. Doris could not begin to question herself now. She had come so far and suffered through so much.

I'm sorry Doc. I really am...

It had not been long before the Doc was able to make his outstanding firewood pile, of course, having the extra hand of Dr. Tracy moved things along in his favor. Together the two of them stood, admiring their large woodpile. Dr. Tracy smiled.

"It will definitely be noticeable when it's ablaze," she remarked. The Doc gave a half smile,

"Well, I must say having you to help made it go by far quicker. It would have taken me at least a month to do it all on my own." Dr. Tracy nodded in his direction. The heap stood to their waists. The wood neatly stacked and was piled carefully tucked away from the elements. Of course, the ground was still wet, but the wood on top remained dry and ready for the flame.

Now, it was only a matter of sneaking Doris away into the night. The Doc had informed her over their many sessions together that he was getting closer and closer to completion, although naturally he left out the part of receiving help. This would be his secret until the time was right. Just as it was his secret that he had seen the Wendigo. And with each instance, came its closer and closer approach.

The last time it reared its ugly head was in the car when he first purchased the wood. He knew, however, that if he were to see it again it would be too late. It would be close enough to touch him by then and the thought alone of its icy embrace made his spine turn to jelly and quiver. He no longer would allow his mind to be occupied with the potential and inevitability of what surely would come next.

"So, when are we going to do it?" Dr. Tracy asked, breaking the prolonged silence between them.

"First, we need to pick a day when it will be easy to get her out. We need to have alibis. We have no room for error." Dr. Tracy nodded. It would not be hard to get Doris out now that the Doc had acquired her help. She could easily be able to distract the guards, telling them she needed them for an emergency. The night guards were usually new hires and eager to flex their small gift of power over the patients. It would not take much for her to be able to coax them away while the Doc grabbed Doris.

"Easy enough. We grabbed a nightcap at your place after a long night's work," she said. The Doc snorted at this.

"In what world, Amelia, are we ever seen as chums? It would be more believable to say we bumped into each other at the 24-hour pharmacy," he retorted back. Amelia shrugged,

"Fair enough. But if people go sniffing, they'll ask the store clerk. We should go there the day before so the clerk will recognize us but might not be able to recall which day." Dr. Vernirelli nodded. The two of them continued to stand in silence, simply admiring their hard work over the last few weeks. It was almost time; the doctor was so close to freedom that he could almost taste it.

I'm sorry Doris. I really am...

—⚬⚬⚬—

"Doris," the doctor said, sitting in his usual chair. His back was beginning to get a more noticeable hunch. He suspected it was from his several hauls of the wood from the car to their secret spot. "Doris, it's ready. When do you want to set it into motion?"

Doris took a sharp inhale; she had not expected it to come so soon. A reasonable amount of time had gone by since the Doc first informed her of his purchasing the wood and bringing it into the forest, but still! He had more remarkable speed than she had imagined.

"So soon..." she murmured. The Doc nodded,

"Yes, I was able to finish everything sooner than expected, but it's all set. I even have a plan on how to get you out. I'll call the guards away on a fake errand and when they are distracted, I will unlock your room and bring you to the spot." Doris did not respond. She knew the doctor was telling her the truth, but still. There seemed to be something underlying. She and the Doc had been tiptoeing around one another since they both seemed to have opposing views on how it would all end; her wanting to run away into the night. Him, wanting her to stay so he would not be blamed for her disappearance. But Doris did not care. She was going to make a break for it. She had fully made up her mind.

"Alright... alright. How's the day after tomorrow? The sooner the better. I'm ready" The determination in her voice gave the Doc a shutter. She had never sounded so strong, so sure, so powerful before. He could feel her bravery radiating off of her. This new side of Doris was certainly a glimpse into her previous life before possession, the one after leaving her childhood home. It radiated what she was like as an independent woman.

The Doc nodded. Proud of how far she had come and all the challenges and obstacles she went through. It was this that reminded the doctor of why he liked her so much in the first place, why he loved her. A *pang* struck the doctor's heart. His mind flashed to the Grinch, stealing Christmas and listening for the cries and wails of the Whos - *And now his heart didn't feel quite so tight, he whizzed with his loathe through the bright morning light.*

Alas the feeling was not one to stay. For just then the Doc felt something cold and sinister through the air. His spine began to crack up straight, his limbs became weak, and he knew what was to come next. He glanced at Doris, eyes widened with fear, but she did not seem to notice. Doris seemed completely unphased. She was talking in fact. Although he could not hear her words flowing from her mouth, he could see her lips moving and her jaw as it gently bounced up and down.

It was the smell that came rolling in after the feeling, one of sewage and grime, of blood and iron, of rotten flesh. There, he stood. Face only a mere inch away. The Doc held his breath. He was not sure if this was going to be it. He closed his eyes tightly, not wanting to see the endless gape of what was inside.

"Doc? Doc!" The doctor re-opened his eyes. It was just him and Doris in the room. There was no uninvited third party. "Doc, are you alright?" Doris asked again. She had known that look on the doctor's face before. It was one she herself had felt many times before. But she knew it couldn't be what she was thinking. After all, she felt nothing. No spooks, chills, or doom.

"Y-yes. I'm fine. Just a dizzy spell." The doctor took a small cloth from his breast pocket and dabbed it across his forehead. Then he knew, he knew what was to happen if the plan was not to be set in motion. His heart no longer felt like it was growing with compassion for Doris, instead, he could feel it beginning to drown. It was heavy in his chest as it sunk further and further into him. Now it was his turn to be determined. To be brave. To be decisive.

———⟶ஒ/ஒ⟵———

The next day drifted by as if it was a dream. It hazed and slipped its way past both Doris and the Doc. Looking back on the day Doris could not remember if she even lived that day. It seemed to fog over her like she was walking through mist. She knew she must have gone through her normal routine. She found herself to be laying in bed.

Her arms rested behind her head, her breathing shallow. She glanced about; the Doc would be coming for her later that evening. She wasn't sure what time he would be able to sneak in and steal her away, but she knew he was coming.

The day after tomorrow she said. Why did she have to pick a day so close? She could have just as easily told him a week or a month from then. He would have waited, right? He would wait until she felt comfortable and ready enough. The day before yesterday she was so certain, so certain of her plan and her escape to the sweet amber grains of freedom. But now, in this bed, knowing any minute she would be pulled from these four walls that had encased her for the better part of 10 months now, she was not so sure.

Doris could feel the fear and self-doubt bubble and roar within her. It seemed to ooze its way along inside her, threatening to break free. A sudden shock shot through Doris's spine, and she felt sick. She swung her legs to the side of her bed and let them hang. They dangled there, almost lifeless as they lazy rotated themselves side to side. She wished she had an antacid, even a small piece of ginger for her to chew on. Something to help her stomach from rumbling out of her skin.

Clinging to her stomach she heard it. The sound she had been waiting for for the last day and a half, the undeniable *click* of her room's lock being turned, and the squeaking squeal of the door swinging open.

⸺◦/◦/◦⸺

The time had come. The doctor had told Amelia that Doris was ready to move forward the day after tomorrow and here it finally was. The two of them had arranged everything. Amelia would call the guards away onto one of the more problematic patients. The doc felt awful throwing another patient under the bus, but there was no other choice.

Amelia radioed in that there was a problem on the other side of the building, and that she needed back up. She wanted the patient taken to her office to be reconditioned in the morning. And while this normally would have been a two-man job, this patient was particularly huge and needed around 4 or 5 just to bring him down.

As Amelia worked on her part the doc slipped into his office and changed. He pulled over a black turtleneck, black pants, a hat, and even gloves. He would not risk showing any part of himself if he did not have to. In his drawer were clothes for Doris. He had gone shopping yesterday and guessed her size. He was sure everything would fit.

Taking one last look around his office, the doctor let out a heavy sigh. This was it. *I will not become the next vessel*, and with that thought, the doctor clicked his office shut.

⸺◦/◦/◦⸺

There the Doc stood. He was not in his usual outfits of sweat vests, khakis, and button up. Instead, he was dressed head to toe in dark clothing. He held in his hand a bag; he reached inside and threw a pair of dark pants and a hooded sweatshirt at Doris.

"Put these on, quickly, we've gotta get out of here." Doris did as she was told. She did not even ask how he was able to pull the guards away. She wasn't sure if she wanted to know. Some small part of her thought maybe the doctor needed to use another patient as a distraction. She hoped he wouldn't have had to stoop that low, but then again, what else could pull the guards away for a long enough time?

Doris slipped the hood and pants over her medical gown. She did not want to waste any time, in case the doctor underestimated the guards, and they were able to take care of whatever business he devised quicker than expected.

As soon as Doris pulled the pants up the doctor grabbed her, he held her wrist too tightly. Doris was a little afraid he would pull it out of place. The Doc turned to leave, but before he made his way out the door he turned to Doris one last time, no words were needed for an exchange, he looked her in the eyes and nodded. She nodded back, she was ready for him to take her.

Slipping out into the hallway the doctor was completely silent. Doris had not noticed it before, but he was not wearing any shoes. He must have left them behind, so they did not make his signature *click clacking* down the halls. She followed behind him, he still had not let go of her wrist as he led her down the dimly lit hallway.

They made a few turned down halls that Doris had not been to before during her time here. She never really paid much mind before, but her life in Tokema only involved, for the most part, the same hallways every day. There was no need for her to break from her usual procedure, and therefore there was no reason for her to make these twists and turns before.

After a short while the two of them came to a back door. The doctor tilted his head toward it, indicating he wanted Doris to go out first. He stepped behind her, blocking her from the hallway they had just crept and slithered their way down. Doris grabbed the handle, taking in one slow and shaky breath she pushed, it opened without a sound. This was the end of all her misery and suffering, this door was the only thing keeping her locked inside, and she now had the power to walk though. And with that, Doris stepped through the door.

⟶◦◦◦⟵

The air nipped at her cheeks, she barely had time to take it all in before the doctor completely pushed her through the door, once more clutching her wrist and dragging her into the dead of night. It was just then that Doris realized she never even bothered to look at the clock outside her room. She had no idea when the doctor came for her.

As she stumbled and tripped her way through the wood Doris looked to the moon. It shined brightly in the sky against its background of velvet blue and silver stars. She held her gaze as best she could without falling. She had not seen the moon the entirety of her time in Tokema. She was never allowed anywhere at night that had a window nor was she allowed outside. In fact, Doris could no longer recall if she even saw the moon during her dreams which led her outside amongst those woods. This is how she knew it was real. Not a dream, but real. She did not realize how much she had even missed it until now.

As the Doc bobbed and weaved his way silently through the trees Doris began to realize, she knew where she was. She had been here before, many times in fact. She knew the spot in which the doctor had chosen. She could even guide him if she wanted. But instead, she let him drag her and pull her away. She hoped she would be wrong on their destination, although she knew she was not.

The moon rays almost acted like a guide, the path seemed to appear and disappear with each passing step. It would shine brilliantly for Doris and the Doc to glide through the forest and then immediately be gone. Coincidence? Doris did not think so, a higher power, she thought, had to be guiding their way. Wanting them to push forward like the tide. And like the tide the moon seemed to be pulling them as well.

Soon it all came to view, the small clearing in the woods, a blue tarp draped across a large, neatly stacked pile. *This is it*, Doris breathed in so immensely it also took her back. As they slowed their strides Doris glanced about. The clearing was exactly like in her dreams. It made a small circle, perfectly hidden and encased by the tree cover. A truly perfect spot for what they were about to do. They were far enough from the vicinity now that she could no longer make out the building's lights. She was certain no one would even hear the two of them if they spoke normally, still, she would not risk it.

"Doc," Doris whispered, "What now?"

"Here," the doctor handed her a small package of matches from his coat. He took out another pair for himself. Together they peeled back the tarp. The wood had been stacked so neatly, so carefully placed. Doris could see different bricks of fire starters all within the wood labyrinth waiting to be set aflame. It seemed nearly impossible that the Doc was able to do all this fine work himself. He must have hauled large loads each and every night. For all Doris knew he could have stayed out there all night some days and showered and got dressed in Tokema before work.

Without exchanging another word, the two of them lit their matches, dropping them in strategic spots that barely showed fire starters. It was not long before the fire was so hot, the two of them needed to take a step back to admire their work.

Doris could feel her skin crawl, it felt uncomfortable and itchy. She took a hesitant step back, tempted to retreat into the darkness and make a break for the woods now. Doris's discomfort was clear. Her eyes bulged and the Doc could see her eyes shooting side to side. Not in an attempt to look for her demon, no, she was going to attempt and run, the doctor thought. He took a step closer to her.

"Doris, Doris get closer. We want *him* to think he's in danger, then he will come." Doris knew he was right. Even if she did attempt to run now, what good would it do? He still would be attached to her. Following her around like gum on the bottom of a shoe.

Doris took a step closer to the flame. Her brow began to sweat. It reminded her of being in the tub, only this time, she felt like she was in true danger. Before she was afraid for herself and the Doc, now, she was afraid for her soul.

Deep from within the wood Doris could hear a distant *snap*. She turned on her heels, kicking mud up from the ground and onto her backside. She frantically looked side to side, desperately searching for the sound. But there was nothing more. The Doc held his breath, then he saw it.

A shadow began to form from the dancing fire's silhouette on the ground. It breathed out of beat with the fire and grew. The shadowy figure began to slowly pull itself from the ground, extending its disjointed limbs as it scraped and crawled from the earth. Instinctively the Doc grabbed Doris's arm, she turned and froze to see the Wendigo emerging from the ground floor.

There, hand-in-hand the two stood. Eyes threatening to pop forth from their sockets and roll from stings along their chests. Chests that weighed so heavily Doris felt as if her ribs would spring from its place, wrenching the rest of her skeleton with it.

There *it* stood. Before the two of them clear as the day. It towered over them; the Doc gave Doris's hand a tight squeeze. She knew it was now or never. She would need to push him in from the flames from which it was born. Not taking another moment to think or be scared Doris lunged at the monster. Throwing her weight into it, flinging it as hard as she could into the fire.

The Wendigo let out an awful screech, it wailed and moaned in such a way that Doris wanted to cover her ears and eyes and fall to the ground. It seized at her, desperate to take hold of whatever it could, an arm, leg, it didn't matter. But Doris was quick, she pulled herself back, stumbling back on her feet and to the ground. She watched as it squealed and spasmed, turning to cremation. And with an ember glow, a fiery haze, back to hell which forth it came...

Doris laid there on the ground. Breathing too intensely she was not sure she would ever catch her breath again. She felt something from behind her reach under her armpits and scoop her up.

"Doris! Are you alright?" The Doc pulled her to her feet. But Doris could not speak, her fear and adrenaline had not worn off yet. She was stunned, dumbfounded even. The doctor pulled her in for a hug. Holding her tight he closed his eyes; he could feel tears rolling down them. She conquered her fear. She overcame it.

"My dear I am so very proud of-" the doctor opened his eyes. Deep from within the flame he saw it. Its fingers were the first to emerge, its black holes where its eyes should have been gleamed like onyx in the crimson and blues. Extending its arm, it began to crawl and lunge its way forward. "-you."

Doris began to shake and cry. The doctor could hear she was now speaking, but her words could not transform into meaning. He was hypnotized by the beast trying to slither and seduce its way out of the ash and flame.

It'll never be gone. Not until she is. She cannot stay, I cannot allow it to live on. I must set her free. I must set myself free. The doctor pulled away from Doris. Tears still in his eyes. "My dear," he murmured, cutting her off, "I am so proud you faced your fear. Now, it's time to face mine." And with that, the doctor took hold of Doris's arm and flung her into the fire.

Doris screamed; her skin almost immediately seemed to melt from its flesh. Writhing in agony, but the doctor could no longer hear her screams. He fell to his knees, *It's a rare thing. An unusual thing. To feel this way about someone. A feeling in which you don't even realize that it is happening. It develops slowly. Creeping up on you like falling asleep. Something you don't even realize you are having until you are dreaming, or suddenly awaken. To love someone in such a way that you are willing to sacrifice everything. And yes, it was worth it. To know the truth. To know what to do. But only love can hurt like this. I know it's love. The only patient*

I have ever loved. And it ends like this? Pity really. But I know it's what's best. Best for everyone really. I'll miss you…

The doctor was not sure how long he stayed on his knees. He felt something rest upon his shoulder. He looked up to see Dr. Tracy standing there. Her eyes glowed with a sick hunger, she seemed to have a slight glimmer in her eyes.

"It's a marvelous thing" Amelia murmured. He was unsure of how long she had been standing there. Did she see him push her in? He could not tell. The doctor could not speak. He felt sick to his stomach. But there was something in the air that seemed lighter now. Something like an unknown weight had been lifted. Again, he was not sure how long they stayed there for. The hours seemed to wipe by. The doctor could not remember how he had gotten home. He could not recall getting into his bed. But there he lay.

———❦❦❦———

It had almost been a month since the fire. Word of Doris Draker missing from the hospital spread not only all around the facilities but to the public as well. The doctor had been interviewed several times but was never once questioned about his helping her escape. A search through the wood had been conducted, but no one ever found that small clearing in the woods.

Neither Dr. Vernirelli, nor Amelia, had joined that search. They both knew their bodies would be naturally drawn back to that spot. The doctor had not even visited it since that night. Part of him wanted to go back. To see if it was all truly there, or only a fever dream he had thought up. Maybe he thought everything up! Doris's face seemed to blur within his mind. The sound of her voice had seemed to fade away as well. A voice he had once heard almost every day seemed to shred itself into nothing.

———❦❦❦———

The doctor had decided that night that he would go back. He would return to that place one last time. He needed to prove to himself that it really happened. That he was not going insane by thinking he dreamed Doris up. He would go back, find the ash pile, and leave as soon as he proved it to himself.

Trudging through the woods the doctor did not even need to think about the placement of his footsteps. He could walk this path blindfolded if he chose to. It was not long before he made his way into the clearing. And there it was, a burned pile of wood and ash.

The doctor slowly crept forward. He was not sure what he was looking for or hoping to find. Originally, he simply wanted to prove it to himself, now, there seemed to be more. Falling to his hands and knees the doctor felt a gravitational pull to sift through the ash. His hands began searching frantically for something, but what? He did not know. He could feel his hands getting closer and closer. Until he felt it. It was cold, hard, and linked.

The doctor pulled a small necklace from the ash. He held it close. He knew it could not have been Doris's, she did not have jewelry to wear. Could it have been Amelia's and it somehow got lost in the flame? No. There was not even a scorch mark upon the thing. The Doc sat there on his knees like he had done just a month before. Sighing, he slipped the thing into his pocket. He would take it home and have a closer look at it there.

Raising himself the doctor turned. And there, only a mere few inches from his face stood the Wendigo. Before the doctor could even scream it grabbed him, forcing the doctor down, and swallowed him whole.

THE END.

Printed in the United States
by Baker & Taylor Publisher Services